ENDORSEMENTS

I really enjoyed reading the book. The book should be read by any manager in plants with poorly performing throughput and high costs before they start any improvement initiative. That would help them better understand what the front-line people in a plant goes through and how they suffer under poor, or lacking leadership.

Christer Idhammar – Founder of IDCON INC

Rob tells a great story with real life wisdom. He reminds us that people are our biggest asset and poor leadership can destroy a culture very quickly

Neil Betteridge, Global Dairy Operations Executive

Every CEO should read this book.

Don Truesdell – Senior Reliability Consultant at 151 plants in 39 countries

BOHICA

WHAT YOU MANAGERS ALWAYS DO TO US WORKERS

ROB PROBST

BALBOA.PRESS
A DIVISION OF HAY HOUSE

Balboa Press books may be ordered through booksellers or by contacting:

Balboa Press
A Division of Hay House
1663 Liberty Drive
Bloomington, IN 47403
www.balboapress.com
844-682-1282

Print information available on the last page.

ISBN: 979-8-7652-4089-2 (sc)
ISBN: 979-8-7652-4091-5 (hc)
ISBN: 979-8-7652-4090-8 (e)

Library of Congress Control Number: 2023906475

Balboa Press rev. date: 05/26/2023

CONTENTS

AUTHOR'S NOTE

The mechanical engineers presented me with the toy bird, shown on the cover, as my Christmas present four months after my appointment as engineering manager at Bay Milk Products. An engineering union delegate, Chris, explained, "This kiwi bird represents us workers, and the carriage bolt is what you managers always do to us." I was momentarily left speechless, before responding, "I look forward to removing this bolt together at next year's Christmas celebration." I was unsure how we would transform our adversarial relationship.

Twelve months later, we unscrewed the bolt and toasted our success. Bay Milk's engineering union members and management had jointly authored a collective employment agreement and reliability improvement plan that incentivized self-management, job-sharing, and breakdown reduction. The new agreement would result in reduced overtime, guaranteed income, improved productivity, and work-life balance. Some years later, Bay Milk Products was recognized for achievement of world-class reliability performance.

This story was intended to be an upbeat tale of our successful organizational transformation, but as writing progressed, I reminded myself that just two percent of organization initiatives are successful, while an additional ten percent get close to best practice, according to reliability experts. The majority of organizations fail as a result of poor leadership. I felt compelled to recount a version of the most likely outcome, what happens when staff and mid-level managers attempt to improve their working conditions and performance under the direction of an unrealistic leader.

A year after publishing the first edition of BOHICA, I led a reliability improvement initiative at a New Zealand forest products company as the newly-appointed engineering manager. I loaned a copy of BOHICA to one of my direct reports, and a month later, he returned the book and enquired, "Rob, are you psychic?" I was embroiled in a nearly identical, real-life portrayal of BOHICA's plot. I decided not to bend over to toxic corporate management and resigned three months later. I resolved to rewrite BOHICA and promote it as a cautionary tale.

This story is dedicated to fellow workmates, through the years of my career, with whom I have shared tribulation and success in pursuit of a more ideal working environment. Sociopathic leaders frequently blocked our path, and we consoled ourselves, rationalizing, "At least we're not in a battlefield situation. We'd be dead."

I thankfully acknowledge the work of several authors and mentors. Their research and contributions to reliability practice and organizational behavior theory have influenced my career and the creation of this story: Christer Idhammar, Terry Wireman, Robert Sutton, Jeffrey Pfeffer, Jim Collins, and Frederick Herzberg.

All the Best.
Rob

CHAPTER 1

Matt jumped at the sound of the workshop door slamming against the wall as though it had swung open hard and fast enough for the handle to break the doorstop and penetrate the gypsum wallboard. He turned from the workbench to see Jim Champion, the Site manager, striding into the center of the workshop. There was fire in his eyes, and Matt could feel his stomach muscles tighten. It was Friday, and he'd hoped they might have made it through the week without any management dust-ups. But, unfortunately, he knew what to expect next.

"Trevor, get your ass down here!!!" Jim yelled as he glanced up the stairway toward the office window overlooking the mechanical engineering workshop.

The Venetian blinds opened slightly.

Matt could see Trevor's eyes peeking through the gap. He wondered why Trevor bothered. He knew what was in store.

Jim looked back at Matt and commanded, "Matt! Get the rest of the engineers in here now!"

Matt headed into the smoko room where the electricians and mechanical engineers were gathered for morning break. He made a silent wrist gesture to the guys at the table to follow him back into the workshop. They had heard the commotion; some looked afraid, while others were resigned to another tyrannical outpouring.

Trevor stumbled down the stairs, grasping for the handrail.

At one of the workbenches in the center of the room, Jim was tapping a two-foot-long piece of 50mm diameter, stainless-steel tubing on the edge of the metal workbench. He stopped tapping the tubing. The workshop was silent. He raised the pipe, slammed it furiously into the top of the table, and then raked the parts off the tabletop and onto the floor. The crashing sound of the stainless-steel tubing on the tabletop was painful. The men stood motionless, frozen as the energy drained out of their legs.

Trevor's knees were visibly shaking when Matt looked at him. He wondered if Trevor was about to wet his pants.

"This workshop is a pigsty!" Jim shouted. He looked up to see if there was any disagreement in the eyes of the trade staff. All of them were looking at the floor. "No wonder my one hundred fifty-million-dollar powder drier is broken down again! You guys have no understanding of discipline, work standards, or ownership!"

Matt looked up. For a split second, he was sure he recognized the hint of a smile on Jim's lips. He shuddered, realizing Jim was enjoying his own tirade.

"The CEO didn't ask the stockholders, the farmers, to shell out their hard-earned profits so it could sit around and look like a shiny Christmas ornament! And I didn't promise Colin Gray I would keep the plant running hard enough to surpass its design specs because I wanted to look stupid!" He paused for effect. "You guys are making me look bad. You are making the site and everyone who works here look bad because you can't keep the drier running longer than three days without a breakdown!" Jim paused again, his eyes moving from one man to the next, finishing with Trevor. "We are supposed to be making powder yesterday, today, tomorrow, and the day after tomorrow, but my operators tell me the cyclones are blocking. You guys can't get the rotary valves fixed to stop the blockages. Trevor?!"

Trevor jerked out of a frozen stupor. Drifting, trying to escape, mentally, Matt surmised.

Now he had been caught off guard. Perhaps he hadn't heard what Jim had said. Things could get worse.

"Trevor!!!? I'm talking to you!"

"Uh……er…….Jim. I'm so, so sorry," Trevor replied.

"Trevor, you are sorry!" Jim paused again, letting the words sink in. "You are the sorriest excuse for a maintenance manager, for an engineer, for a human I have ever seen!" Jim eyed Trevor's reaction, cruelly.

"But, Jim. It's not just our fault. The operators aren't following their SOP's. They're partly to blame for the blockages. Fifty percent of the downtime is caused by operator faults. Some of them aren't even trained."

Matt was surprised to hear Trevor challenge Jim. It was a pitiful attempt.

"I don't bloody give a rat's ass, Trevor!"

Matt couldn't hold back any longer. "He's right, Jim. And not only that, half of our breakdowns are a result of the crappy startup commissioning by the contract engineers and the substitution of sub-standard parts, like the rotary valves."

Jim turned quickly to Matt. His fingers tightened on the stainless tube.

"Matt's right, Jim. I told you that too."

Jim turned back to Trevor. "I want the drier back online in an hour, or I'm going to seriously start thinking about contracting out maintenance!" Jim looked around at all of them, menacing, assuring himself the staff had received the impact of his threat. Only Matt looked him back in the eye. "Matt. I want to see you and Trevor in my office in an hour. I want a report on the actions you are taking to get back online and stay online."

Trevor piped in, "Okay Jim. We'll get onto it. I'm sorry you had to come over here. We'll do whatever it takes to get the drier back up."

"Trevor. I don't want you to do whatever! You're already over budget. Just do what's necessary and do it fast." Jim didn't wait for a response as he tossed the tubing on the metal bench top and spun toward the door. He was out of the shop with a few quick strides, heading toward the administration block.

Nobody moved. Jim's smashing of metal, his tirade, his threat, the abuse of Trevor, had left them drained. They stood in silence for a few seconds until Moke piped in with sarcastic cheerfulness.

"Is this what you call ….uh….Deja Vu, or something?

Some of the tradesmen giggled as they began shuffling back to the smoko room.

Matt reflected on the tirade. Like so many other similar incidents, the Maintenance, or "Site Services Department," as they were designated on the organization chart, was again the scapegoat, the dumping ground, not only for Jim Champion but for the plant managers and anyone else looking for an excuse for their reduced performance. He remembered another recent outburst when Jim had said they were just a necessary evil because people were required to fix the kit when it broke down. If it never broke down, they would be the first to go.

Once in a while, when one of them got a piece of the critical plant up and running following a breakdown, they would get a pat on the back from the supervisor or plant manager.

They were heroes for five or ten minutes. That was how things had always been around the plant: one minute, a hero, the next minute, the biggest assholes on the site. The hero feeling was measured in minutes, and the asshole feeling was measured in weeks. Matt turned to look at Trevor and gauge his reaction.

"Okay. Matt! I want you to get the boys and get those rotary valves replaced now. Get Peter to send two control techs over to check out if there are any program faults. The operators may have locked up the program again. Tell Chris to make sure the instruments are set up correctly on the cyclones."

"Trevor! This is all knee-jerk stuff! We don't even know why the drier is down this time," Matt snapped.

"Matt! Don't say that! I know what's wrong. It's always the same thing!"

"No. It's not. And if we go over there and run around like guys at a house on fire we'll look even worse if the drier doesn't get back online."

"Yeah, Trevor. I don't want those production jerks mouthing off at us as well," Crazy Andy piped in. He was backing Matt, but he wasn't sure what Matt was proposing.

"We should be doing a root cause analysis on these cyclone blocks. When are we going to use the training we got last year?!" Matt was insistent.

"We don't have time right now. We've got to get into action."

Matt felt like picking the pipe up and hitting Trevor with it. Seeing him in panic mode was so bloody frustrating.

Half the guys left the shop while Trevor and Matt were arguing. They had their own ideas about what to check for. Matt was the Leading Hand, but Trevor had overridden him once again.

Matt took after them, hoping to direct them to places where he thought they'd have a better chance of solving the problem.

He turned to Trevor as he left. "Trev, you go up to Jim's office on your own. I don't want him to think I had anything to do with the solution discussion because I didn't." Trevor's expression was almost blank, totally distracted. Onto the next knee-jerk response plan, Matt guessed.

"Okay, Matt. I can handle Jim."

"Bloody hell," Matt thought to himself. He's right off his nut. He walked out of the shop and into the mid-morning heat.

Matt glanced at the surroundings as he crossed the milk reception area toward the powder plant entrance. It was a pretty setting, a thirty-acre powder and cream plant site set amid farmland, five miles outside Mornington. The dairy site processed the milk from the surrounding three thousand farms on a good day, when it wasn't broken down. It was one of the largest sites in the Dairy Cooperative, and it had grown steadily over the past fifty years as dairy farming became more lucrative. The new milk powder drier Jim was ranting about was the third to be built on the site, and the financial returns to the farmers had increased.

Most of the farmers had family members working at the processing site, which meant you had to watch what you said or did since any disparaging remarks or more than frugal spending would get back to a farmer, who would then pass his complaint up to the local board member or the CEO and back it would come, to you. Around four hundred fifty people were employed, mostly as production operators or tanker drivers, who worked shifts that covered around-the-clock, seven-day-a-week production. The manufacturing operation turned out nearly a billion dollars of product every year, and each time the plant went down, milk had to be shipped somewhere else for processing, and the farmers lost profit.

It was strange. The farmers seemed happy to tolerate the breakdowns. Matt figured it must have something to do with how they ran their farms. Even though they had the money to spend on preventive maintenance, the bulk of the work on their farm equipment happened only when the equipment broke down. He knew from experience since he had worked as a mechanical engineer on farms for a couple of years, servicing equipment.

He got fed up with the farmer's attitudes and applied for a job at the plant. The farmers always thought his repair work cost too much and wanted to argue about a price reduction. He couldn't convince them they could save half their repair expense with a simple preventive maintenance program. They weren't in the habit of doing preventive maintenance and since they had established the manufacturing plants, they weren't much in the habit of demanding preventive maintenance work at their plants, either. The cheapest, fastest fix possible was acceptable.

The rest of the people on the site worked in operations and the laboratory, or in the administration building at the entrance to the main powder plant. They were a mix of folks, including university graduates doing research and technical work, accountants who always wanted to chop more out of the maintenance budget, and administration staff. The production season lasted ten months. Then, during the winter, when rainfall was plentiful, and temperatures dropped, the farmers dried off their cows.

The Mornington site was kept in a pretty tidy state; no potholes in the pavement like some of the other sites in the cooperative. Jim Champion splurged on landscaping, with a small bonsai garden near the administration entrance to impress Japanese customers. The buildings were repainted once every two years.

Matt pushed through the entrance to the main powder plant. He realized he no longer appreciated or even noticed the cosmetic appearance of the plant and surroundings. The reactive, breakdown, panic-stricken culture had dimmed its natural beauty beyond recognition.

A few hours later, Matt looked up as he walked up the steps to ground level from the Powder plant entrance. He spotted Jim at the entrance of the administration building. Trevor was standing behind him. Matt hesitated. It was nearly "home time." He and 'the boys' had gotten the drier back online an hour earlier. Jim might be lining him up for another thrashing because they had taken longer than an hour to unblock the cyclones. Fortunately, the operators hadn't blocked the plant with wet milk powder.

It would have taken them five more hours to get the abseilers into the plant to dig out the powder.

"C'mon Matt! Get your butt over here. You'll like this," Jim yelled, waving him to approach.

Matt couldn't believe Jim was smiling at him. He was amazed at how quickly Jim could shift moods. He reluctantly headed toward them.

"Matt. I want to send you and Trevor on a training course." Jim explained as Matt approached.

Matt and Trevor followed Jim as he turned and walked into the foyer.

Matt looked at Trevor in disbelief, wondering if Trevor had a clue. Trevor didn't respond.

"I've already explained this to Trevor," Jim said as he turned to face them both.

Matt cringed. "What?"

"Yeah, Matt. It sounds like a good idea," Trevor piped in.

Jim handed Matt an advertisement brochure. It had glossy photos with large bold print and a list of industry experts speaking about topics that were either disinteresting or over the top from his point of view. However, Matt could see it was a brochure for a maintenance training program.

"Matt. Catch the title?! KISS or KICKASS; Transformation to Maintenance Best Practices!" Jim announced excitedly. "This is a course on how to motivate your crew. You and Trevor, so you can learn how to kick some ass, get your crew off its duff, and save us millions."

"You're kidding?" Matt replied.

"No, I'm not." Jim explained, "This is coming straight from North America. A Canadian expert from a heavy equipment manufacturing environment is presenting it, in New Haven."

Matt glanced at the title and the brochure. KICKASS, he thought to himself. So typical. Jim was trying to get them to adopt his management style.

"It's not just about kicking ass; it's about maintenance best practice concepts and how to kick asses into doing it."

Matt held his tongue. It wasn't his perception of the course title.

"I want you two guys at this conference on Monday. You got a stay of execution for getting the drier back up today. This conference may answer my frustrations and be an opportunity for you both." Jim peered over his reading glasses into their eyes. "I've already asked Kay to book your rooms and another in case you want to take somebody else from maintenance. She's arranged a rental car and your conference fees too. So, pack your bags!"

"Great! Jim. I'm looking forward to it already." Trevor was beaming.

Matt thought he could see some dried saliva at the corner of Trevor's mouth. God, he could be disgusting.

Trevor suggested, "Matt, how about we get Dave to come along too? It would be good to have him on board."

"Yeah, that's fine, Trev. Did you talk to him yet?" Matt turned to leave. He was growing weary of the conversation, and it was past quitting time. "Anything else?"

"Yeah," Jim smirked, "How about a thank you, Jim?"

Matt thought for a second about just ignoring him. "Thanks. I hope it's better than most conferences. They're usually only worth attending for the free lunch."

Jim patted him on the back and turned toward his office. "Come and tell me about it as soon as you get back."

"See. He's not such a bad guy," Trevor said as he turned to head back to the maintenance shop with Matt. "I'll pick up the car and come by for you and Dave around 6:30 am Monday. Okay?"

"Yeah, fine. I'm going to check on the cooling water pump." Matt intentionally turned and took the long way back to the shop, around the cooling tower, so he didn't have to walk with Trevor.

As he walked, Matt took stock of his situation and what might or might not have been. He had just turned thirty-three. As a teenager, he had dreamt of cycling as a professional and doing the Tour de France. As a junior cyclist he placed well in National Secondary events, but financial considerations prevented him from following his dream. Instead, he needed to find employment. Nevertheless, he continued cycling to maintain his fitness, cycling the forty kilometers to work and racing with the local club when possible.

He wasn't the biggest of the men in the workshop at six feet in height, but his strength and athletic ability made him an equal to the others. He knew his workmates trusted him to work safely and to carry more than the average load when things got physically demanding. He also knew that he was one of the tradesmen his colleagues came to for help with problem solving and motivation.

He was pleased when his mates had supported him to take on the Leading Hand role several years earlier.

The "boys" knew that he could be trusted to have their interests at heart and to have thought through alternatives before taking action.

Despite the stressful work life at the plant, Matt was reasonably comfortable with his lot in life. He was making good dosh, had the respect of his workmates, and was in a position of influence. As he continued along the footpath, he once again realized a missing element in his life could be the daily anticipation of seeing his son or daughter as he headed home. After three years of marriage, Jan reluctantly agreed to get pregnant, but they were unsuccessful. Matt had convinced Jan to quit her full-time position and take on a position as a substitute teacher in anticipation of her transition to motherhood. While waiting for the good news, he was dismayed by Jan's change of taste. She had become house-proud, insisting on the latest fabrics and fashions around the house and extending her wardrobe to match. It created financial stress since they had lost her income. As he opened the door to the workshop, Matt was confident everything would fall into a comfortable space once Jan got pregnant and they moved into the family way at home.

CHAPTER 2

"Hey! Matt. Look at this. It's unbelievable!!" Dave was trying to get Matt to look at the screen of his cell phone. He was bored with the maintenance seminar so he was searching the internet with his cell phone browser.

"SSSHHH! Dave! I'm listening to this guy." Matt was intent. He was following every word of the Canadian maintenance expert.

"Look at her boobs Matt. You got to!" Dave was holding the cell phone screen up so high now the guys behind them could see the internet browser photo of the naked woman he had found on a porno site.

Matt glanced over. "Get stuffed! I'm listening to this guy!"

Dave pulled back and dropped the cell phone down to lap level.

"Hey! Mate! Pass it back here so we can get a close-up!" The guys behind were obviously more interested in what Dave had found than his best mate was. He turned and passed it back to them.

"You're gonna get us thrown out of here!" Matt hissed.

Dave was oblivious, since he had now turned around and was whispering instructions to the two guys on how to operate the cell phone.

"So anyways......that's the bottom line. Reliability reduces costs. You need to focus on improving the reliability of your plant and the costs will drop automatically, not the other way around."

Matt jotted down some more notes as Jack, the Canadian maintenance expert, wrapped up his presentation. Matt had at least five pages of handwritten notes from the day long presentation. "That's it!" "Reliability reduces costs, not cost reduction programs!" Matt was so excited he was talking out loud to himself.

"Aw who gives a stuff?" Dave responded. "And the bloody lunch was lame. Too much green stuff. Not enough greasies and meat."

"I give a bloody stuff, but I'm not going to sit here and argue with you. I want to talk to Jack some more." Matt stood up as Jack finished

There was moderate applause from the fifty attendees and Matt joined in as he moved to the aisle to make his way toward the speaker's podium. He was intent on getting some further insight and maybe a plan from Jack on how to help the dairy site back in Mornington.

The day had been amazing. Matt had arrived expecting to hear about kickass motivation rules as Jim had believed, but instead they had ended up listening to a down to earth guy from the paper industry in Canada who talked common sense. The guy was a hockey coach in his spare time. He had a great manner about him and impressed all three of them with his knowledge of the systems they were trying to run at the site. Matt realized the maintenance systems approach Jack was proposing had the potential to significantly reduce breakdowns, improve site performance and most importantly, his personal life. It could mean fewer after-hour callouts, reduced social event cancellations, and a happier Jan. It might even result in some respect for the maintenance department once they got the plant running more reliably. He was more excited about this than anything in a long time.

Matt could see Trevor making his way up the aisle behind him. Trevor had missed the last half hour of the lecture and other lengthy bits during the day. Trevor's cell phone went off frequently and he had rushed out of the lecture hall to respond to what he thought were emergency requests. Matt knew most of them were people at site, like Mandy, the stores clerk, calling up for authorization to release spare parts, supplies or some other permission from Trevor. He wouldn't delegate anything to them. Matt pushed up to the podium where five or six other men were standing around Jack.

Jack finished answering a question as Matt arrived.

"Mr. Clark! Sorry to interrupt, but I've got a quick one for you." The other men turned toward Matt, so he carried on, "What's the first step in getting my site on track with this reliability focus? We need it bad!"

Jack turned to Matt and gave him a knowing nod. "Well, that's a very important question my friend, and it has several answers depending on where your site is at."

"We aren't anywhere, Mr. Clark. We're in a total "circle of despair," as you called it; Tarzan mode, swinging in on the vines from one breakdown to another with a site manager who wants to cut more R&M costs!"

"Please. Call me Jack." He extended his thick hand for a warm handshake.

"Matt's the name."

"Well Matt. Here's what I'd recommend." The five other guys were all listening intently. "You need to figure out where you are right now, and everyone on your site needs to be part of the process."

"Well how do we figure it out?"

"Weren't you paying attention?" Jack jokingly reprimanded him.

Trevor had now pushed alongside Matt and put his hand on Matt's shoulder, whispering, "Matt we've got to go."

Matt shrugged him off. "In a minute, Trev. Listen to this!"

"You and your mates need to do an audit, a maintenance survey, to figure out where you are right now. It's an educational process and it will wake up people in other parts of your business."

"An audit?" Matt realized he must have missed part of Jack's presentation. He hoped it didn't show.

"Yes Matt. I suggest you find someone to conduct a benchmark audit, like I mentioned shortly after we came back from lunch." Jack hesitated, a wry smile crossing his lips. "Or did you nod off on me after all the food?!"

Matt looked down.

Jack continued, "Or you can invite me to your site to conduct the audit, and then we talk about the next steps to reach your goals."

Matt turned to Trevor with a knowing nod. "Trev, you hear this?!"

Trevor was distracted, looking directly at Matt and Jack, but consciously on another planet. "Matt! We need to leave. I've got to pick up the kids from music practice today."

Matt turned back to Jack, ignoring Trevor's plea. "This is good stuff Jack. Just what I think we need to do back at the dairy plant. When could you come by and talk to me, Trevor and the rest of the guys plus the site manager?"

Trevor responded with a long sigh and stomped his right foot angrily.

Jack jerked in surprise, but Matt's reaction was indifferent. He was used to Trevor's tantrums

"Matt! We don't have permission to organize an audit!" Trev protested.

"Shit, Trevor. Jim's the one who sent us up here in the first place! He wants to see some action out of this trip."

"Sounds like you gents need to sort things out first." Jack said with a calming tone of voice.

"Yeah, you're right Jack, but I'm sure we can get it organized. What's your schedule?"

Trevor was practically pulling Matt away now.

"Cut it out Trev!" Matt turned back to Jack. "Can you get to Mornington this Friday noon?!"

"You're in luck Matt. I've had a last-minute cancellation for a paper mill visit near Mornington. So, I could come by. Here's my card with contact details."

Matt took the card as he turned to leave with Trevor. "Count on it, Jack. Friday morning ten o'clock kickoff. I'll get back to you tomorrow."

Trevor was moving rapidly toward the back of the auditorium, where Matt could see Dave waiting near the double door exit.

The drive back to the plant was fairly uneventful, following the initial five-minute discussion when they got to the car. Trevor had reminded Matt, once again, they did not have permission to invite Jack to the site on Friday. Dave reminded Matt they had better put on a better feed than the conference center, or none of the boys would be interested in the program, no matter what Jack had to say. Matt told Trevor they could get the improvement initiative underway there would be an opportunity for Trevor to stop getting all the late-night breakdown phone calls which would keep his wife happier, and Trevor could then roll the program out to other dairy sites around the company and make a name for himself.

Trevor reminded Matt he wasn't interested in making a name for himself and abruptly stopped talking.

Matt spent the remainder of the trip thinking about how Jack's philosophy could make life easier for himself and the boys. Jack was talking about some concepts completely the opposite of the way they did maintenance in the dairy business. Things like "reliability reduces costs," instead of "cost cutting reduces costs." Cost cutting was Matt's reality. Each year in the autumn, when the farmers were expecting an increased payout, or return for the milk they had produced, every manufacturing site went through a cost cutting exercise. It wasn't as if there was a lot of extra cost to save either. Each year, management screwed the budget down tighter than the previous year, and each autumn they expected the site maintenance crew to cut into expenses even further. During Project Blowtorch, some site managers had required maintenance engineers to get permission from the site manager to requisition a light bulb from the stores. Toilet paper was dispensed by the roll instead of by the box. They had stopped doing any maintenance except breakdowns for a period of three months. It drove the payout up as planned, but it was all just a delaying tactic, because when they started up the following season, the neglected plant broke down on a regular basis and the cost of repairs was triple the budgeted expense.

The breakdowns at work were also contributing to the breakdown of Matt's marriage. Matt had been married for four years to Jan, and every year he worked at the plant resulted in less quality time between the two of them. Matt had lost track of how many broken social dates he had instigated at the last minute when he had to "stay back" to help with yet another equipment breakdown. He had missed their anniversary, her birthday, and even Christmas Eve last year. Jan blamed his workaholic habits for their lack of family. She said he was too busy or too tense to make love to her properly and it was the reason they had been unable to have children so far. Matt wasn't sure about her conclusion, but he had to admit he was usually too tired to even think about having sex after finishing a sixty-hour work week.

Matt was amazed by Jack's stories. He told the audience about a plant in Canada where operations treated maintenance staff as equals, where ninety percent of the work the tradesmen did was planned. The opposite of Mornington's performance where they had ten percent planned work which was only during the annual shut. The rest of the year it was one hundred percent breakdown maintenance, sometimes they even had to prioritize amongst simultaneous breakdowns. Jack also talked about reducing breakdowns to one percent or even a half percent of all the work they did. Simply unbelievable! Jack's story sounded too good to be true. It would be interesting to see what Jim thought of Jack's approach and the payback. Matt pondered the dilemma the rest of the way home and imagined a different workplace, as Jack described. It was difficult to fathom, but the clarity of Jack's vision and his sincerity convinced Matt of its potential for the Mornington site.

Matt was busy arranging the chairs in the social club rooms into a theatre style seating arrangement for thirty people. The maintenance engineers were standing in the back of the room near the bar area. The screen was still locked so there wasn't any alcohol available. They were due to knock off at 4:30 pm which meant there was only a half hour for Jack to go over the results of his visit. "Trevor! Are you sure Jim's coming?"

"He said 'Yep.' Ten minutes ago!" Trevor replied.

"Well, we're going to start without him."

"You guys! In the back! Come up and grab a seat we're going to get started."

"Aw….Hell, Matt! Why don't you get Trevor to open the bar?! We'll promise to stay till five if he puts on a few beers now."

"BS! You guys will make a bee line for the parking lot at 4:29 p.m. Don't do it Matt!" Mandy, the Engineering Stores Head Clerk, piped in.

Matt smiled. She was lovely to look at, but displayed a barbed wire tongue for those she didn't like. She sat down in the front row to set a positive example for the rest of the maintenance staff. The tradesmen moved into the back three rows.

"The social club will lose its license if we open early," Trev piped in. He escorted five of the operations managers to seats in the front near Mandy. Trevor turned to Jack, who was waiting near the front of the room, "Ok. Jack. Let's start without Jim."

Jack stepped to the center-front. The wall behind him was a decent substitute for a screen. "Ok. Well. Good to see you all could make it. As you know, Matt and Trevor have invited me to your site to conduct a quick maintenance best practice audit. I'm here to tell you how you scored today, and the way forward, if you choose to go there."

Matt relaxed as he saw Jim Champion duck into the back of the room and move to one of the aisle seats. Jack had a soothing, fatherly way of talking which put people at ease, and he knew the maintenance staff would find his presentation interesting and humorous.

Jack carried on for the next twenty-five minutes, telling stories about best practices companies and situations he'd been involved in, and the difficulty of moving down the path toward a best practice environment. He said it was eighty percent people and paradigm changes and twenty percent technology improvements. He explained everyone, particularly the site manager and CEO and board of directors needed to be committed to the process because it would take additional money and resources to break through the "circle of despair" where the maintenance staff simply responded to breakdowns, did a band aid repair job, and then were doomed to return and repeat the repair over and over without any opportunity to solve the problem and make a proper job of it.

Matt could see the tradesmen were surprised by the stories and examples Jack provided because they were a close description of maintenance practices at the site.

Jack flicked through "before" and "after" pictures of maintenance workshops which had been improved as a result of reliability improvement initiatives. None of them had seen anything like it. Jack finished with an explanation of a typical implementation plan. Getting to an "excellence" ranking would require a commitment of five to seven years because the Mornington site was starting at the beginning. He said there were millions of dollars to be saved by improved R&M efficiency, reduced grade, yield and energy losses, and increased throughput and product mix.

"So, what the hell is our ranking?!" Jim Champion shouted out.

"Sorry Jack. I'm Jim Champion, Site Manager. Just wanted to make sure we were all awake!"

Jack hesitated for a minute.

Matt wondered what Jack was contemplating.

"Ok Jim. Nice to see you here. Well…. I was saving the best for last."

"Are you sure it's the best or the worst?!" Jim retorted.

"I'm sure it's the best you can do with your present leadership and resources."

Ouch! Matt thought. Jack's words had a bite. Good. Jim deserves it, and Jack doesn't act like he cares. He's probably got plenty of other work lined up. It would be nice to be able to tell people to get stuffed. Matt noticed Mandy was beaming at Jack's response.

"What I mean is you must have made a conscious decision to minimize maintenance activities and the pursuit of best practices here because you've scored 19% out of a possible 100%, which puts you in the lowest range of the survey. I've been told the Mornington site has always operated in this manner?"

"Well Jack, I'm not surprised. It's about the score I would have estimated." Jim stood and faced the attendees, "And you're right. We have made a conscious choice to run maintenance at this level in the past."

"Do you have any idea how much the lack of maintenance is costing you?"

Jim cut him off. "Yep. We know exactly, and it had been the price we needed to pay in order to save money for acquisition of other dairy companies."

"But you could have saved more with a reliability focus, and put yourself in an even better position."

Jim looked around the room, gauging the mood. He wondered whether they thought he had the upper hand or whether he should just shut down the discussion. He glanced at his wristwatch and realized it was time for the trades to split. "Hey. Trevor! Why don't you open up the bar? First round is on me! Jack and I will continue this discussion since it's quitting time for the boys."

Matt jumped to his feet, incensed because Jim had cut off Jack's finishing remarks. "Jim, I was hoping the guys here might have some questions for Jack?!"

Jim stared bullets at him, implying the open forum was finished. "Trev, hop to it mate! I can see the boys are thirsty! Jack, I'll join you and Matt for a beer and wrap up of this discussion."

Trevor moved to the bar area in the back and opened the screen guard with one of the fifty keys on his key chain. The trades staff disdainfully rose to their feet at Jim's announcement. The senior tradesmen knew Jim had used the drink offer as a ruse to cut off the discussion.

The operations managers quietly moved out the door and headed back to their offices, happy to be out of the strange, mixed operations and maintenance environment. They seldom worked or talked with the maintenance crew, and they certainly weren't going to socialize with them.

Jim moved to the front of the room and shook Jack's hand as he patronizingly remarked, "Impressive presentation Jack!"

"Thanks Jim, but it's not rocket science."

"So, seriously, Jack. How come it takes so long to get there? We don't have money to burn on a five or seven-year trip to the moon here!"

"You can accept it or not, Jim, but you won't get there any quicker, because you are talking about a lot of change for people around here, and they won't get on board with the program as rapidly as you hope."

"What do you mean?! I'll just tell them and they'll be on board. It's simple!"

"It's not simple, and if you try that approach, it will fail." Matt was surprised to see Jack turning slightly red. "The first thing you have to do is see if you've even got a ghost of a chance."

"And how is that?" Jim had moved closer to Jack, within two feet. He was in his face, invading Jack's comfort zone.

Jack was stoic. "You have to assess whether you've got a culture open to changing their maintenance practices."

"Culture?!"

"Yeah, like whether your maintenance folks are afraid to come up with new ideas, or try a new planned maintenance program. Or even share information with their operations counterparts."

"Well of course they're afraid! If they don't get the job done they'll be down the road! Right Matt?" Jim was smiling again.

Matt wasn't sure if he was serious or messing with Jack. Matt was certain of one thing. People <u>were</u> afraid at the Mornington site. They were afraid of Jim and afraid to try anything new since it might fail and put their job in jeopardy.

"So. What else Jack? What other cultural requirements are there?"

"There's only four more." Jack hesitated.

Matt wondered if Jim would answer before Jack could explain. He was hanging Jim out. Jim didn't bite; he just stared at Jack, smiling.

"Whether you people talk about doing things, and walk the talk."

"Yeah Right! That's two."

"Whether or not you are stuck in the past or are open to new ideas," Jack continued.

"How's that any different than the fear thing?!"

"Way different. You can have a work environment where people aren't afraid of trying something new, but they just never do anything new because they're stuck in a rut of always doing things the way they've always done them." Jack hesitated, waiting for Jim to chime in again.

Matt could see Jim was stymied.

"OK Jack. That's three. We're running out of time. What are the last two?"

"Simple, Jim. Whether you've got performance measurements to encourage change and the right behavior."

"Such as?"

"Such as whether you are measuring your plant managers by the amount of the planned work they promise to complete every day, or whether you are measuring your maintenance and operations people together on a single measure like OEE that drives them to work together."

"OEE?"

"Overall equipment effectiveness. It ties plant availability, quality and plant speed all together. If you measure operations and maintenance people on this, it'll force them to work together not against each other. Which brings us to item number five."

Jim was thinking about Jack's examples.

Matt knew they weren't practicing any of Jack's recommendations.

"The last one is whether or not you are turning friends into enemies."

"What's wrong with that?! A little competition stimulates performance." Jim's answer was no surprise, Matt reflected.

"I'll give you an example, Jim. Mandy, your stores girl, is being measured on how many stock items she can reduce in order to reduce the value of inventory holdings."

"What's wrong? The engineers have put way too much stuff in the store!"

"How do you know how much inventory you should have in there?"

"We've got plenty of local suppliers who can deliver in the middle of the night if we have a breakdown!"

"Just my point. You may not have the time, or that time may cost you a lot more than holding the spare part. The bottom line is what you're asking Mandy to do is making her an enemy of your trades staff because she will be getting rid of parts they need."

Matt could see Jim was getting aggravated with what he regarded as a lecture about incorrect management practices.

"Listen, Jack. It was nice to meet you. I like what you're talking about, the plant running at ninety-nine percent availability, fewer surprises, better quality. I'm just not convinced about the time it takes." He hesitated, glancing at his watch. "I've got to run." He extended his hand to shake Jack's. "We'll be in touch!"

Matt could see it would be futile to try to convince Jim to stay. He knew Jim had a short attention span, and it was Friday. Jim had a favorite pub in the town of Mornington where he could hook up with some of the other dairy executives and board members.

Jack and Matt watched Jim head for the door and exchange a couple remarks with one or two of the trades staff before ducking out.

Matt turned to Jack. "So, what do you think Jack? Have we got a chance here?"

Jack looked down at the floor for a minute, before responding. "Matt, my boy. You've got an uphill battle on your hands here."

"But things could change!?" Matt was deflated by Jack's assessment of Jim's position even though it matched his own. He wanted to salvage some inkling of a chance for the site, for the maintenance department, for his lifestyle and his relationship with Jan.

Matt realized Jack had done his best. The short audit had shown the gap they had with maintenance best practices. Jack's commentary on the cultural challenges at the site was disturbing. Matt didn't fully understand what Jack was talking about, but a couple of the points clearly made sense. The culture would have to change for the program to succeed. Matt walked Jack out to his rental car. He was heading for the airport in New Haven and the eighteen-hour return flight to British Columbia.

Jack tried to encourage Matt, but he suggested Jim was unlikely to endorse or initiate an MBP program on the site. Jack offered Matt a warm handshake and knowing nod as they reached his vehicle. "I'll keep in touch with you, from Canada. I'd like to clarify some of the availability numbers with you as well." Jack climbed into his car and rolled out of the car park leaving Matt standing alone, wondering what would happen next.

CHAPTER 3

Matt heard Moke before he saw him. Matt approached the bottom of the Drier One chamber, and the muffled cursing led him to a well-worn pair of steel-capped boots protruding from under the two-meter diameter duct.

"You sound happy in your work, Mate!"

"Huh?!" Moke grunted. "Bloody Hell! I'll be happy if you are the fairy Godmother who's going to wave a magic wand! I need a day off to go hunting."

"In your dreams, Moke. What's the problem?"

"You know the problem. We keep patching this thing up, making temporary parts, and then the bloody operators don't follow the start-up procedure and wreck everything."

"Haven't the new spares arrived yet?"

"Nope. I stopped in to see Mandy. She said she's trying. And nobody can accuse Mandy of not be a 'try-her,' he added with a chuckle.

Matt smiled. Rumor had it Mandy had posed as a calendar girl for a biker magazine a few years earlier. Looking at her, it was easy to believe her reputation. Now, in her early thirties, the sex appeal was still there, though a broken marriage and two kids had blurred the edges. Matt knew a few of the boys had tried their luck and discovered Mandy was harder to get your hands on than parts for Drier One. "Did she give any indication of when they might arrive?"

"Nah! She just said something along the lines of If Dickhead Trevor had signed off the order earlier, we wouldn't be having this conversation!"

"Okay I'll go and see her. Meantime, what's the situation here?"

"I reckon it's going to take a couple of hours to get this up and running."

Matt looked at his watch. It was just after 5:00 p.m. The machine had been down for an hour and a quarter. He left Moke, and decided to discover the impact of the breakdown on the production schedule. As he walked into the control room, he was greeted by one of the operators.

"Hey! Here's the Tea Boy!" All the operators burst out laughing and raised their mugs in a toast to Matt.

Matt smiled sarcastically.

"We like you maintenance boys. Every time we see you, we know we are in for a nice, long, tea break."

Matt ignored the jibe. "It looks like the drier will be down for a couple more hours. What impact is that going to have on your production schedule?"

"Not good, Matt," Graeme, one of the senior operators, replied,. "We're late on a production run due for shipment tonight. If we miss it, all hell will break loose. We were late on the same customer's last delivery, and he complained directly to Jim. Scott got a real roasting. He's sweating already and won't cover your backsides again."

"Thanks heaps, mate! Just what I wanted to hear." Matt hesitated, making mental calculations. "How soon do we need to get it up and running to make the deadline?"

"Now would be good. 18:00 at the latest."

"Okay. We'll do our best."

As he walked left the control room, Matt reflected on Jack's comments the day before about a 'cycle or circle of despair.' "Hell!" Matt said to himself, "We've got the whole Tour de France cycling through here!" The thought reminded him he had hoped to make his cycling club's 6:00 p.m. evening race. He realized he'd be lucky to get home in time to avoid the wrath of Jan.

Matt phoned a couple of extra tradesmen and between them, Moke and himself, they got the drier going at 6:15 p.m. Matt thanked the boys for staying late and phoned Scott, the Powder Production Manager, at home. "The drier is online and your team are getting it back into operation."

"That's a relief, Matt. But, if we don't get the order shipped tonight, we are in for the high jump."

"From what I hear … our jumps will need to qualify us for the Olympics."

"You're not joking. Is it a permanent fix, Matt?"

"'No. We are making the spares ourselves. Still waiting for the original equipment manufacturer's parts, with the correct metallurgy. It's a miracle it's running at all. I'll talk to Mandy tomorrow to find out where the spares have got to. Meantime, can you talk to your guys about using the standard operating procedures for start-up? They are taking shortcuts which puts extra pressure on the system and increases the likelihood of more breakdowns."

"Yeah, sure, Matt. What if it breaks down again tonight?"

"Get the operators to contact the shift tradesman."

"Matt, you know as well as I do that the shifties can't fix this machine quickly. That only happens when you're here."

"Okay, I'll tell the shiftie to contact me and I'll come out."

"Thanks, Matt. Your blood's worth bottling! Here's wishing you and me an undisturbed night, and let's hope to God we make the deadline."

Before leaving the site Matt stopped by his desk and fired off an email.

Subject: spare parts
From: matt
To: Mandy

I need an urgent update on spare parts for D1. When will they get here? Much more delay and you and I will both be history.

Matt arrived home at 7:20 p.m. He walked through the door and called to Jan. "Hi. Sorry I'm late."

"Where have you been?"

"'I got held up in the plant, fixing a problem with the drier."

"What's new?!" She replied sarcastically. "What I don't get is you are supposed to be the maintenance team leader, which means you should be leading, not fixing? What are those guys doing while you are doing their work? I bet Dave isn't working late? I bet he's down the pub, drinking with his mates."

Matt steeled himself. He could do without an argument with Jan. He knew she had a point, but she didn't understand he felt responsible for the plant and the guys.

Dave was a constant source of irritation to Jan, but Matt was obliged to defend him since they were best mates. He and Dave had grown up together. Their fathers were mates, as well. When Matt's mother died of cancer, Jukka, Matt's father went to pieces, and Dave's father stepped in to support Matt and his family.

Matt and Dave got on at school, but weren't best friends. Dave was the class clown, quick-witted, and a practical joker. He was known as a fixer, able to fix or source anything from bikes to dirty magazines, alcohol, drugs, and party invites. Matt, in comparison, was quiet and kept a low profile. The school principal tried to fix Dave. Corporal punishment with his cane didn't work, and he could never pin anything serious enough on Dave as grounds for his dismissal. Dave left school with no academic qualification, but the life skills to survive.

Matt completed his school certificate, and Dave's dad got Matt hired as an apprentice tradesman after Matt gave up on his professional cycling aspirations.

Dave went bush, making his living trapping possums, hunting, and dealing in a bit of this and that. One deal got him in some hot water with the police. His father bailed him out on a promise he would get a proper job, and it was at that point he joined Matt as an apprentice at the Northland dairy plant.

Matt had accepted a leading hand role at Mornington five years later and Dave quit to work in the bush, once again. A couple of years passed without seeing much of each other and Matt learned that Dave was married with two kids and another in the oven. He needed a job with more stability and income. Matt asked him why he had left the Northland plant, but Dave explained it was best Matt didn't know the circumstances, implying he had learned one of life's lessons.

Matt was reluctant about recommending Dave for a position at Mornington. In Northland, while working at the dairy plant, Dave ran a profitable sideline business doing 'homers,' personal projects, making and fixing anything mechanical, during company time. Dave's practical jokes and irreverent sense of humor challenged the patience of anyone who attempted to manage him. Fortunately, he had a genuine talent for fixing things, and no one could match him as a tradesman.

Unsure about making the recommendation, Matt had turned to Jan for her opinion. Jan disliked Dave, particularly for the practical joke he played on their wedding day. Her elegant departure from their reception had been ruined when the wedding car had backfired, sputtered, and started billowing smoke from under the bonnet. Their departure came to a halt, a direct result of Dave's handiwork. The last thing she wanted was Dave living near them, and she made it clear to Matt that he should discourage Dave's employment at Mornington. Matt countered, explaining the support he received from Dave's father, and that he owed Dave every consideration. A row between him and Jan had erupted, and it still simmered to this day.

Matt let the comment from Jan drop without responding. Instead, he ate the cold dinner she left sitting on the table and fell asleep on the sofa while watching a rugby game rerun. He spent the night there, partly because he wanted to stop any middle-of-the–night calls from the plant awakening Jan and partly because he felt unwelcome in bed. Before nodding off, he reminded himself to remember Jan's birthday party the following Friday. He awoke at 5:30 a.m. and headed to work.

Matt found an email response on the workshop computer when he logged on.

Subject: Spare Parts
From: Mandy
To:Matt

Matt,
Thanks for your chatty email. I wouldn't mind making history with you whilst checking over your spare parts.
The problem has been signed off with Trev the Rev.
Come on over and I'll explain the problem and show you my spare parts.
Mandy x

Matt re-read the email, smiling and groaning simultaneously. He liked Mandy and admired her cheerful outlook and work ethic. But, right now, he needed an answer to his question instead of a flirtatious response. He dialed her number, got the engaged tone, and cursed silently. Looking up from his desk, he saw Moke passing. "Hey! Moke!"

Moke stopped in his tracks and turned toward Matt so he could hear his boss, clearly. Working without ear protection for fifteen years had permanently damaged Moke's hearing, something he was reluctant to admit. "Hi Matt. Good night's sleep last night?"

"Not exactly. I slept with one ear open, waiting for the phone to go."

"I gather it didn't. Did the order get out on time?"

"'I don't know. I haven't got the production update, and I've got a meeting with Trevor, which probably means bad news. I need an update from Mandy on the spare parts, but I can't get hold of her. Could you shoot over to the stores and find out latest?"

"No worries, mate. I've got your back."

"Thanks Moke, and give me a call on the mobile as soon as you get some feedback."

Jim was walking away from the engineering storeroom as Moke approached. He could see Mandy leaning on the counter, glaring at Jim's back. He sensed she was ticked off, and figured he knew the reason. Jim had unsuccessfully tried to have his way with Mandy for yonks.

Mandy was a charmer and loved to get a rise out of Moke or any other tradesmen who came by for spare parts or a chat. When she was angry, everyone knew to give her a wide birth. This morning, her long, lustrous brown hair was tied back, accenting her long neck. She was dressed casually, in tight jeans and a denim shirt with the top three buttons intentionally unfastened. She intentionally leaned forward, exposing her ample cleavage, when she felt like giving the boys a rush. She noticed Moke examining her breasts and gave him a quick wink, shifting out of her angry countenance.

He turned slightly red, realizing she had noticed his gaze "So what do you want sunshine? You know I'll do anything for men with brown eyes!"

Having been caught in the act, Moke replied sheepishly, "Matt asked me to come by and find out when the rush order for the Drier One parts will arrive?"

Dave walked up alongside Moke as Mandy worked with the computer mouse, scrolling on the screen for information about the order. "Hi Mandy. How's it hanging?"

"Hey babe!" Mandy responded, then turned to Moke, "You tell Matt I'd lie on my back to get the order in here faster, but it's not going to be here until Sunday, and we'll have to pay double shipping costs to expedite a Sunday delivery." She could see Moke's mind working and continued, "Tell him I'm sorry, but Trevor's got me between a rock and a hard place. If the plant didn't break down so much, we might have enough stock on hand. Trevor's trying to keep inventory to a minimum to satisfy the accountants."

"Yeah, two or three times out of ten, you're out of the stock you're supposed to have anyway!" Dave piped in.

"Who asked you to show your face so early in the morning? Like, I have time to do a stock take anyway, and you guys are as much to blame as me, and you know it! Every time you come in here, when nobody's minding the store, half of you don't write down what you take. So you guys contribute to the problem as much as anyone!"

"You're right." Dave admitted.

"Matt! Please! You've got to listen to me!" Trevor was frantic, pleading.

Matt was sitting in Trevor's office. He had expected Trevor to ask about last night's breakdown on D1. He figured production must have made the midnight deadline, or Trevor would be squealing for answers. "Trevor, I'm listening to you, but there are more urgent issues to deal with. D1 went down late yesterday and again last night. They lost two more hours of production time. Moke and I patched it up, but it's the last time. If the parts don't arrive before the next breakdown, we are stuffed. We'll be pouring raw milk down the drain!"

Matt carried on before Trevor could reply, "Trevor, I've got to get down to the shop and check on the D1 parts. Moke was supposed to call me, and he hasn't." Matt shut the door firmly and moved quickly down the hall as Trevor stopped halfway around his desk, stammering, gasping for air.

Matt wondered how Trevor ever got to a management position? He knew the answer. Trevor got the role because Jim, and the previous manager, wanted a Yes Man, a human whipping post to beat on when the plant broke down. They wanted someone to muster the maintenance troops to repair breakdowns without complaint as they cut maintenance budgets and demanded service whenever production required.

Jack, the Canadian expert, had explained the repair and maintenance expenditures at the plant had been whittled down below benchmark level. There weren't any other dairy manufacturers, the size of Mornington, operating on such a small budget. He said they were in 'Budget Jail,' since the maintenance department was responsible for the budget, but couldn't control the expenditures.

Halfway to the shop, Matt received a page to the boiler house. Unfortunately, the backup high- pressure feed water pump had failed and the primary pump was unavailable since it had been sent off-site for an overhaul. "Okay. Okay." Matt tried to calm the boiler operator. "I know this is going to shut the site down." Matt walked back to Trevor's office and barged in. Rachel, his administrative assistant, was with him. "Thought you might like to know the reserve feed water pump is down, and the whole site's going down." He held Trevor responsible for this failure since Trevor refused to support an overhaul of both boiler pumps earlier in the year, during the annual winter shutdown. The primary pump had failed two weeks prior, as a result.

"Oh No!" Trevor jumped to his feet and started pacing, frantically. "I'm gonna get screwed over for this!" He hesitated then turned toward Matt. "Matt! I'm holding you responsible for this!!"

Matt was incensed, but didn't want to frighten Rachel with an outburst. He could see she was scared by Trevor's emotional reaction and accusation. "Yeah? Well, that's crap Trev, and you know it. I've got to get up to the boiler house."

Dave was at the boiler house pump platform when Matt arrived. He'd done a preliminary assessment of the pump. "She's stuffed, mate! Bearings are shot and one or two of the impellor stages feel like they're probably rooted. Your maintenance guru, Jack, would be shaking his head."

Sometimes Matt hated the timing of Dave's sarcasm. The boiler house was the heartbeat of the site, and when it failed it brought the driers and the rest of the production lines to a halt.

"We break it. You fix it, and then tea time everywhere!" Dave continued, in mock despair. "Feels great to be on the losing end again, eh, Chief?"

Matt realized Dave was feeling stressed and needed to maintain a sense of humor to calm himself. It was a Northland personality trait. "Can you call Mandy about spares availability, and get a couple more fitters up here to help? Get some bodies up here, while I tell Trev the possible timeframes. It's gonna be eight hours minimum, even if we can Gerry-rig a repair on the impellers and we've got the bearings. I was supposed to be home for Jan's birthday party tonight. Never gonna make it."

Dave took off as Matt walked toward the power house office.

All Matt could think about during the brief walk to the control room was Jan's reaction when he told her the news. She would accuse him of being a workaholic, once again, taking the entire responsibility for maintenance of the plant upon himself. She would suggest the company bury him under a cement slab on the production floor after he dropped dead while in service. It was her usual response following similar last-minute disruptions. No matter often he explained his responsibility, as the leading hand, to ensure a rapid, adequate response, his explanation was unacceptable. She couldn't see his point of view.

Matt sat down with Dave and Moke three hours later in the engineering break room.

"How're the contract pump fitters going on the repair?" Moke asked.

Matt replied dejectedly. "Looks like it won't be back on line till midnight."

"Mate, don't look so sad, it could have been a lot worse," Dave countered. "We did well to get guys who know our gear."

Matt shrugged his shoulders. He was thinking about Jan

"Hey Matt. Why don't we put this place behind us for four or five days?" Moke sensed Matt needed some time with the boys as well as some laughs. "I've got a boat jacked up to take the three of us plus a couple of the boys on a pig hunting trip, up the river. We leave tomorrow at dawn. By morning tea time, you'll have forgotten about this place. A few beers with the boys tomorrow night, and a little sing-song. Trevor and Jim will be a distant memory."

Matt heard what he was saying. Both Moke and Dave had happy-go-lucky attitudes. So what was wrong with them? Or was there something wrong with him? They worked to live, while he seemed to live to work. That's how they'd explained it to him. He imagined Moke strumming the guitar by the campfire, out in the bush, a rabbit or wild pig roasting on the spit and the cold beers, cooled by icy river water. The laughter and camaraderie were tempting.

"Are you guys nuts? Jan is going to roast _me_ when I get home tonight, if she's still there. I was supposed to be at her birthday party hours ago. I was lucky she didn't answer the phone when I called about the breakdown. No way, guys."

"You got to change your attitude, mate." Moke countered.

"Or your missus," Dave added with a knowing nod.

"Yeah. You guys know the score. Maybe next time. Why don't you take off? I'll watch over the contractors. At least only one of us will be in the doghouse." Matt tapped them both on the shoulder as he passed by and dumped what was left of his coffee into the sink as he headed back to the boiler house.

"Hi, Babe." Mandy greeted Matt with a smile as he arrived at the stores' window. She was making preparations to close up for the weekend.

"Have you got the bearings I asked for?"

"Why so serious, Matt?"

"Because you haven't been able to deliver about half the things I've asked for lately. You told me you had them when I phoned a half hour ago!"

Mandy's smile disappeared. Her brown eyes turned steely cold. If Matt was challenging her commitment and ability to run the stores, he was in for some tough feedback instead of the gentle support she was planning to offer. "Now listen, mate, your tradesmen are the ones responsible for most of the stockouts in this store. I do my darndest to cover for their slipups, but I won't allow you to accuse me of not doing my job!"

"You still haven't told me about the D1 parts delivery either."

"Your bloody fitter was in here asking me about it earlier today. What's wrong with you guys? Don't you talk to each other?! I told him it would be Sunday, and he said he'd tell you."

Matt decided to back off. Moke had never told him about her response.

"Ok. How about the bearings?"

Mandy handed them over without another word, and pulled the security fencing down to the window counter with a bang.

Matt walked away with the parts. He didn't have time to smooth things with her. He had to get the parts back to the fitters.

After he left, Mandy stopped at the computer long enough to knock off an email:

Subject: Rotate
From: Mandy
To: Matt

She attached a jpg. of an attractive, clenched, female hand with an extended index finger. She hit the SEND button, and angrily switched off the computer.

Six hours later, a half-hour after midnight, Matt slipped quietly under the sheets. He was relieved the house was dark when he arrived home. Perhaps she wasn't angry? His heart was pumping as he tip-toed inside, slipping off his shoes on the outside porch and undressing in the front room before making his way to the master bedroom. He didn't dare brush his teeth or use the toilet since the noise might wake Jan. She was lying in their bed, facing away from him as he entered the room. Her breathing was deep and regular. He was sure she had been asleep for some time.

Matt felt terrible about letting her down at her birthday celebration. She had turned thirty-two and they were once again the same age, for six months of each year. God! How could he have stayed at work? He should have turned the problem over to Dave instead of feeling obligated to stay on. Maybe he wanted to be a hero, a 'Maintenance Tarzan,' as Jack described? He was thankful Jan was here and not out late. He had to figure out how to resolve the work demands and get his life back in balance and into her good graces.

The pump repair had been miraculously successful, he thought to himself as he settled into the bed. The boiler house was operational, warming up a half hour ahead of schedule, which meant the driers would be back online by sunrise, a fifteen-hour production loss. Diversions costs were probably around fifty grand, but it had been worse on previous occasions.

Maintenance best practices could prevent these events, in the future, but it was an adrenaline rush to get these major breakdowns knocked on the head so efficiently. His chest had swelled several inches when Scott patted him on the back in front of the rest of the operators in the powder plant control room after reporting the boiler house was operational a half hour early. Scott had stayed late, as well, to ensure they were back online as soon as possible. Matt guessed Scott knew his operators would lengthen the breakdown with extra tea breaks, delaying the start-up if he wasn't present.

Scott had explained Jim had been absolutely out of his tree when he heard about the boiler failure. Matt figured there would be a deep reaming for Trevor and repeat threat to contract out maintenance. The contract companies claimed they could improve performance and save money. Matt was sure he, Moke, Dave and the others would be kept on, in any event. They were the ones who knew the plant, and it was only people like Trevor who would get the bullet if maintenance was contracted out. It couldn't be any worse than things were now, he thought to himself, as his eyes began to close.

He felt the sheets rustle as Jan rolled over to face him. His eyes opened, feeling her stare. Her voice was icy, piercing. She hadn't been asleep, just waiting for him to come home and get settled so she could blast him. Though he couldn't see her expression clearly in the darkness, he sensed her rigid, cold anger.

"We were supposed to go out tonight for my birthday. I booked dinner with Kathy and Steve at The Pyrenees Restaurant." She paused for several long seconds. "I'm seriously thinking about leaving you, Matt." She got out of bed and pulled the covers off him as she walked out of the room and down the hallway to sleep in the guest bedroom.

Matt felt chilled to the bone, short of breath. He left a message on her cell phone. When he didn't hear anything back, he thought things would be ok. He was unprepared for her reaction. A sense of dread replaced his feeling of well-being about the breakdown repair. His stomach felt empty as he rolled over and stared at the wall.

CHAPTER 4

Subject: Rotate
From: Mandy
To: Shane

Well Shane, if you don't like my emails, maybe I could just "rotate" on you!

Mandy chuckled as she hit the Send button and fired off her reply to Shane. "Why are all these IT guys such nerds?" She thought to herself. Shane was the site Information Technology support engineer. "That ought to make him blush!" She said to Moke and Dave, who were sipping a cup of coffee at the stores window, early Monday morning.

"Maybe you should take his warning a little more seriously," Dave cautioned. "You know Jim could make trouble for you."

"Oh, heck! He'll never hear about it. Shane wouldn't rat on me. I've got him wrapped around my little finger."

Dave and Moke smiled at each other, knowingly, as they left to deal with the first breakdown of their workday.

Mandy smirked. Shane was a sweetie. Too bad he took offense at the photo and message she had sent to Matt. He was easier to embarrass than anyone on site, and Mandy took pleasure making him feel uneasy, especially with a bit of sexual content added to the exchange. She figured he couldn't be as shy as he suggested. He had a wife and two kids, but like most IT types she had met, he was uncomfortable around other people. Perhaps the reason he was uneasy about chasing her up for violating the company policy.

Christ! Didn't he have anything better to do? She was certain the company created the policy to be politically correct, not because they were planning to enforce it. She was convinced Shane was overdoing it and shouldn't be bothering her.

Shane walked into his office with his morning cup of coffee and pressed the start button on his computer, an act he regarded as essential as the sun's rising. Shane loved IT and working at the site, troubleshooting problems and new projects. He counted himself lucky to have a permanent job at Mornington, after the contract IT company he was employed by for the previous five years went bankrupt. The site IT manager, Ralph, cancelled the contract with his former employer, Computer Cares, and offered Shane a full-time role as a company employee. Ralph had offered Shane the role a year earlier, but he felt guilty considering the option. He thought it was wrong to work direct for the site, when Computer Cares, his employer, would lose out if he took the job. However, it was a moot point, now CC was out of the picture. Ralph was a great guy and he told Shane he was impressed with Shane's performance. On several occasions, he told Shane he was as close to a genius as anyone he'd ever met.

The first item to appear on Shane's morning report was a copy of the email from Mandy to Matt sent the previous Friday. The email had automatically appeared on Shane's daily report due to the filter Shane had installed on all internal IT traffic. Any email with profanity or lewd pictures is automatically routed to Shane and put on hold, preventing delivery to addressees. He decided the message to Matt was important enough to be released, but he also knew he had to talk to Mandy before she got them and his boss, Ralph, into trouble with head office. He scrolled down to the following email from Mandy and turned red when he saw the content. He needed to talk to her immediately. Shane's palms started to sweat, and the computer keys seemed slippery as he typed a response to Mandy.

Subject: I need to talk to you about your email to Matt. I'll be over to see you later this morning. Please don't send any more emails till I see you.
From: Shane

To: Mandy

Hesitating, like a teenage kid calling a girl for the first time, he considered deleting the email before hitting the Send button. Instead, he would call in at the engineering stores window to follow up with Mandy face to face.

Matt walked into the Monday morning production meeting at the same time Shane was wrestling with his fear of confronting Mandy. Scott, Trevor, and several other plant managers were present. Jim, who normally chaired the meeting, was absent. Matt hated the daily meetings because they consistently departed from the agenda instead of dealing with exceptions during the previous twenty-four hours, a fifteen-minute task. The meeting often turned into a bitch session with Jim talking about his latest pet peeve or attacking attendees or others, who weren't present.

Scott started by celebrating the achievement of the D1 shipment, but the good news was offset by the boiler feed water pump failure and fifteen hours of resulting downtime. The entire month's performance was in jeopardy. Jim had gone to head office to plea for additional raw materials in an attempt to increase production output and offset the shortfall.

Trevor stopped tapping his pen on the table top and interrupted Scott. "This sort of thing wouldn't have happened if we were improving our maintenance practices. Like I said on Friday, I'm holding Matt responsible."

Matt looked down as his face flushed. He was incensed. Jan hadn't talked to him for the entire weekend after he stayed late to deal with the breakdown. Trevor never bothered to thank him, and now, in his typical fashion, he was attempting to shift accountability for the failure to Matt. Matt jumped to his feet. "Listen, Trevor! You are the one responsible, not me! We told you both of those pumps were overdue for major overhauls six months ago! You refused to authorize the work because we were over budget!"

Scott piped in, sensing things were going to blow. "Hey guys. Let's chill."

"No way, Scott. Trevor is driving me nuts, and this place is threatening my marriage. I'm not going to allow him to shift the blame!"

"I'm sorry Matt, but the truth hurts sometimes doesn't it?!" Strangely,

Trevor sensed he had the upper hand in a discussion that shouldn't have happened in front of other managers.

Matt got to his feet, fists clenched. He was close to hitting Trevor, but quickly realized Trevor was too pathetic, too pitiful to warrant an attack and loss of his job. It would be unpleasant, unsatisfying. Instead, Matt delivered a more profound blow, "That's it! I've had enough. I'm finished!"

The room's atmosphere instantaneously became heavy, thick with emotion, and an uneasy silence prevailed as Matt backed away from the table. Finally, he turned and left the room leaving the door ajar.

Scott's expression of disgust mirrored the reaction of those who remained. Trevor had blown it. He had surpassed his pitiful reputation for mucking things up.

Trevor's expression dissolved into a half-smile as he glanced nervously around the room, searching for at least one empathetic face. Finally, he heaved a nervous sigh and addressed Scott, "Guess I better try to get him back." He rose from the table, folding his meeting notes, and walked out the door. The remaining staff watched, dumbfounded by Trevor's behavior and the potential of losing Matt.

The workshop normally clanged with the noise of equipment being disassembled and repaired. Hammering and filing sounds frequently drowned out the constant repetition of adverts played by the local radio station. Trevor found the silence chilling as he pushed through the workshop door. He noticed the door of the adjoining smoko room was open where several pairs of blue overalls were thrown on the benchtops indicating the maintenance team was taking a break. Trevor hesitated. Should he go into the smoko room, talk to the guys, or go and find Matt? Going to his office, closing the door and hoping would be the easiest option, but would Matt come to him? He heard the sound of a pair of steel-toe-capped boots heading across the workshop floor towards him. He turned and was startled to see one of the fitters approaching, a wrench tightly grasped in one hand silently pounding a beat into the open palm of his other hand. Trevor stiffened. His tongue felt dry. Unable to speak, he braced himself. A pair of steely cold eyes bored through him, and he flinched as the man lifted the wrench to strike. Instead, the blow was delivered verbally

"Trevor, you are an absolute wanker!" The tradesman known as Crazy Andy turned and walked through the workshop exit and slammed the door shut.

Trevor caught his breath and turned back toward the smoko room, but before the air had reached his lungs, it was knocked out of him by a metallic crash from behind. Involuntarily he swung around, expecting a second confrontation with Andy. Andy's wrench clattered harmlessly after impacting the exterior, corrugated metal wall. Trevor knew the other tradesmen must have heard it, and he felt their watchful eyes, awaiting his next move. Instead of entering the break room to face them and enquiring about Matt, Trevor climbed the stairs to the sanctuary of his office. He closed the door and pushed his desk in front of it, blocking access, before slumping into his chair.

Matt was already gone. A myriad of thoughts spun through his head as he drove home. Should he have quit? What will Jan say? She'll hit the roof, but he didn't care. No. He did care. She wasn't responsible for his work situation. To his surprise, he found himself driving through the gate at home without remembering the drive home. He noticed, with relief, Jan's car was gone.

Walking into the foyer, he saw his cycle helmet lying on the floor. That's what I need, he thought. I need to get on my bike and ride, and ride and ride. Anxious to avoid seeing Jan and the need to explain his presence, he headed to the bedroom to change, as quickly as possible. Five minutes later, clad in lycra riding gear, he loaded his water bottles on his bike, clipped into his pedals, and headed onto the highway.

Three hours later, Matt coasted into the driveway, arching his back, feeling the muscles tighten in his back and legs as he unclipped and leaned the bike against the interior wall of the garage. Peeling off his cycle helmet and running his fingers through his damp hair, he realized his head felt clearer. He headed for the shower.

Matt heard Jan entering the house as he toweled himself dry, fifteen minutes later. He called to her, from the bathroom, "Hi darling, how was your day?" He hoped the tone of his voice didn't betray his trepidation.

"Oh. Hi Matt. What are you doing home so early?"

"I thought I'd get away early and make it up to you, for the birthday botch-up. How about going out for dinner?" Matt knew further explanation would be required.

"I can't. It's my yoga night."

Matt walked down the hallway with a towel covering his athletic, muscular body. He put his arm around Jan's shoulder, pulling her close, and kissed her. "How about giving it a miss and practicing some positions with me?"

Jan pushed away from him. "Your luck's out, mate. Wrong time of the month."

When would she forgive him, he wondered? He badly needed some comfort. He wanted to tell her about the day's events, his feeling of rejection. He needed to talk, but didn't know how to broach the subject. "Oh. Well. Dinner? At least?"

"Matt, I don't want to miss yoga. You can't just come home and expect me to drop what I'm doing. When you are supposed to be here, you are at work and when you are supposed to be at work, you're here. How do you expect me to plan my life?"

"You're right. I'll cook dinner and pick up a bottle of wine by the time you get back."

"Ok," she responded, disbelieving. "That sounds good."

After she left, Matt remembered his mobile phone had rung on the way home, and he had switched it to silent mode without answering. He was curious. He assumed Trevor had called. Switching the mobile on, the familiar electronic voice announced, "You have seven new messages."

The automated voicemail operator recited the familiar introduction, "Message one. Received today at three o'clock p.m."

He sighed at the sound of Trevor's voice.

"Matt. It's Trevor. Matt, I think your decision was a bit hasty. Please call me."

Matt clicked the delete button.

"Message two. Received today at four o'clock p.m."

Matt perked up as he heard a different voice on the recording.

"Matt. Hi. It's Scott. I am sorry about the mess with Trevor. Listen, we know you are doing your utmost. We also know we will sink without you. We don't want you quitting Matt. Trevor realizes he's stuffed up. Give me a call, and let's have a talk about it."

"Message three. Received today at four zero seven p.m." Trevor again. Matt's finger quickly moved across the keypad.

"Mmm …att."

Matt hit delete before message playback was completed.

"Message four. Received today at four twenty p.m."

Matt paced across the room. It was Dave.

"Hey Matt. You missed some action this afternoon. Mad Andy was threatening Trevor with his wrench. The boys are keen to sort him. Trev, that is, but they'd like their Leading Hand's permission. What d'ya reckon?"

Matt smiled. He could hear the grin in Dave's voice. He listened to the message again. Did the team know what had happened? Had Trevor told them? Was that why Mad Andy was swinging wrenches? He tried to picture what might have happened. Trevor had once asked Matt if he thought Andy was a psychopath. He had assured Trevor that Andy was socially withdrawn and under-skilled, but was an extremely diligent tradesman. He had earned the name Mad Andy for occasionally exploding into uncontrollable rage because he had difficulty expressing himself until he was at his wit's end. Matt could only recall it happening twice, and on both occasions, he had endured significant prior provocation. He wondered what Trevor had done to provoke Andy?

"Message five. Received today at four fifty-five p.m."

"Mmm…att!" Matt hit delete again.

"Message six. Received today at five fifteen p.m."

"Hey Matt. I heard you quit. Is that right? Was it because of the parts? Matt, you are the only decent leader this place has. If you go what's the hope for the rest of us? Don't do it, babe. Call me!"

Matt smiled again. So, Mandy was up to speed. She was a very solid stake supporting the networking grapevine If she knew, everyone else would.

"Message seven. Received today at six ten p.m."

"Mmm…att!!!!" Trevor's voice had gone up several octaves. As he thumped the delete button the phone rang, and Trevor's name was displayed as the Caller ID. He quickly switched the phone off.

An hour later, Matt and Jan were halfway through the bottle of Barossa Shiraz and the entre he had prepared for dinner when the house landline rang. Matt cursed as he realized he had forgotten to turn it off. He didn't want any interruptions.

Matt put his hand on Jan's, cautioning. "Let it ring Jan. It's probably work."

"I told Shelly to call tonight. To let me know about a shopping date," Jan responded. "Work would be calling you on your cell phone."

Matt hadn't told her he already switched off his cell phone. "Just wait anyway," Matt said with a nervous tone. "You can call her later. She'll leave a voicemail."

"No. I'll get it. If it's work, I'll tell them you're out, and I don't know when you'll be back."

Matt felt his heart palpitate as Jan picked up the receiver. He knew Trevor would call on the landline after so many unanswered attempts to his cellphone.

"Oh. Hello Trevor," she answered.

Matt's heart missed another beat. He sat motionless; listening to Jan's responses, hoping Trevor wouldn't mention his resignation. He knew he should have been upfront with her, earlier in the evening, but the timing hadn't been right. Another confrontation seemed imminent.

"No, he's not here." There was a pause as Jan continued to listen to Trevor. "Yes, he's been home"

"I don't know when he'll be back, but I expect it will be late. She glanced at Matt and winked.

"No, I don't know where he is. What is this Trevor? Twenty questions? Can't you fix the problem yourself?" Jan paused, listening to another lengthy statement from Trevor.

"He did what?!" Jan exploded, turning to Matt with an astonished look.

Matt cringed.

Jan paused again, listening intently. "No. He did not tell me! If you want to speak to him you can do so, yourself!" She thrust the handset towards Matt, shaking her head.

Matt, stood up, taking the handset from Jan. He whispered, "I'll explain in a minute."

Raising his voice as he spoke into the handset, "Trevor, I am not talking to you now. I'll talk to you in the morning." Before Trevor could reply he placed the handset onto its cradle.

"You quit!?" She blazed. "You quit and you didn't have the nerve to tell me?!"

"I was going to tell you."

"When?!"

"I just wanted"

Jan cut him off, "What? What did you want? Oh, I remember, sex, wasn't it? You told me you had come home to 'make it up to me.' You lying bastard! You came home because you had walked off the job."

"Jan. Let me explain."

"What are you going to explain? Are you going to explain how we can pay the mortgage and hire purchase agreements now that you don't have a job?"

She paused for what seemed like minutes to Matt, and then walked out of the room, slamming the door behind her. The reverberation from the door had not subsided before another crash joined it as the bedroom door slammed shut.

Matt slumped into his chair and reached for his glass of Shiraz.

Ten minutes later the phone rang. "Yes?!" Matt's tone was harsh.

There was a pause, on the opposite end of the line, before a female voice responded.

"Matt? Is that you?" Matt took a deep breath as he recognized Shelly's voice.

"Hi Shelly." Matt took a breath. "How's it going? Sorry about the tone. I thought it was somebody else."

"That's alright. Something wrong?"

Matt forced a laugh. "No. I'm ok. Just been getting a lot of calls from work tonight."

"Oh. Ok. Is Jan there?"

"Yep. She told me you were going to call. Hold on." Taking the handset with him, Matt headed down the hallway and stopped at the bedroom door. He looked at the handset and pushed the mute button. He didn't want Shelly picking up what was going on. He tapped gently on the door. "Jan?"

"Go away!"

"It's Shelly."

The door opened just enough for Matt to hand the phone through.

"It's on mute."

She took the phone without a word and closed the door.

He could hear her talking, animatedly but not loud enough to make out her words. Her tone was aggravated. He returned to the kitchen to clear up the dinner dishes and a night on the couch.

Matt stretched. The combination of a night on the couch and yesterday afternoon's ride left him feeling sore and stiff. He picked up his mobile to check the time, 6:15 a.m. The phone flashed 'new messages.' What to do? Matt asked himself. Start looking for new jobs or go back? He thought about asking Trevor to reinstate him. Nope. Not an option. He thought about finding a new position somewhere else. It could take a while, but he might get some contract work while he was looking. How would he pay the mortgage and hire purchase agreements? Jan was right, again.

His mobile rang. Scott's name showed on the display. He hesitated before answering. "Hi Scott. If you're phoning to tell me D1 is down, I have to remind you I don't work there anymore," Matt attempted a joke.

Scott humored Matt. "You are up early for a man of leisure. How's it feel?"

"Oh, just great," Matt replied sarcastically.

"Not so great here." Scott was sullen. "The best maintenance guy we have just quit. The maintenance manager stuffed up. Even admits it. He asked me to help him get the maintenance guy back. Any suggestions?"

"Yep. Tell <u>him</u> to quit"

"Tempting, but we all know nobody else will employ him and Jim won't sack him. Any other ideas?"

"Nope."

"Seriously Matt. Trevor knows he's wrong and he's prepared to admit it. We need you here." Scott paused, waiting for Matt to respond.

Matt was silent.

"Look. I've arranged a meeting with Trevor for seven-thirty, and I told him I'd try and get you there. Come in and let's talk about it."

Matt was silent for a few seconds before responding, "Scott. Nothing's going to change. Trevor's will whine, moan and grovel and then I'll come back and it'll be the same ole same ole. I want a job where I can control what's happening around me, where I can see results." After a pause he added bitterly, "And where I have a life outside work too."

"I know what you mean. I called the maintenance consultant after you left yesterday."

"Jack?!" Matt was surprised.

"Yes. He phoned from Canada. He wanted some data about plant availability and he couldn't get a hold of you or Trevor, so the receptionist put him through to me. He talked to me about MBP? Maintenance best practice? He said we are in the circle of despair. I told him, he wasn't wrong there! He's got some good ideas about how to get out of it. It's not just about maintenance; it means us production guys have got to get our act together as well. I'll happily support it, but we need someone like you to drive it."

Matt sat up on the couch, in disbelief. Scott barely knew about the program and had left Jack's audit review early with the rest of the production guys. Now he was talking as though he was sincerely interested, volunteering his support. "You forget, driving things is Trevor's job. Fixing his cock-ups is mine."

"I know, and I reckon this guy Jack knows Trevor is a problem. He talked about ensuring the guys who need to make the decisions are allowed to make them. I think with his help, we could work around Trevor."

"It won't happen, Scott. It will just be another flavor of the month and Jim or Trevor will be on to another improvement initiative."

"It won't happen, if we don't try. What have you got to lose? You already quit your job. If you come back, you can give it a go and, if it's not working, at least you can buy yourself some time to find a new position. Come to the meeting at seven-thirty and hear Trevor out?" Scott waited for Matt's response. There wasn't any. "What else have you got planned for this morning?"

Trying to repair my marriage, Matt thought to himself. He knew he didn't have any choice, and this was his opportunity to get back into work and Jan's favor. "Okay, I'll come to the meeting, but right now, I'm not making any promises."

"Great! I'll let Trevor know. We'll meet in my office. That way you don't need to go to the workshop which is buzzing right now."

"Thanks Scott, see you then." Matt stood up and stretched. Should he go and talk to Jan? Was she asleep, or was she awake and brooding? He checked the time. It was 6:50 a.m. He didn't have time for a long discussion with Jan if he was going to get to the dairy site by 7:30. Before leaving the house, he left a note.

Jan,
I'm sorry about last night. I seem to be stuffing up everything. We need to talk. I am going into work to talk to Trevor and Scott. How about meeting for lunch? 12:30 at The Bean? Call me, if it doesn't fit with you, otherwise I'll see you there.
Matt x

When Matt walked into Scott's office both Trevor and Scott were waiting for him.

"Hey. Matt! Good to see you. Do you want a coffee; I was just going to get one?"

"Thanks Scott, that would be good." As Scott walked out of the room Matt turned and looked at Trevor without verbally acknowledging him.

"Matt, I tried to contact you on your mobile."

"Yeah. I know." Matt slid into one of four chairs at a small round table. He sat on the opposite side from Trevor.

"About yesterday, I didn't mean what I said. I mean, I just want to see maintenance best practice go ahead. Please Matt, stay on and be part of it. We can make it work," Trevor pleaded.

Matt thought Trevor had dressed with special care. His shirt was neatly ironed with the collar buttoned down. Even his shoes looked polished. His clothing contrasted with his ragged, pale and drawn expression. His eyes seemed slightly sunken surrounded by two dark circles. I hope I don't look as rough Matt thought to himself.

"Trevor. I need a life. Jan told me she's had enough of my late nights. I don't blame her."

Trevor nodded, "Matt, we can fix it. Why don't you take Jan away for the weekend? The company will pay. You choose where you want to go and enjoy it."

Matt was irritated, "Typical! Another maintenance patch up. Rather than figuring out the root cause of the problem. My marriage requires more than a quick fix!"

"Hold on Matt! I'm offering you a weekend away along with your job back. I could be disciplining you for your behavior."

Scott walked in the room, alerted by the increased level of tension. He warned Trevor, "Don't go there!"

"Trevor's just reminded me he could be disciplining me. He forgot I don't work here anymore," Matt retorted.

Scott realized Matt was about to walk out again.

Trevor, about to speak again, was cut off by Scott. "Matt whether you go or stay is your choice. You know we would like you to stay. What would it take for you to stay?"

"Convince me things are going to change around here."

"I think the guy who can help us find a way to change things is Jack. Why don't we talk to him on the phone and see what he has to say?"

"Okay, but I want to involve a couple of the tradesmen in the discussion. At the end of the day, they're the ones who make this plant tick."

Trevor, leaned forward to speak, but Scott cut in quickly, "Good idea. Who do you want to involve?"

"Dave's the Union Rep. Without his buy-in the guys won't follow. Any of the others will be fine. Andy's an option." At the mention of Andy's name, Matt saw Trevor's expression tighten.

Scott responded, sensing Trevor's anxiety. "Andy tends to be pretty quiet in meetings. How about Moke? He'll say what he thinks and he knows the problems as well as anyone?"

"Moke will be fine, but Andy's got to come along as well." Matt was insistent.

An hour later, Jack was re-iterating the key concepts behind maintenance best practice on the speaker phone to Trevor, Moke, Dave,

Matt, Andy, Scott and several of Scott's assistant managers. Scott tried to get Jim to attend the conference call as well, but was informed Jim was not on site.

Matt queried, "Sounds great. Can you tell me again who's lifestyle we're improving and how we do it, especially if we don't have Jim's support?"

Scott intervened, "You're right Matt. We don't have Jim's support, but some of us production managers do support it, even though we left Jack's presentation early. Graham, from the cream plant, and Colin in the packing area both know things should be running better and they're willing to support the MBP initiative and get Jim on board." He turned to direct his question into the speakerphone at the center of the table, "Jack. What's your perspective?"

Jack responded as though he could read their body language over the phone line. "Let me answer the first question first. We are improving your lifestyle at work and home, and Scott's, and Colin and Grahams, and........even Jim's. Though he may not want it improved. If your plant availability was at 100% or close to it......Would you need to be on call? Would you need to work nights, weekends, or unsocial hours?"

"Hallelujah!" said Dave lifting his hands in the air. "Of course, you wouldn't expect us to work for less than we are now?! After all, we need to be paid more, as we will have more time to spend it. Eh Moke?"

Moke smiled and picked up Dave's thread. "Yeah, there would be helicopters to be paid for so we can go deeper into the bush, new guns, fishing rods ..."

"Okay you guys!" Jack laughed. "You may think I'm joking, but I'm not. The plant availability at your mill is shocking. In theory you produce twenty-four hours a day, seven days a week. In practice, the plant is down twenty-five percent of the time, which means you are actually only producing eighteen hours a day. If you improve the uptime, you would increase your productivity and in turn increase profitability, so there is really no reason why your pay rates shouldn't stay the same even though you are working fewer hours.

"Hey!" smiled Moke, "I am beginning to like this man!"

Jack continued, "But nothing worth doing is easy. Only you guys can make this thing happen. It means changing the way things are done around there."

Moke piped in again. "That's right Jack. And there are some guys around here who like emergency repair work. They get a buzz outa being the hero, and they like sitting around reading the paper when they're not on a breakdown."

"Well, my boy, that will have to change." Jack was resolute.

Looking pointedly at Trevor, Dave cut in again, "Well, it's about time changes were made to the way things are done around here!"

Seeing Trevor lean forward, Scott quickly interrupted and directed his comment to the speakerphone again. "Jack, you didn't answer the second part of Matt's question. How do we improve plant availability?"

"I'm not sure I'm the right person to answer that question," replied Jack. "The guys who are best able to answer it are the people who work on it, day in and day out like Moke and Dave. What do they think?"

Dave retorted leaned forward toward the speaker, for emphasis. "Seeing as you have asked, here's my thoughts. The problem at the moment is we just go from one job to another based on who shouts the loudest, or what has broken down. We get to a job and we don't have the parts, so we can't do anything, or we do a temporary fix. Then we get called to another part of the plant for another breakdown. We walk miles every day, back and forth. It keeps us fit but it doesn't get us anywhere. We never get any time to do any preventative maintenance; it's like running a car, but never checking the petrol, oil or water levels. We just wait for the car to stop running and then fix what's broken as a result of not checking. We have an annual shut, when the plant stops running and we should do a major overhaul, but there is no plan so we spend half the time working out what should be done and the other half trying to get parts. I bet we even fix a bunch of things that don't even need fixing and then they break down on startup because we haven't done the repair right, or it wasn't even needed!"

Moke nodded his agreement.

Jack summarized, "So, from what you have told me you are in a vicious circle that keeps feeding on itself?"

Moke and Dave nodded back and then Dave said, "Yes," remembering Jack couldn't see them.

Jack continued, "You need three things to start with. A good planning system enables you to routinely do preventative maintenance without interruption. A plan for your annual shut, which is developed prior to the shut, so parts can be ordered in preparation and you do the right work on the equipment that needs work. Parts readily available when you go and work on a piece of equipment you take the parts with you."

"Choice," Moke said sarcastically. "Matt did get a planning system in place for routine preventative maintenance, but it didn't work. When Production see you in their area, they grab you and give you a whole list of things to do instead. Before you get to doing what you went up there for, you have a heap of other jobs."

There was a pause while Jack waited for a response. Nobody said anything.

Scott piped in. "Carry on Jack. We're all in agreement here."

Jack resumed. "That's good to hear Scott, and I am sure you have often asked the maintenance guys to do work, without a work order?"

Scott nodded and replied, "I have to plead guilty, but in my defense, it's easier to grab them while they are there than submit a work order and wait."

"Understandable, but the problem is while they are dealing with a low priority job, they aren't getting time to do preventative maintenance, which in turn leads to major failure and off we go into the circle of despair."

Scott replied, "I understand. But if we submit a work order for a non-priority job, we can wait for weeks to get it done. Most operators put it as a high priority just to make sure something happens."

Jack interrupted. "The question is how do you break the cycle? I've got a presentation here showing how a manufacturing plant in Minnesota has reduced their plant breakdowns from 20% to less than 3% of their work orders. Too bad I'm not there. I'd like to show it to you. You would appreciate how they did it."

Scott broke in again. "Jack, it sounds like there's quite a bit of support here for the Maintenance Best Practices program."

"Yeah. More than I thought when I left your site."

"I suggest we cut this conference call short and talk about support from Jim Champion to get you back here."

Everyone around the table nodded their agreement except for Trevor, who looked agitated.

"That's fine Scott. Let me know when you're ready and I'll jump on a plane."

"Ok Jack. We'll be in touch."

The rest of the men shouted their farewells and Scott punched the 'Off" button on the speakerphone.

He turned to the rest of the group. "I like what I've heard, and I think Dave and Moke would agree. If we had those systems in place, we could make this place fly. But to get there we need resources, people to deal with the backlog of work and develop the systems. We also need someone to drive it. All that means dollars and time and investment in maintenance which has never been a priority."

"Too right, mate!" Dave agreed.

"I've already spoken to Jim. He's agreed to support the project," Trevor broke in.

Up to this point in time, everyone in the room had forgotten Trevor was present.

"What are you talking about Trevor?" Scott couldn't believe what he was hearing.

"I had a quiet word with Jim after Jack's presentation here on site."

"He hasn't said anything about it to the operations managers." Scott challenged.

Trevor leaned forward confidently. "I told him I needed to get you guys and Matt on board first, before he made any announcements. Jim gave me a week."

Trevor was disgustingly smug, as though he had orchestrated things.

Matt hated Trevor and his unwarranted self-confidence.

"Jim wanted me to get some more data on our plant availability and the payback. Jack emailed the info to me yesterday," Trevor explained. "The numbers will show this project needs to go ahead. Jack said we could save over two million dollars a year once the program was in place. It will take us several years to put the foundation in place to get the improved performance. I didn't want to broadcast this till we knew we had a case."

The bloody weasel! Matt thought, he was about ready to leave again. Two million a year! He reckoned it was possible based on the other examples Jack had discussed at the seminar, probably twice as much.

"You say Jack's numbers leave no doubts the project should go ahead, but has Jim seen Jack's latest estimates? How are we going to pay for the high-priced consultants and other project expenses?" Scott was challenging Trevor again.

"I've got some money I've held back in the maintenance budget, which will help get us started."

Dave opened his mouth to challenge Trevor, but before he could say anything Matt shook his head.

"When do you expect to meet with Jim, Scott and the rest of us?" Matt queried sarcastically.

"Jim's scheduled a meeting for tomorrow at 10:00. Jack can phone in to support the discussion," Trevor replied.

"Well, things are moving a lot faster than I was aware." Scott pushed his chair back from the table, checking Matt's reaction along with the rest. "Matt. What are your thoughts? If Trevor and Jack are able to get Jim to commit funding and support will you support it, along with Dave, Moke and the rest of the guys? You've got operations management behind you, at least at my level." Scott was hoping Matt was ready to come back to work.

"Yeah, it's worth a shot. We've never had operations support before. We shouldn't let the chance pass."

"We need you to lead us." Dave was applying direct pressure. He playfully pushed Matt on the shoulder.

Moke caught Matt's eye and nodded, "If you don't it's going to be another Bohica."

"Bohica?" Scott queried.

"Yeah. Bohica. Bend over. Here it comes again," Moke explained.

Dave and Matt looked away, slightly embarrassed at Moke's remark in the presence of Scott and Trevor.

"It's what managers do to us workers. Ask us to do something without enough resources, time or money. Setting us up for failure."

"Moke's right, Matt. They all need you," Trevor piped in.

There was silence as everyone in the room waited for the impact of Moke's explanation to sink in, and for Matt to make a decision.

Matt looked downward, pondering the options. There was a hint of hope. He despised Trevor for making a secret approach to Jim. Returning to work at the site would alleviate some of the tension at home. He didn't have any confidence Trevor would get Jim's agreement, but Scott was committed and he respected Scott and his ability to get the other operations managers on board. Jack's involvement was essential. He pushed back from the table, heaved a sigh and said, without looking up, "Alright."

There was a palpable sense of relief amongst some of the men.

"I need to get on to another meeting," Scott said as he got to his feet, directing his comment toward Matt instead of Trevor. "Keep me in the loop and I'll support you any way I can."

Dave stretched and turned to Moke, "Come on bro, we have things to do." Turning to Matt he added, "You heading back to the workshop then?"

Trevor interrupted. "Matt, I'd like to have a word with you before you go."

Matt rolled his eyes at Dave and Moke. "I'll catch you later."

After everyone had left the room, Trevor stared at Matt imploringly. "Matt. We can make this work."

"Trevor. That's easy for you to say. You accused me of incompetence in front of the entire Production Team when, as you know full well, the situation was completely outside my control. I work endless hours to keep this plant running. I stuffed up the weekend with Jan. She is threatening to leave me and I don't blame her. I may have to live with being made an idiot here at work, but I don't have to look like an idiot at home as well." He caught himself and checked his watch as he remembered his lunch date with Jan. 11:45....Shit! He needed to wind up this discussion.

"Matt. With MBP it will all be different. Jack's going to come back and help us. Please. Take a long weekend this weekend and I'll pay. It's time you were recognized. I'll get fifteen hundred paid into your account. Take Friday and Monday off and you and Jan go away and do something special."

Matt was half out the door. He turned quickly to respond, "I'll stay, for now, but I'm not making any promises. Meantime, I'd like the rest of the day off, I've arranged to meet Jan for lunch."

"You go Matt. I'll see you tomorrow. Give my regards to Jan."

Matt nodded and left the office. The hell he'd give Trevor's regards to Jan. Heading out of the office and across the car park he switched on his mobile, hoping there would be no messages, confirmation Jan would be meeting him for lunch.

His phone beeped signaling waiting messages as he hustled toward the parking lot. He pushed the voicemail retrieval button.

"Message received today at 10:27 a.m. "Hi!" Matt froze for a second, hearing a female voice before the word "sexy" followed. He was relieved and disappointed simultaneously. Relieved it wasn't Jan canceling, but disappointed it was not Jan calling him sexy.

"How are you, mate? I hear you are on site, does that mean you're staying? Come on over and I'll give you a good reason to." A throaty chuckle followed. "I've got something here you want badly." Matt smiled. Mandy was incorrigible, but it was good news if the spare parts had arrived.

Driving into town, Matt thought about the conference call discussion and Trevor's revelation. Jack had made a lot of sense and it was interesting to hear about the results achieved at the Minnesota plant in the USA. Dave and Moke had been impressed. They would get the other tradesmen behind them. Where had Trevor come up with money? The guys were desperate for tools, and Trevor had argued they were short of discretionary funds. Now he wanted to give Matt fifteen hundred dollars as well as having funds to pay Jack. No wonder Dave had nearly jumped across the table. Matt's thoughts returned to the bonus. Part of him wanted to throw it back at Trevor, but why shouldn't he take it? He had earned it. If he had been a tradesman he would have earned it in overtime just this month.

Pulling up outside The Bean Café he was pleased to see Jan's car parked nearby. He combed his hair and checked himself in the rear-view mirror. He was a bit dark around the eyes but apart from that, he looked okay. He thought about the weekend, the money and the fact he had his job back. Jan would be pleased. Standing tall, he pulled his shoulders back tensed his firm stomach muscles, smiled to himself and walked through the café door.

The first thing he noticed was the sound of Jan's laughter. He spotted her across the room sitting in a corner alcove. As he crossed the room, he could see her talking animatedly to someone who was out of view. As he rounded the corner, he noticed her companion was a guy wearing a track suit.

Jan moved her focus from the stranger toward Matt as he approached. "Hi. Matt. This is Wayne. Wayne. Meet Matt."

Wayne didn't bother standing up and offered Matt a limp handshake. "Hi. Matt. How you doing?" He had a lazy, confident manner.

"Uh, fine," Matt replied, looking quizzically at Jan.

Jan explained, "Wayne's my personal trainer."

"Oh. I didn't know you had a personal trainer."

Jan's eyes rolled to the ceiling in a rapid, exasperated expression. "I told you I had a personal trainer a month ago." She looked apologetically at Wayne and then back at Matt. "As usual you were probably preoccupied with some work issue and didn't hear me?!" She looked back at Wayne and got an acknowledging wink Matt didn't catch.

Matt recovered slightly, "I'll get myself a chair." Turning back towards the door, in search of a chair, Matt contemplated walking straight out of the café. Bullshit! If she had told me about her <u>male</u> personal trainer he would have remembered. He walked to a nearby table and picked up a spare chair and turned back to join them. "So, umm have you and ......ordered anything to eat?" Jan's trainer's name had gone clean out of his head.

"Wayne and I had a smoothie when we got here. We've got a gym session at one o'clock so we won't have anything else, but you go ahead."

Buying a bit more time, Matt walked to the counter. He looked at the food in the display case and pretended to glance at a menu. He had lost his appetite. 'Wayne' and 'smoothie' were sticking in his throat.

The girl behind the counter interrupted his thoughts, "Can I help you?"

"Yeah! Black coffee; double shot please." He paid and returned to the table.

Wayne leaned forward toward Matt. "I hear you work at the dairy plant."

"Yep."

"Rather you than me." Wayne responded with a lazy grin. "From what I hear it's pretty grim."

"It's not that bad," Matt said defensively, but at a loss to explain why he was defending Wayne's criticism. "We've got a great bunch of guys and the pay's good."

"Well. I prefer being surrounded by gorgeous chicks, myself," Wayne replied giving Jan an appraising look.

Matt noticed Jan blush. He had just about had enough of this guy.

Jan could see Matt was biting at Wayne's baiting comments, and decided to deflect the conversation. "What happened at work this morning?" she demanded, taking the offensive. "You and Trevor make up?"

Matt was irritated she was bringing up the subject in the presence of Wayne. "Yep. Old happy chappy and I have made up. What are your plans for this afternoon?" He was trying to deflect any more discussion about the work situation.

Jan ignored the enquiry. "After my gym class, I'm meeting up with Kathy to do some shopping. I'll be home around five. What time will you be home?"

Matt hesitated. No point in telling her he had the afternoon off now. It would make him look like a loser. "I'm not sure, should be around the usual time."

"Okay." Jan replied, looking at her watch and then Wayne. "We'd better get going. I don't want us to be late for our session."

"I'll hitch a ride with you." Wayne didn't offer his hand to Matt as he turned to go with Jan. "See you around Matt."

Matt watched them head out of the Café. Did he see Wayne put his hand on Jan's waist as they went through the door? No! He was imagining it. He was certain. After they left Matt ordered himself a second coffee, double shot. What the hell was that all about? Is Jan having an affair with the joker? Smooth, alright. Surely Jan could see through it. Was it a ploy to avoid talking to him or a ploy to make him jealous? What next?!

CHAPTER 5

Jim Champion's daughter, Candace, could hardly contain her excitement as she walked out of Libby Galwaith's office at VFM. She was energized by her conversation with Libby, her new boss at VFM's Contract Maintenance Services division. Not only was Libby a drop-dead gorgeous woman in her late twenties, she was also an expert in her field, maintenance best practices and financial analysis. No wonder VFM had picked Libby to head their regional office. Candice planned to call her dad as soon as possible. She was certain he could use Libby's help to improve performance at his dairy plant.

Candace owed her good fortune, like so much else in her life, to her dad. She had graduated from university as a mechanical engineer a year earlier and was already employed in a consulting role with VFM, one of the most prestigious engineering firms in the country VFM did a fair bit of business with her dad's company and her dad had organized an interview with VFM's managing director following her graduation. The interview lasted about fifteen minutes before Candace was offered the job. She figured the director must have been impressed with her grades and a degree from one of the best engineering schools in the country.

Candace felt on top of the world as she returned to her cubicle in the central engineering offices. If she could talk her dad into using Libby's services it would be another kudo for her fledgling career at VFM. She would call her engineering mates from Uni to celebrate with a bottle of champagne or two if she could pull it off. She opened her notebook to review the things Libby had outlined for a pitch to her dad and picked up the phone.

Jim Champion turned toward the ringing phone on the credenza behind his desk. Kay, his personal assistant was seated on the opposite side of the credenza. He motioned for her to pick up the phone and she quickly rose from her chair to rush around Jim's large desk to the phone which was within Jim's reach. Jim's office furniture was intentionally arranged in a configuration to put visitors at a disadvantage. The chairs on Kay's side of the desk were six inches lower than Jim's chair, and the rimu desk was set in the middle of the office facing the door, a barrier between him and those seeking his approval. Behind his high-backed leather chair was a matching rimu credenza placed against the wall with an assortment of ornamental gifts from vendors and company customers.

The phone was placed next to an ornately painted vase, depicting Japanese garden scenes, a gift from one of the company's Japanese customers. Jim felt the vase represented the elegance and grandeur Jim associated with his role. He planned to ask his Japanese customers for a pair of samurai swords the next time gifts were exchanged. Mounted on the wall, above the vase, they would convey a powerful, intimidating effect.

"Hey mate, how's the new job?" Jim answered cheerfully at the sound of his daughter's voice as Kay handed the phone to him with a whisper about the identity of the speaker. He waved Kay away with the back of his hand, and she nodded obediently and left the office.

"Dad! You're not going to believe what's going on! I'm working for the most fantastic woman I've ever met!"

"Is she a knockout?"

"No, dad! I mean yes! Yes, she is a knockout, but that's not what I mean. She is the most intelligent, persuasive woman I've ever met, and I think she can help you at the plant."

"And what makes you think I need help here, babe? You know I'm the greatest!"

"Dad, I know. But I also know you get a lot of calls at home and on the weekends when the plant is broken down. Libby, my manager, she's the head of VFM's contract maintenance division. She's an expert on reliability. She has helped companies in the UK increase their plant availability to world class levels of 99% before she came here six months ago. She knows what it takes; preventive maintenance, planned and scheduled maintenance, root cause analysis, everything!"

"Ok. Ok." Jim cut her off.

"Seriously Dad, all you have to do is talk to her on the phone. I know you can use her there. Please, just have a chat with her."

Shit. Jim thought to himself. He had Scott, Trevor and his Canadian mate, Jack, talking to him about maintenance best practices tomorrow morning, and now his daughter was bugging him about it. Libby sounded yummy though. Out of the corner of his eye, he could see Kay trying to catch his attention through the glass side-panel at the doorway. Scott, the powder manager, was standing behind her.

"Dad! Listen to me! Libby has not only increased plant availability, but she has saved twenty-five percent of maintenance costs in the first year at three of the UK sites where VFM was the contract maintenance provider. The principles are the same here as there. You really need to talk with her. It could help you."

"Listen Sweetcakes. I hear you, but I've got a busy schedule. I'll think about it. Maybe we can talk some more this weekend when you come over to the house. Are you bringing Graham? I saw him walking by my office yesterday. He seemed kinda down."

"Yeah. No, Graham's ok. Ok you promise we'll talk about Libby this weekend ok?"

"Yeah mate. Gotta go now. Love you."

"Ok dad. See you this weekend. Bye"

Jim waved Kay and Scott into his office. Twenty-five percent reduction in R&M costs in one year. Sounded too good to be true, he thought to himself.

Jim spun around in his swivel chair to face his visitors.

"Scott thought you should see this."

Scott was standing alongside Kay and explained his interpretations of the memo as Kay handed it to Jim. "It's a press release from the board. They've announced a ten percent reduction in payout to shareholders due to the commodity price drop in the international market and the strengthening of our dollar. It's probably going to result in some pressure to cut costs."

Jim glanced at the memo and spun onto his desk, like a frisbee. He was ticked off Scott and Kay had the information before he did. He was supposed to get all important memos first, before anyone else on the site. He decided not to growl Kay for the slip-up. The note must have come through from the Board Chairman while he was driving back from Mornington earlier in the morning. Funny, the CEO hadn't mentioned it while he was in town. Jim wondered if the CEO, Colin Gray, was withholding information from him, intentionally. "Hmmm, sounds like you could be right, Scott. What's the fuss? What's the rush? We've heard things like this before." He intentionally minimized Scott's assessment.

Kay was backing out of the office as she sensed there might be a confrontation, which occurred frequently in Jim's office.

"Yeah. Usually, I wouldn't have reacted as quickly, but my first thought was about the impact of cost cutting on the maintenance best practice program approval you gave Trevor last week?"

"Oh Shit! He finally told you? You guys need to trust me."

"Yeah, Jim. But for the first time in my working life at Mornington I actually believe we can reduce all this reactive behavior around plant breakdowns. Jack's got some pretty interesting data about turnarounds at sites he's worked at, in North America, but it's going to take four or five years, not twelve months."

So, Scott is a convert Jim surmised. "Hey, I know all about this stuff. You don't have to remind me." Jim couldn't believe people kept forgetting about the breadth of his experience. "I told Jack and Trevor I was committed to the MBP work. I wouldn't pull the plug just because of a memo like this. We'll hold fire till I hear something from the CEO in person. If they want to cut costs, we'll look elsewhere. I promise. I'm the guy who sent Trevor and Matt to meet Jack in the first place. Remember?"

Scott relaxed, slightly. "That's great to hear, Jim. I was worried we'd cave in too quickly if the command to cut costs comes through. I've got some of the supervisors in powder excited about the MBP program and I made a personal promise to Matt to promote and support this to get him to come back to work. I don't want this to look just like another flavor-of-the-month program.

"Matt coming back to work? Did I miss something?"

"No big deal. Just Trevor ticking Matt off, again." Scott didn't want to go into detail about how close they had come to losing Matt permanently. "I'm glad to hear of your support," Scott finished.

Jim smiled to himself. "That's right Scott, just hold fire. Keep up the good work. Good job meeting the powder delivery in spite of the breakdown on the drier." Jim turned around to face his computer screen on the credenza as he spoke.

"Thanks Jim, but it was Matt's who got the problem knocked off in time to complete the order."

Jim had completely turned his back to Scott as he clicked on an email from his daughter. "Ok Scott. Anything else?"

"No. I think I'll head over and reassure Trevor, Matt and the guys before they see the memo from the board and start jumping to conclusions. Conference call with you, them and Jack tomorrow at 10:00 a.m. still OK?"

"All right mate, you do that. Yep. Ten tomorrow morning." He waved to Scott without turning around and leaned forward, toward the computer screen. He clicked open the email from Candace as Scott closed the door.

Subject: Libby's Phone Number
From: C_Champion@VFM.com
To: Jim Champion

Dad. Here's Libby's number; 03 434 2962
Email: Libby.Galwaith@VFM.com
Call her!! You'll be glad you did! See you this weekend!
Hugs. C

CHAPTER 6

Subject: Parts Order
From: Mandy
To: Matt Polaski

Hey babe. No emergency part requirements? No emergency "services" required for you from me?! I miss you. See the attached for how much.

Shane was at his desk, looking at Mandy's email which had been identified automatically in the email management system as a violation of company policy.

Mandy's attachment showed a photo of a striking blonde model standing next to a roll-away tool box with mini-short cut-offs, high spike heels and her body posed in an inviting position with bare breasts exposed. It was an advert for the roll-away tool box company which Mandy must have picked up from one of the sales representatives.

"She can't be doing this again! Not after I told her." Shane was incredulous. He'd warned Mandy about the company policy and potential dismissal a week ago. Shane picked up the phone and dialed Mandy's number.

"Shane! Come and give me some loving babe!" Mandy was prepared after seeing Shane's name on her phone's caller display.

"Mandy!! I just saw the photo you attached to your email to Matt!"

"So! What? You're not supposed to be looking at my emails, anyway! What are you some sort of pervert?!" She tried to dismiss his warning.

"No, I'm not! And if you keep talking to me like that, I'm going to turn you in."

"What are you talking about babe?" Mandy softened her tone.

"I'll come down and show you myself. Obviously you aren't getting the message."

Five minutes later Shane was standing next to Mandy at the engineering stores counter. She was pressing her breast against his side, feigning innocence, as he logged onto her computer with his own log-in credentials.

"See. This is what comes up on my screen when I log on and auto-alerts come through on emails like yours."

Mandy leaned closer, pressing. "So, what is it?"

Shane stepped aside, intentionally removing himself from contact with her and pointed to the screen from behind her. "It's IT alerts I have to respond to and the ones on top are always the ones who have to do with miss-use of the company's system."

Mandy acted concerned. "So, what do you do when you see these?"

I'm supposed to check them out and see if there are any policy violations or if it's just an error generated by the automated mail management system."

"And if it isn't an error?" Mandy was now gently clasping Shane's right forearm, in a gesture of contrition and concern.

"Then I decide whether it's a violation of the company standards and I refer it to the HR manager."

"And then what?"

"And then the person either gets a warning or gets the sack." Shane turned to look Mandy in the eye and pushed her hands away. "I can't protect you on this, Mandy. I'm risking my own job by ignoring it. You remember what happened to the cream plant operator who was logging onto porn sites last month don't you?"

Mandy nodded. "Poor Joker."

"He got the sack," Shane reminded her.

Mandy sat down on her chair. Lucky no one was at the counter to hear this conversation she thought. She would have cut it off earlier if there had been. Shane was sweet for covering for her. She appreciated his protection and concern especially since he wasn't interested in getting into her pants like most of the blokes. The company was blocking what little fun she thought she could have. How would she be able to 'wind up' Matt, test him for a response to her interests, if she couldn't do it on the email system? It didn't work trying to do it directly with him, face to face. There were too many other eyes watching. Emails seemed to be the only avenue where she was going to be able to let Matt know she had a crush on him and wanted to do something about it, especially since things weren't going so well at the house, with Jan. "A girl just wants to have fun!" Mandy exclaimed.

Shane turned to leave, dejected since she had fobbed him off. Again.

Mandy jumped up and grabbed him by the arm. "Hey."

Shane stopped, listening.

"I really appreciate what you've done for me."

She seemed sincere, but he hesitated.

"I'm serious. You've been taking a risk for me, Shane. I didn't really understand how much."

"Well, I hope you do now."

"I do. I won't put any more attachments like this in the system, and I'll try not to say things that are wrong. Thanks for watching over me. Mandy sensed Shane had accepted her apology. She pressed her body up against his in a warm hug. "Friends?" She asked.

"Yep." Shane gulped, pulling back. His face was bright red.

"Thanks Mate!" Mandy smiled and gave his shoulder a pat as he turned to leave.

"Hey!" Shane remembered, "Don't forget to restart the computer with your logon. I don't want you trying to snoop through any other stuff." He should have logged off, but was too embarrassed to turn around and go back to the workstation.

"You got it." Mandy smiled as Shane turned toward her as he stepped out the exit.

CHAPTER 7

Subject: Shareholder Dividend Announcement
From: Colin Grey — CEO
To: Site-wide Distribution List

As you all are well aware, the shareholder dividend reduction of 10% is going to create severe pressure at the Board level for action. I would appreciate your thoughts.

Jim pushed back from his computer and spun around in his chair. The office door was closed, but he noticed Trevor and Scott walking by in the hallway, gesturing energetically. They didn't look through the window toward him. "Limpdicks!" Jim said out loud. "Those guys don't have a bloody clue!"

He'd just finished an hour-long conversation with Libby Galwaith about Mornington's maintenance best practices program. He was convinced VFM was a better choice than Trevor and Jack's approach. Libby suggested a twenty-five percent reduction in maintenance costs was achievable in the first year, worth two million dollars. A huge offset to the proposed ten percent dividend reduction. Libby sounded hot, as well. She was confident, sophisticated, and professional with youthful enthusiasm and energy. Jim found her English accent and extensive vocabulary sexually appealing.

Jim had been thinking about ways to get a jump start on cost savings at the plant since Kay and Scott had confronted him earlier in the day. The site manager who came up with the most aggressive cost savings program, at any of the company sites, would receive substantial recognition from Colin Grey and the board of directors. Jim's VFM idea would be the most aggressive suggestion, and he needed to act immediately. He was convinced he could persuade, or coerce, the other Site Managers to contract out to VFM once he proved its success at Mornington. He would run a trial of the concepts at the Mornington site, and then convince Colin to move it to other sites. He would be recognized as the person who had come up with the single biggest cost savings idea which could increase his chances of stepping into the General Manager's role when the incumbent GM, Graham Chambers, retired. At present, Graham wasn't supporting Jim's ascendency to replace him. This initiative would clinch it with or without Graham's support.

Jim reflected about his daughter's advice. She was a champ. She had finally come through for once, instead of draining off money or asking for advice about what to do next. He reckoned there was hope for her. Maybe she wasn't such a wimp after all, like her mother.

Jim propped his feet up on the table, cracked his knuckles and indulged himself in further reflection. He had been married to Sharon for twenty years. They had one daughter, Candace, and a son, sixteen-year-old Brent. Both of the kids held him in high esteem. They were spoiled, enjoying a childhood full of life's advantages as a result of his success in the dairy industry.

Jim hadn't always enjoyed a successful lifestyle and he wondered if some intentional deprivation for his own kids would help them develop more grit. His high school grades hadn't been crash hot, and his dyslexia contributed to a failure on university entrance examinations. He kept the dyslexia a secret at secondary school through an elaborate process of plagiarism and networking and continued using the same strategy in his professional career. He disliked university graduates. He had spent a couple of years at the local polytechnic institute and then pursued an extra-mural business certificate program which he promoted as a master's degree equivalent. During the course of his business studies, he was arrested while driving under the influence of alcohol, and subsequently had to be driven to the extra-mural night courses. His personal assistant provided the chauffeur service and assisted him with course work, typing papers from recorded dictation or directly from himself, during working hours.

He realized his children were puzzled by the fact their father was unable to help on their homework assignments, particularly written exercises. He always made a point of telling them it was their mother's job to help them with their school work. He had been busy most of the kids' lives. They had taken family vacations twice in twenty years, a trip to Aussie and a trip to Fiji. He had been unable to shake his apprehension about plant performance during both trips. When he returned a week earlier than planned he found his fears justified. It was difficult to find people he could trust to perform at his level. He let Sharon do the book keeping, cheque writing for the household. She also wrote all the Christmas cards single-handedly. The kids learned these things are not a man's work.

Jim participated in a number of extra marital affairs, which he knew Sharon was aware of. He was entitled to have these affairs as they were part of a powerful man's world. He always came home to her, so she had nothing to complain about. The dairy business was a good life in spite of the demands and challenges. He was required to be at the office six days a week and to call into work on the seventh day to ensure his site was getting the maximum amount of milk to meet or exceed production targets. He bullied tanker dispatchers into sending milk to his site ahead of other sites.

Jim had missed fifteen of twenty wedding anniversaries along with children's birthdays and other family events because of plant crisis he needed to personally resolve. He always told Sharon he would make it up to her, which simply meant a dozen roses delivered the following day from the florist, arranged by Kay, including the writing of the sentiment on the card.

He had staunch opinions regarding personal decorum. He believed wearing a tie engendered respect from subordinates. He insisted his direct reports wear ties as well. He'd never taken a sick day and on occasion, had arrived at work with heavy flu symptoms in spite of dairy hygiene restrictions. He was proud of the fact he had accumulated more than two years of outstanding leave.

Jim was also a firm believer in the concept of professional conduct. He discouraged joking and laughter in the office areas, which he believed gave people the impression his staff weren't serious about their work. Of course, there was a double standard for him, particularly when the joke was at another's expense. His biggest laughs were about stuff-ups by managers he was competing with from other dairy sites. He was determined to take over the General Manager's position and the million-dollar annual salary. Afterwards, he would go for the CEO role along with an investment in a dairy farm or two.

Jim congratulated himself about his personal ruthlessness, his ability to do anything to enhance his position. He had the nerve to sweep into a business, cut headcount and costs, and then move to another role after demonstrating a bottom-line benefit. He turned to his computer monitor and keyboard to hunt and peck a final email for the day.

Subject: Maintenance Best Practices Support
To: Trevor
From: Jim Champion

Please be in my office to discuss above at 10:00 am tomorrow morning. I look forward to supporting the program

Trevor was nervous. He had seen the email first thing in the morning after an early arrival to follow up on a 350kw motor bearing failure. A replacement motor was required for the drier exhaust system after the bearing failure had twisted the motor shaft and shut the site down. Raw milk diversions had resulted.

He couldn't help thinking Jim might have some new motive or concern which would challenge support for the MBP program. Scott, the powder plant manager, had come by for a pep talk the prior afternoon, just after Colin Grey's memo on cost savings. Scott had explained the renewed statement of support from Jim. It was nearly ten o'clock and Trevor wanted to be on time for the meeting. He packed his notebook and rushed out of his office in a cold sweat. Scott had assured him Kay would get Jack on the conference call and he'd told Matt to come along as well.

Trevor detected a perfume scent in the air as he pushed open the door to Jim's office. A woman was standing next to Jim. She moved toward him as he entered the office, and he felt his palms go clammy as she extended her hand, confidently.

"Hi Trevor, I'm Libby Galwaith. Nice to meet you."

Libby was dressed impeccably, wearing brown high heels, a beige skirt and business jacket with the skirt cut off at the knees revealing shapely legs. Her teeth sparkled white, gleaming in a perfect smile. Her blond hair was pulled back in an attractive, plaited, French roll. Large black-pearl ear-rings complimented a black pearl and gold pendant at the top of her crisply pressed white blouse.

Trevor could feel his sphincter muscles almost totally relax. He caught himself before he made a mess in his pants. "Uh. Good morning," he sputtered. He looked at Jim but received only a confident, reassuring smile from him. He had no idea what to expect, but he knew it wasn't going to be good.

Jim explained, "Libby's here to talk to us about the maintenance best practices program. Have a seat."

Trevor sat down in one of the two seats in front of Jim's desk. Jim was leaned back in his chair, pressing his fingers together, smiling, peaceful and glowing. Libby walked to an electronic whiteboard where there were a large amount of colored pen markings, figures and $2 Million written in red, circled boldly.

"Jim! Trevor exclaimed. "Where are Matt, Scott and the others? I thought we were going to have a conference call with Jack?! What's going on?!" Trevor was starting to freak, moving forward in the lowered seat about to jump to his feet.

"Trevor," Jim said firmly and forceful. "We don't need them. I've had Kay tell Scott the phone hook-up with Jack is canned for the time being. We've got something else to consider first." Jim waited, staring at Trevor. When Trevor had settled back in his chair, Jim continued, "Libby is with VFM. She has been working in the UK up until last October, when they brought her down to head up VFM Maintenance Best Practices."

Trevor stiffened.

Libby's eyes widened as she watched Trevor's reaction, then she smiled at him, supportively and smoothly cut in. "Trevor, Jim has explained the excellent work you and your men have been doing to put together a maintenance best practices program. I am highly impressed at what you've accomplished so far, getting your production and maintenance teams to open up to the idea after so many years of reactive work."

"That's right Trev. Libby and I are both impressed. What we want to talk to you about is an opportunity to accelerate the payback for the program."

"But Jim!" Trevor could barely speak. His face had turned bright red. He was in danger of choking. "You know MBP can't be accelerated! Jack's told us. I thought we were supposed to be talking with Jack about this today?"

Jim leaned forward, glaring at Trevor. He was sick and tired of Trevor's behavior, and he was worried Trevor was going to lose it here, in front of Libby. He didn't want him making a scene and bringing his own reputation into question. "Trevor! Listen up!" Jim commanded. "I'm not challenging Jack, or you, on MBP. We're going to do it! But we can't wait for three or four years to get a payback. Libby says she can help us get a twenty-five percent return now. This year! I told Scott we'd catch up with him later, after the three of us discussed the VFM option." Jim paused, estimating Trevor's potential for another uncontrolled outburst. "Trevor, this is your chance to accelerate the program. Make a name for yourself. Earn some respect. Listen to what Libby is suggesting!"

Trevor was deflated.

Libby was surprised by the exchange and Trevor's reaction. Her expression remained constant, and her caring, supportive, empathetic smile remained. She was ready to provide eye to eye contact and support if Trevor looked her way.

"Trevor. Libby and I have been through the numbers here this morning. She will guarantee a two million dollar reduction in repair and maintenance expenses in the next twelve months. You've seen the memo from Colin haven't you?! We can't afford to wait. The shareholders need our total support on this MBP program."

Libby piped in, directing her comment to Trevor. "I know we can make this a success! I know I can support you on the initiatives you've already started and I can bring experience and expertise from my international organization to support. We have thousands of people working on MBP programs world-wide and there are opportunities to cross-pollinate and leverage on VFM experience. It'll be transparent, as though your own program was simply continuing but with some new powerful enhancements."

Jim nodded, admiring Libby's persuasive commentary and her

supportive tone and gestures. She was a pro! He piped in, "We will also avoid Jack's long distance travel expenses and North American consulting rates."

Trevor was lifeless. He was looking at the floor, withdrawn. He had imagined something might happen, but not this dramatic. His worst nightmare had come true, again. He was no longer in control of the program, whatever program, this woman was proposing.

"Trev......listen! We're going ahead with Jack's ideas. We're not cancelling the MBP program, just chipping in the VFM enhancements!"

Trevor said nothing. He was almost catatonic. Jim looked at Libby and shrugged.

"I've told Libby to work up a contract for us to look at. I've made the decision to go with VFM. It's in our best interests and I expect you to support Libby and her strategy, to work with her, to mold your program with hers so we get the two-million payoff this year. Got it?!" Jim winked at Libby as Trevor gathered his papers and stood up, head down, without looking at either of them.

"Ok Jim. When does Libby start? Where is her office?" Trevor's voice was filled with resignation.

"She's already started! You can organize a meeting with her to review strategy at one o'clock this afternoon, in the site meeting room. I'll be there to support. Kay is organizing an office for her in the administration block."

"Ok." Trevor got up and left without another word.

CHAPTER 8

Driving into work Thursday morning, Matt reflected on the past few days with Jan. After the

incident on Tuesday at The Bean things had gone badly. He'd gone for a ride and ended up at Dave's place late in the afternoon. A few beers on a Tuesday night? Not unheard of, for Dave. Matt enjoyed the odd beer, but seldom got the opportunity to drink much due to being on call twenty-four-seven. Moke had turned up with his guitar, wife and five kids. It was as though it had been planned, like the guys knew Matt needed support. Matt knew they didn't know the half of it.

Along with Dave's three kids they enjoyed an impromptu game of touch rugby until it got too dark and the kids disappeared to play computer games. It was warm and they sat outside on the back patio, entertained by Dave and Moke's hunting stories accompanied by the occasional song from Moke.

Matt felt the tension drain away and at eight o'clock Moke's wife announced it was time they headed home and put the kids to bed. Matt felt light headed as he stood up to leave and grabbed hold of a chair to steady himself. Moke noticed and insisted on giving him a lift home.

Jan silent treatment made it clear she was unimpressed, when Matt arrived home. She cooked dinner and they sat on the sofa watching TV like two strangers occupying adjacent seats on an airplane flight to nowhere. He had the same feeling when they went to bed. They avoided physical contact. He had considered how to broach his feelings about Wayne and what appeared to be more than personal training, but said nothing.

Wednesday had been a blip, with heaps of breakdowns. He received a phone call from Kay, Jim's personal assistant, telling him the conference call with Jack was postponed. He was disappointed, but figured Jim must have been unavailable. There wasn't any point in having the discussion with Jack if Jim wasn't on the line. He hadn't seen Trevor for the entire day. Matt figured he'd ask Trevor when the conference call with Jack would be rescheduled at the morning toolbox meeting. Matt felt positive. He was back at work and confident the maintenance best practice project would help him to get his life back in control.

The toolbox meeting commenced on time with the twelve attendees scattered amongst the workbenches. Under the harsh fluorescent light, it was hard to distinguish expressions which would indicate who was coming off night shift and who had arrived for the day shift. Everyone looked pale and tired. The purpose of the meeting was to update the incoming shift about problems experienced by the outgoing shift and any safety or environmental incidents. All maintenance team members were expected to attend. Matt normally chaired the meeting except for Mondays when Trevor liked to make his presence felt.

Attendance at the meetings was dropping off and Trevor had instructed Matt to find out where the missing people had been and ensure they attended in future. It was a routine they followed almost every week. Trevor baled up Matt. Matt agreed and ignored the instruction. The last person Matt had chased up had responded "Piss off, Matt! I'm not wasting my time listening to that frigging idiot Trev!" Matt silently sympathized.

The situation had become untenable a few months earlier when one of the apprentices fell asleep. People falling asleep during the meetings wasn't uncommon, but the more experienced team members knew how to prop themselves up against the various pieces of equipment in the workshop. Rowan, an apprentice fitter, had moved to a sitting position on the workbench, wedged between a vice and a small electric motor. As he dozed off his weight shifted and the motor started sliding very slowly towards the side of the bench. A few tradesmen noticed and watched with amusement. Finally, the motor tipped off the bench, crashing onto the concrete floor. Rowan recoiled, and caught off balance, followed the motor to the ground, gashing his head open on the edge of the bench as he fell.

Trevor was outraged someone had fallen asleep during the safety meeting and been injured as a result. He formally disciplined Rowan.

Dave, the Union Delegate, challenged Trevor's action. The Health and Safety Manager subsequently conducted several meetings with Trevor, suggesting Trevor drop the disciplinary action. Trevor refused. Finally, the Health and Safety Manager wrote to Trevor telling him he would not defend Trevor's actions and copied the letter to Jim. The next day Rowan was told he had clean record.

Following the incident, Matt suggested the Monday morning stand-up meeting be limited to fifteen minutes. If a longer meeting was necessary, it should be held in one of the meeting rooms where people could sit down. Trevor had curtly replied it was a short meeting and there was no reason why people couldn't stand up and pay attention.

Matt looked around. Most of the scheduled technicians were present, bleary eyed while they sipped coffee. A couple guys were missing; Mad Andy and Moke. Matt queried Dave, "Any idea where Moke and Andy are?"

"Moke was heading to the Store, when I saw him. As for Andy, who knows?"

One of the fitters called across the room. "Hey Matt, when's this meeting getting underway? There's a problem up on the packing line and they are moaning like stuck pigs."

"What's the problem?" asked Matt.

"Not sure," replied the fitter. "But it's got to be more important than listening to the daily burble."

Matt looked at his watch. It was seven-fifty. "Just give it a couple more minutes. Trevor said he'd be coming along for today's meeting. If he's not here soon, head on up." As he finished, Matt heard the workshop door open.

Trevor walked in, followed by a woman. The men, who had been chatting lazily, perked up at the sound of a female voice and the unusual spectacle of an attractive, well-dressed woman in their midst.

"Good morning gentlemen," Trevor said with a tone that implied he was reminding them to be on their best behavior. Receiving no reply, as expected, he continued "This is …. Err…"

The woman broke in. "Libby Galwaith, from VFM."

"Yes," Trevor recovered, "She's going to be running the MBP program."

Matt was shocked. He immediately challenged Trevor. "What's happened to Jack? What about the conference call yesterday?!"

Trevor shook his head at Matt. "Jack's out of the picture. Libby and VFM are running the MBP program now."

Matt turned to Libby, "I don't mean to be rude," as he turned and addressed Trevor, "But why the change? We were making good progress with Jack. I thought we had a plan? You said you had Jim's approval to work with Jack?"

"I think I can answer that question," Libby cut in. "In order to do so, I'd like to show you a presentation I have set up in the board room. It will take twenty minutes. I know some of you are coming off night shift and I hope you can stay. I've organized coffee and bacon and egg sandwiches for you all."

"Let's get one thing straight before we head anywhere," Dave demanded. As the union delegate, whenever he was confronted by a contractor he was immediately wary of potential outsourcing of their jobs. "VFM is a contract maintenance services outfit, isn't it? Are you going to tell us maintenance services are going to be contracted out?"

All eyes were on Libby. Dave had pushed a sensitive button and she knew it. "VFM have a maintenance excellence program. We know the best people to deliver results are you guys. We work with you to get results. When you see the presentation you'll understand some of the results we have achieved across the UK, and it'll put you at ease about contract out question."

"What happens if you don't get the results?" asked Dave.

"Don't worry. We will," she replied, emphasizing We, for effect.

"You contracted out maintenance at the timber processing plant in Riverdale……….. fifty crew members made redundant." Dave challenged.

"That was different. There was a history of poor industrial relations on the site and a lot of management problems."

"What was different?" One of the electricians mumbled, sarcastically.

"Sorry, I didn't catch that?"

"Nothing." replied the sparkie.

"Well," continued Libby, "I'm sure there will be lots of questions and I think my presentation will answer quite a few of them. I wouldn't want those bacon and egg sandwiches to bet cold, so why don't we head for the

Boardroom?" Turning towards Trevor she nodded and they both headed for the workshop door.

Matt looked at Dave.

Dave shrugged. "Better go and listen. Something tells me Jim has had a hand in this!"

As the crew filed out of the door, a couple of the tradesmen hung back. "What about the packing line?" asked the fitter who had spoken to Matt earlier.

"You go to the meeting with the guys. I'll go see what's up." Matt turned toward another tradesman. "You need to get away Adrian?"

"Yeah, Matt. My mum has my little one, when I'm on nights, but I always pick her up and take her to daycare. I need to be there for her."

"Ok. You head off."

Adrian's wife had been killed in a car accident and he was bringing up their three-year old on his own. "Thanks Matt. And Matt …. What's going on? Are we going to lose our jobs?"

Seeing his concern Matt put a reassuring hand on his shoulder. "Adrian, I don't know what's going on. But this place will never survive without good tradesmen and you are one of the best, so I don't think you need to worry. Go home, spend some time with Sophie and then get some sleep. Give me a call on the mobile when you wake up and I'll update you if you can't wait till you're back on site to hear the story."

"Thanks Matt."

Matt phoned the Senior Operator on the packing line. After hearing a quick description of the problem, Matt assured him it was an easy to fix and after he picked up the part from stores he would be there. As he put the phone down and picked up his toolbox he heard melodic whistling.

The workshop door opened and Moke appeared. "Hi Matt, where is everyone? Did I miss the meeting?"

"They've gone up to the Boardroom."

"What the bloody hell for? Has Rowan fallen off the bench again?"

"No. It's more serious. Some woman from VFM has turned up and says she is taking over the maintenance best practice program! She's fronted up with some tucker."

"Now, you're talking" said Moke. "But I thought we were going to run the deal with Jack, the guy from Canada? I don't get it!?"

Matt shrugged his shoulders as he left Moke.

As Matt walked into the Stores, a courier driver brushed quickly passed him from the opposite direction. Matt could hear Mandy laughing.

"Hey! My day just got a whole lot better!" She shouted toward Matt.

"By the look of him, you were having a good day already."

"He's a kid. I like my men real, like this man of the month." Mandy gestured up at the calendar on the wall. It had been produced by the volunteer firefighters as a fundraiser and it was their answer to 'Calendar Girls.' This month's fire fighter looked like a body builder who was fully exposed except for a strategically placed fire hose.

"Maybe you should sign up too," Matt challenged.

"As a firefighter? They don't make them like that around here. Look at Moke. He's one of the volunteer firefighters, and you can't find a six pack on him."

"Well, if it's six packs you want, you'd better join the gym."

"Nah. Too many women, wearing make-up, falling all over their personal trainers. Makes me sick!"

Matt was suddenly reminded of Wayne. He felt his stomach turn and wondered whether Wayne had added volunteer fire fighting to his resume.

"Anyway, you come to check on my spare parts?" she said, leaning over the counter and giving Matt a clear view of her cleavage.

Matt ignored her tempting gesture. "Yep. I need a pneumatic valve for the packing machine. You should have one in stock."

Mandy made a number of rapid key strokes on the computer keyboard to pull up the part number which she appeared to have memorized. "Your luck's in. I do. You want to come round here and get it?"

"Mandy!" Matt replied sternly. "Just get it for me. I don't have time to mess around."

A few hours later, Matt was cleaning up his tools on the packing line when Dave appeared.

"Moke told me I'd find you here," he shouted over the noise of the machine. "Got a minute?"

"Hold on mate. I need to tell the operators what I've done so they can start-up the line." Matt shouted as he walked toward the control room.

Having updated the operators, Matt and Dave walked out of the plant and headed across the yard to the workshop. "So, what's the story?" Before Dave could reply Matt's mobile rang. Matt looked at the number and pushed the Reject button. "Trevor."

"The story is, this pommie tart is coming in to run a maintenance excellence program, which sounds to me like the same maintenance best practice Jack was talking about." He paused for emphasis, "Except she reckons VFM can get a payback in the first year. I don't like it, Matt. VFM have a history of contracting out maintenance services and her figures don't stack up."

"Who got her in? Trevor said he had convinced Jim that Jack knew what he was doing. The team was ready to work with Jack. Why has Jim booted Jack out and brought in this woman?"

"I think I can answer that. Jim was at the meeting and did a formal introduction of … what's her name. He was smooth as. I reckon the lech is planning on tweeking this one's G-string."

Matt shook his head. Dave and the rest of the guys had one track minds. "She doesn't look like the G-string wearing type to me."

Dave nodded. "No. You are probably right, mate. She's not my type either. Too buttoned up, but Jim was drooling."

Matt continued, thinking out loud, "It still doesn't make sense. Where did she come from? How did Jim meet her?"

"I don't know, but one thing's for sure. I better get John Grimley involved."

Matt groaned inwardly. John was the national organizer for the Engineering Union. Involving the Union official meant scheduling time for the guys to meet with him. It would mean time off the tools just when they were going to start talking about maintenance best practices. In any event, it was a distraction to their day-to-day work routine. "Don't worry the guys unduly," Matt cautioned. "I mean about the contract out threat. Don't you think we should wait a bit and see what this woman has planned?"

"Alright. I'll back off for a few days, but I'm not letting those bastards sell us down the road without putting up a fight."

"I know, Dave. I'll go and see Trevor and find out what the next steps are. Meantime you might like to go and tick off some of your work orders."

Matt checked his cell phone for voice messages as Dave headed into the planner's office

"Message one. Message received today at nine-twenty a.m.
Hi Matt. I've been thinking about the weekend. Vulcan Lane's annual sale starts on Friday. Could we head off on Thursday evening? Then we can be there for opening. Call me on my mobile and I'll book the accommodation."

Matt groaned. He was almost sorry he'd mentioned Trevor's reward weekend away to Jan, now that it was looking like a shopping excursion. Vulcan Lane, the most exclusive shopping area in New Haven! He pictured himself standing around outside the changing rooms in the various boutiques, while Jan tried on one outfit after another. Worse still, she would come out wearing an outfit and ask him questions which were impossible to answer correctly, like 'does this make me look fat?' He would be lucky if the fifteen hundred dollars lasted the day, let alone the weekend. Their relationship was just starting to get back on track and he couldn't risk pushing it apart again. He would deal with the shopping challenges. Friday shouldn't be a problem. Trevor had told him to take it and Monday as well. He dialed her number and got her voicemail.

"Sounds great Jan. Go ahead and book somewhere for Thursday night."

He thought about suggesting they get tickets to the Friday evening rugby match, but decided against it. He hit the cell phone voicemail button again.

"Message two. Message received today at nine-twenty-five a.m.
"MMmm ..att! I need to talk to you. Come to my office, as soon as you can."

I need to talk to you too, Matt thought, deleting the messages and heading for Trevor's office. The workshop was empty as Matt walked through it toward the stairway. Glancing toward the smoko room he noticed several of the tradesmen taking a break. He checked his watch.

Eleven a.m. He felt a flash of irritation that they had still taken their break, despite starting late and having bacon and egg sandwiches earlier at the discussion with the VFM woman.

He climbed the stairs two at a time. Trevor's door was open, but Trevor was gone. Papers were spread around his desk and a plastic sandwich box with 'Trevor' written neatly across the top sat on top of a pile of daily reports. Matt smiled to himself. The lunch box was a standing joke with the tradesmen who knew the day of the week by what Trevor was eating in the daily grind of the maintenance department it was the only thing guaranteed to be consistent. Moke had made up a song about it once, Matt tried to remember it.

> Monday, starts with Sunday roast
> Tuesday comes with eggs, no toast
> Wednesday, if you please
> He likes to have a little cheese
> Thursday comes with luncheon meat
> Which makes him fart, oh what a treat
> Friday, we know the end is nigh
> The sardines make his bottom sigh
> Saturday and Sunday we like the best
> No box, no Trevor, ahhhhh… we can rest

Matt was tempted to look inside the box to see whether the lyrics held true. He noticed a document written on VFM headed paper underneath. He shifted the box to see more detail. It was addressed to Jim and had been photocopied. Someone had circled key words including, maintenance excellence project, savings of $2 million, immediate benefits, impress shareholders. Hearing footsteps, Matt quickly pulled the lunch box back over the document and started browsing through an equipment manual on top of a nearby pile.

"Mm…matt, where were you this morning?"

"There was a problem on the packing line. I went to fix it so Neil could attend the bacon and egg meeting. What's going on Trevor? I thought we were running an MBP program with Jack?"

Trevor closed the door behind him. "This woman from VFM is coming on site to take over the program. She's not going to use Jack's approach."

"That's what I was afraid of. Is there any way to back track? Go back to Jack's program instead of VFM's?"

"Jim wants her."

"But …why? Jack's program was going to provide benefits. You told us it was worth two million a year!"

'Yeah. But not as fast as Libby promised. The Board needs the two million now."

"What did you tell Jack then? On the conference call?"

"We never made the call. Jim made the decision. He told me Jack wasn't needed. I tried to argue but he wouldn't listen."

"So, you've terminated the agreement with Jack?"

"Didn't need to. There wasn't any formal agreement."

Matt wondered if Trevor was inventing the story but allowed him to carry on with the explanation. "Did you even call Jack? What did he say about it?"

"Yep. After the meeting with Jim, I called him on my own. He said something like nothing surprises him, and he said he'd send you an email. Have you received it?"

"I don't know. I haven't got to my desk yet this morning." Matt was tempted to head to his computer before talking any further. "Trevor this is a disaster. We convinced the guys MBP was the way to go. They liked Jack and respected him. They won't buy in to a new program, especially one run by VFM, let alone, a woman." Matt hesitated, then added, "This was the reason I said I'd come back to work."

"I know Matt. I'm sorry. It's out of my hands."

"What are VFM really up to? Is it a plan contract out maintenance? You had better be straight up with me, Trevor."

"No …. Jim wants to make savings. There's been a memo from Colin Grey."

"How does he expect to make these savings?"

"I don't know. That woman says she can save twenty-five percent this year on the repair and maintenance budget with her maintenance excellence project."

"Well, if you don't know. You sure as hell had better find out fast.

Dave is edgy and wants to contact John Grimley. Once it happens, one thing is for sure, we will lose more than twenty-five percent of our labor to union meetings."

Trevor groaned. "Matt … I don't need him coming out here now and pushing me around. Can't you stop Dave?"

"Dave's role is to protect the guys. Right now, I don't know whether they need protection or not. If you want to stop Dave, you talk to him."

"But!"

"No buts. I am not doing it."

"Alright, Matt. What if I get the VFM project stopped?"

"What do you mean?"

"What if VFM decided to leave or something like that?"

"How would that happen?"

"Leave it to me. You'll see."

Was that grim determination in Trevor's voice? Matt wondered. He certainly hadn't hesitated. His jaw was stuck out as he turned to his computer screen.

"Good luck," Matt muttered. It would take more than luck to change the situation.

Trevor obliviously replied, "Leave it to me."

Matt left the office.

Trevor stared at his computer screen, hoping to find the answer. Trying to stop Jim would be like trying to stop a runaway train. The likely outcome was he would get flattened in the process. He thought about the analogy. It was an old one, but a good one. What did they do in those old black and white movies, when the heroine was tied to the tracks? The hero flagged down the driver at the last minute or untied the ropes and lifted her to safety. In this case though, Jim was the driver. Nothing would flag him down. He wracked his brains. Another black and white movie scenario played. The hero de-railing the train, or switching it to a side track at the last minute. How could he de-rail the VFM project?

He thought about the players. Matt might help him, but Matt was too honest, too straight. Matt's words about Dave came back to him. Dave was a villain lurking in the background. He needed to keep him out of the way. Or did he? Could the hero and villain work together? Or better still, could the hero get the villain to derail the train? He smiled to himself. It shouldn't be too hard to convince Dave that VFM planned to contract out maintenance services, even though Libby hadn't mentioned it. Quite the contrary; she said VFM would work with the existing staff.

Feeling hungry he opened his lunch box. Biting into a cold beef sandwich he noticed the copy of the VFM letter to Jim outlining their proposal. He read it again. The letter was written by Libby and explained, in broad terms, the VFM Maintenance Excellence Project. It detailed how the project would create immediate benefits and realize two million in savings in the next twelve months through a reduction in repair and maintenance costs. It gave examples of how this had been achieved in other manufacturing organizations and the positive shareholder reaction.

It's a shame it doesn't suggest contracting out maintenance services, Trevor thought. What if it did and …. what if I could leak the letter to Dave? He looked at the letter again. It was written in standard Times New Roman font and was already a photocopy. He could re-write some paragraphs, stick them over the original and photocopy again. Then he could contrive a way of getting Dave to discover the letter. Once Dave had seen the letter he would derail or delay the project by calling in the Engineering Union representative with a threat of strike action. They'd be up for months of consultative discussions. Maybe the MBP program with Jack would be re-instated while the union discussions continued, and he could regain control of the initiative.

Wiping his hands on his trousers he opened a new document on his computer. He needed a new paragraph, which could be inserted on the second page. After several attempts he sat back and reviewed his amendments to the original letter, putting in language about redundancies and re-deployment as though Libby had written them.

I agree with your assessment of the current maintenance workforce. It lacks the commitment to make this happen. I have had a look at your Collective Employment Agreement. Your pay rates are at least 20% above the norm for tradesmen and penal rates and agreements are not commercially viable. Attempting to negotiate changes to the Agreement will be an arduous process, indicators suggest it will take five years to realize the benefits outlined above.

As discussed, I recommend services are contracted to VFM following a three-month lead in period. We will manage the redundancy and re-employment of selected staff on new rates, as part of the contract to provide services long term.
Libby Galwaith
VFM Maintenance Excellence Project Manager

That should wind Dave up, Trevor thought. All I need to do is get it photocopied into the letter and get him to read a copy. The photocopier was located in the corridor. He decided to do it after 4.30 when the day staff had gone home.

At 4:50 p.m. when Trevor headed for the photocopier, clutching a pile of documents with his original copy containing the new paragraph. He noticed the photocopier had been switched off. He cursed silently. While waiting for it to warm up he felt his heart pounding in his chest. He looked up and down the corridor. Opening the copier lid, his hands started shaking and half the bundle dropped on the floor. Papers spread in all directions. He was on his hands and knees trying to extract a couple of pages from under the copier when he heard footsteps coming down the corridor.

"Hi Trev. Need some help?" Scott had come out of nowhere and bent down to help him.

"Uhhh … just photocopying some papers."

"So, I see." Picking up the VFM headed paper and passing it to Trevor, he added sarcastically, "And how's it going with the lovely Libby?!"

"Good," Trevor lied. He didn't want to start a conversation with Scott.

"Personally, I was gutted about the decision. Jim told me about it before your meeting with him. I tried to get him to reconsider but his mind was made up. Wish we could roll back the clock and have another go with him."

Trevor feigned interest, "Yeah. I tried to argue with him too!"

"Bloody aggravating," Scott continued. "One day we're all onboard, the next day it's a new bus and direction! I had the other ops managers semi-committed to Jack's approach and this move to VFM has set me back behind square one. I didn't see it coming."

"Yep," Trevor replied distractedly, having retrieved all the papers. He was unsure of his next move. He switched the copier off.

Scott looked at him sideways. "I thought you were going to do some photocopying?"

"Uhhh… Yep."

Scott laughed, "You haven't got your resume hidden in there have you? You look guilty enough. Anyway, I'll leave you to it."

Trevor sighed with relief and nodded his head, still preoccupied. "I mean No. I don't have my resume in here."

Scott shook his head, partly at the events and partly at Trevor's inane response. "I've got to run Trev. Tell Matt thanks for fixing the packing line this morning. That's why I came over here."

"Sure thing, Scott."

Scott was already out the door.

Trevor turned back to the copier. He took a deep breath and switched the machine on. He aligned the letterhead of Libby's original with his revision. He gently closed the copier lid and pressed the copy button. Two minutes later he hustled back to his office with two copies of his counterfeit version of the letter. Once inside, Trevor leaned back on his office door and took a deep breath. Now what? How could he get Dave to read the fake letter without implicating himself? Matt had raised the issue. What if he showed Matt the letter in confidence? Matt might tell Dave. Then again, he might not. It was hard to know where Matt's loyalties lay at times. Perhaps he could leave the letter somewhere in the workshop where Dave would find it. No, too obvious. What if Dave found it in his office? That would be the ideal solution, but why would Dave be in his office? He only came in for meetings. I need to ask him to come to my office when I'm not here, to do something for me while I'm out. Checking the roster, he saw Dave was rostered on for night duty for the following evening. An idea began to germinate in Trevor's mind.

Trevor spent the following day in nervously anticipating his next move, mostly alone in his office. He had taken both copies of the letter home the night before and left one copy at home when he returned to work. As he prepared to leave his office, he placed the counterfeit VFM letter under a couple of memos on his desk ensuring the VFM letterhead could be easily spotted by anyone glancing in the direction of the papers. Turning to his notice board he unpinned his list of key contact numbers from the board and placed it on the desk near the counterfeit VFM memo. The trap was set.

It was just after 9:.00 p.m. when Trevor phoned from home.

Dave answered his mobile on the second ring.

"Dave. It's Trevor."

"Trevor?" Dave was surprised to get a call from him when nothing had gone wrong so far. "What's up?"

"I've had a call from the manager at the cream plant," Trevor lied. "He said he tried to get you but no answer?"

"Oh. Really?! I'm surprised cause my cell phone has been on all evening."

"That's OK Dave, but he's got a problem and he needs the contact number for the refrigeration contractor. It's in my office. Could you get it for me?"

"I'm up at the Drier at the moment. How soon do you need it?"

"Well, he needs it now. Can you head back and get it?"

"Okay, I'll head back as soon as I can. Give me his number and I'll phone it straight through to him."

"No!" Trevor almost shouted. "I mean, there's no need for you to do that. Call me back and I'll do it. Ok?!"

"No worries, but it's just as quick for me to phone him. No need for me to disturb you at home." Dave was curious about Trevor's strange instructions.

Trevor felt the beads of sweat breaking out across his forehead. Why did every encounter he had with Dave have this effect on him? Why couldn't he just do what he was asked for once? "Dave, I need to speak to him again, anyway. Just call me please! The number is on my desk." He hung up without waiting for further response from Dave.

Dave looked at the mobile in his hand after Trevor cut him off. Strange behavior, he thought, shrugging his shoulders. Everything about Trevor is strange. Packing up his tools, he called into the control room and notified the head operator he'd be back in twenty minutes after he took care of Trevor's request.

Inside Trevor's office he looked on the notice board for the list of contact numbers, but it wasn't in its usual place. He remembered Trevor's instructions and spotted the list on his desk. He dialed Trevor's number after finding the refrigeration contractor's details. Glancing at the rest of the papers on Trevor's desk, he saw the VFM letterhead on a memo. He was about to take a look when Trevor answered the phone.

He gave Trevor the refrigeration contractor's number, replaced the phone and decided to look at the VFM letter. He didn't hesitate for a second as he slipped the paper out from under the other memos on Trevor's desk. He felt a flush of anger as he read the letter. So, he was right, there was a plan to contract out maintenance to VFM! Jim and his new advisor Libby were behind it. What was Trevor's involvement? Obviously he knew about it. Did Matt know?

He replaced the letter and started to walk out of the office. As he turned to close the door, a thought came to him. A copy of the letter could be useful. It was 9.30 p.m. and he was on shift until 6.00 a.m. Plenty of time to take a trip via the photocopying machine.

Trevor's night had been so fragmented by nightmares he was relieved to see daylight. Mary, his wife, asked him if he was okay when he staggered into the kitchen for breakfast. He muttered in the affirmative and added he had a busy day ahead, at work. He forgot his lunchbox and she chased him down with it as he walked to her car. She told him not to overdo it at work and watched him drive away, deeply worried. She knew his blood pressure was already elevated and she had never seen him as stressed as he seemed during the past few days.

Trevor's stomach churned as he pulled his company-supplied sedan into the dairy site's parking lot. He was surprised to find everything as normal in the workshop. Matt was finishing the Toolbox meeting and the guys were making their way out of the workshop. A few of them grunted a greeting as they passed. Trevor going the opposite direction.

Matt approached as soon as he noticed Trevor. "Good morning Trevor."

"Hi Matt. Everything okay?" His tone was tentative.

"Seems to be. Looks like the guys had a quiet night and managed to complete some to the preventative maintenance routes for a change."

"Good stuff." Trevor turned away quickly and climbed the stairway to his office. He gasped as he entered his office and found Libby sitting at his desk, typing away on his computer keyboard.

"Trevor! Just the person I need. There's something I want to talk to you about. Close the door behind you."

Trevor's heart stopped.

"I'm trying to find a detailed breakdown of your maintenance expenditure. Where do you keep it?"

Trevor could see she was scrolling through files in Microsoft Explorer. "It's not there" Trevor replied, frantically. It's in the filing cabinet." He gestured frantically toward the cabinet attempting to distract her from any further search of his computer files.

"Don't you keep a copy on your computer?"

"No," he lied.

"Why ever not?"

"I don't trust the guys. If they see any unspent money they want it."

"What do they want?" asked Libby curiously.

"All sorts of things."

"Like?" She asked, raising a questioning eyebrow.

"New tools. Uniforms." Yesterday's coffee mug on his desk inspired another example. "Coffee machines," he finished.

"I see. Well, it's one of the reasons I wanted to see the budget. I'd like to spend a bit of money on smartening things up around here. New uniforms, decent toolboxes and a coffee machine would make a very good start. Raise a requisition and I'll go and have a word with the girl in Stores, who incidentally could do with a new uniform. She is attracting a little too much attention. What's her name?"

"Mandy."

"Right. Can you do that now? And give me a copy of your budget for the year to date," she commanded.

Trevor was on the verge of blowing a fuse. He managed the maintenance budget! How dare she come to his office and demand requisitions? Matt had been pressing him for new toolboxes and uniforms for some time. How would it look if she suddenly got them for the boys? As for a coffee machine, didn't she realize this was a maintenance workshop! "Yep. I'll do the requisition and run off a copy of the budget later."

"Just give me the budget report now, and I'll copy them on my way back from Stores," she countered.

Trevor fumbled through the filing cabinet, pulled out the reports, and passed them to Libby, and then excused himself from the office.

Libby remained seated at Trevor's desk, opened her handbag, pulled out a yellow highlighting pen and began a careful inspection of the reports.

Five minutes passed before Trevor returned from the restroom.

Libby turned to him as he entered the office. "Trevor these figures don't stack up. You are under-spent by twenty thousand dollars. I understood from your latest budget report you were overspent by $150K?"

"Uh. Yeah. That's right. We are overspent. The budget you're looking at doesn't include season to date committals which are one hundred and seventy-thousand."

"Why aren't the committals included in the report?"

"The maintenance computer system doesn't have committals capability. We can't load the committals in until they're receipted."

"So, you're $150K over budget season to date for sure?"

"Yes." Trevor hoped the news would deter her spending spree.

She perused the figures a moment longer, then stacked the papers together and placed them neatly in a manila folder which she slide into a sleek, leather, designer briefcase. She stood slowly as though she was going to ask Trevor another pointed question.

He braced himself.

"Ok Trevor. I'm disappointed about the budget figures and the state of affairs with your computerized maintenance management system reports, but it'll have to do for now. If I have any questions I'll give you a call. I've got a meeting with Jim in fifteen minutes, so I've got to run." She brushed past him and left the office.

Trevor slumped in his chair. His nerves were shot and it was only 8:15 a.m. He picked up the VFM letter from its hiding place and checked its accuracy once again before quickly folding it and pushing it deep into his trouser pocket. He reviewed the situation. Libby being in his office was a near miss. What if she had seen it? He felt nauseous at the thought. He wondered if Dave had seen it. God, I hope not, he thought to himself. I should never have got myself in this mess. He felt an urgent need to go to return to the restroom. He made a run for it, barely making it in time. He sat, bent over, head in hands. He flushed the toilet and remained on the stool, taking the letter out of his pocket he started tearing it into small pieces, flushing them away.

Dave had followed his normal pattern when he got home the night before, in spite of his discovery of the contract-out threat. It could wait he reminded himself. He kissed his wife as she headed out the door to work. He saw the kids off to school and then grabbed a cold beer and watched the breakfast program for fifteen minutes before heading to bed. It was just after one o'clock in the afternoon when he woke. Normally, he would lie in bed and try and drift back to sleep for a bit longer, but he had union work to do.

As he cooked himself a fry-up of eggs, bacon, sausage, potatoes on an extra large skillet with plenty of butter and oil, he contemplated his next move. He thought about talking to Matt before calling John Grimley. Matt had denied any knowledge of VFM's intentions. Either Matt doesn't know, or he is not telling me, Dave figured. If I tell Matt, what will he do? What can he do? Was he trying to keep the Engineering Union organizer out of the picture? Jim is behind this and Matt won't stop him. A call to Grimley would shake things up. Should he tell Matt he was going to call John, and why? No. Matt would try and talk him out of it, again. He called John after breakfast and left a brief voice message.

Two hours later, John returned Dave's call. John was incredulous. "Are you sure, Dave? Do the other guys know about it? Like Matt?"

"I'm sure alright and I have a copy of the VFM letter. Matt may know, but he's holding his cards close to his chest if he does. I think he would've told me if he did. We're pretty tight. He doesn't want you in the picture though."

John let out a long, slow whistle "Geez this is big! If they're planning redundancies and haven't entered into any consultation process we've got them! I need to get down there and meet with you guys so we can put an action plan together!"

Dave remembered John always spoke in exclamations, as though every move management made was a crisis and an opportunity for a fight. "When can you get down here?"

"Tomorrow's out, but I could re-schedule Friday and be down there at ten o'clock. I suggest we call a stop-work meeting. I'll contact Trevor to give him the twenty-four-hour notice period. Can I leave it to you to organize the guys?"

"No worries. I'm on nights again tonight. I'll do a bit of a phone around to inform people on days off, and catch the day shift before they leave this evening."

"Nice work Dave, and you can fax me a copy of the letter?"

"Yep. I'll do it tonight."

"Thanks. If anything else comes up, give me a call. Otherwise, I'll see you Friday."

It was the right thing to do, Dave thought, as he hung up the phone. He felt relieved he had called John and re-enforcements were on the way to deal with the VFM crisis. Once again, management had proved they couldn't be trusted and it was important for the Engineering Union to be vigilant and prepared to fight when the managers over-stepped the line.

Trevor's stomach had settled enough for him to eat his cheese sandwich before John Grimley's call. Now, he was back in the restroom again. John informed him he was informing him about a stop-work meeting on Friday morning at 10:00 a.m. to discuss the lack of consultation regarding the VFM Project. Trevor had lamely tried to prevent it, asking John for the source of his information and why the meeting was necessary.

As usual, John refused to divulge his source. He assured Trevor he had written proof of VFM's plans to reduce staff levels and force redundancies which was against the Engineering Union contract since the consultation process had not occurred. Trevor relented. John was correct and had the right to call the meeting, particularly if Dave had faxed him the doctored VFM letter.

The slight sense of satisfaction about the success of his scheme was over-ridden by the chilling fear of the potential outcomes. What if Jim realized Trevor was behind it? Jim was pretty good at ferreting out the sources of rumors and plots. Another stomach cramp gripped Trevor. There was no way he could be implicated. He had deleted the email document from his computer and flushed away the copy. Dave knew where he had found the memo, but Trevor figured Dave wouldn't divulge the location because it would implicate him in an act of misconduct, snooping in Trevor's office and copying material unintended for his eyes. Besides, he could deny it was in his office and accuse Dave of manufacturing the letter after copying the original. Dave would be twice over the barrel. There was no evidence of its existence apart from the copy at home. He finished up and headed back to his office with a renewed sense of confidence.

Trevor re-checked the budget figures he had supplied to Libby. His computer figures had the committals included, but he hadn't given Libby a copy of the spreadsheet. He smiled to himself. It would take her the rest of the day to sort out the committals with the accountants which would keep her off his back. His thoughts were interrupted by Matt.

"Hey Trevor, I thought I should let you know Libby asked for the list of tools we need to purchase for the guys. I told her you already had it, but there wasn't any money in the budget to buy tools."

"Well, we might be able to free up some," Trevor replied.

"That's good. Mandy tells me Libby was also asking for information on uniforms and a coffee machine?"

"Yes, she seems to think we need some."

"Where is the money coming from?"

"She mm…must be getting money from Jim," Trevor lied.

"Unlike him to give anything away. Wonder what he's getting in return?"

"Matt. I've just had a call from John Grimley. He's calling a stop work meeting at ten o'clock on Friday morning."

"What?!" Matt exploded.

"A stop work meeting," Trevor repeated.

"Why?!"

"I don't know."

"Well, what reason did he give?"

"He said lack of consultation regarding VFM."

"What does he mean? We don't have to consult to use consultants."

Matt paused. "If this place needed to consult every time a consultant was called in, we'd never produce anything."

"They seem to think there's a risk of contracting out," Trevor replied.

"But there isn't, is there?"

Trevor looked straight back at Matt. "No!"

Matt stood motionless his hand on his chin considering the options. "I'll give Dave a call and find out what the hell is going on."

"Good idea," replied Trevor.

Matt walked into the workshop office and dialed Dave's home number. It wasn't time for him to be at the plant yet, and Matt figured he'd be watching the All Blacks greatest re-runs.

After several rings Dave picked up the phone with an irritated tone. "Hullo!"

"What the hell is going on?" Matt countered.

"Good afternoon….. Dave. How are you this afternoon? Did your night shift go well? I'm so sorry to wake you." Dave's voice dripped sarcasm at Matt's directness.

Matt gritted his teeth. "Good afternoon Dave. Did your night shift go well and did you have a good sleep?"

"No and yes."

Ignoring the answer Matt continued. "Can you tell me why the hell John Grimley has called a stop-work meeting for Friday morning?"

"Why don't you ask Trevor?"

"I just did and he told me it was due to lack of consultation on the VFM project. You, I and John Grimley know we don't need to consult to use external help," Matt replied tersely.

"You, I and John Grimley know you do need to consult if you are planning to contract out and make people redundant." Dave's voice was as tense as Matt's.

"Dave! I told you there is no plan to do that!" Matt shot back.

"And I believed you! But, now I know there is a plan!"

"What the hell are you getting at?"

"I know there's a plan in the works, and I tell you something else. Trevor does too." Dave's tone relaxed slightly as he sensed this truly was a surprise to Matt.

"Trevor just told me there is no plan to contract out maintenance."

"Who do you trust Matt? Me or Trevor?"

Matt weighed up the question. He and Dave went back a long way. He wouldn't put it past Dave to bend the truth a bit at times but, when it came to important issues, he could trust Dave to be completely honest. Trevor talked a lot about honesty and integrity, but when it came down to it, his actions didn't match his words.

"Look Dave, I think there has been a misunderstanding here. Why don't you and I meet with Trevor and sort it out?"

"Matt, there has been no misunderstanding. Mornington's upper management are planning to contract out and Trevor knows it. I am not sitting back and letting this happen without a fight, even if you want to."

"You know full well I wouldn't let maintenance services be contracted out without a fight myself, but you've got to tell me what makes you so sure, this is going to happen?!"

"I'm keeping that to myself for the moment, but you can bet your last breath that I have the evidence." Dave countered, adding "It's probably better if you don't know anyway."

"Thanks heaps mate! What am I supposed to do?"

Dave chuckled. "Just wait till Friday and listen. The reaction from the guys will be louder than a powder drier explosion."

"The way our preventative maintenance program is going at the moment, it wouldn't surprise me to hear one of those as well," Matt replied, resigning himself to the union meeting.

"Yeah. Well, one of your fitters is going to be late for work, if you don't get off the phone now."

"Ok mate. See you this avo." Matt hung up the phone and stopped to ponder the situation. It was bad enough losing Jack's program, but now there was a potential union confrontation on top of it. He was also concerned about the impact of the Friday Union meeting on the three- day weekend he had promised Jan.

Libby was ticked off as she left Trevor's office. She had walked across the site from her temporary office in the main administration block to confirm they would be having a full briefing of the maintenance crew tomorrow morning. She planned to update them on the maintenance excellence project. Trevor informed her there was a conflict with an Engineering Union stop-work meeting at 10:00 a.m., for at least two hours. They wouldn't be in the mood to hear about maintenance excellence from VFM prior or after the meeting. Trevor warned she might be dodging a bullet by postponing her presentation, based on his conversation with Dave. He explained Dave had some inside information about the company's failure to consult. Libby asked Trevor if Jim was aware of the developments with the Union and what else he knew about it. Trevor feigned ignorance and blamed Dave and John Grimley for stirring things up without justification. Figuring Jim was probably unaware, Libby made a beeline back to the administration office block and knocked on his door.

"Yeah come on in Libs. I've always got time for a beautiful woman."

He was busy with a pile of documents. She noted he didn't seem to be reading them, just shuffling them from one stack to another. "I've just heard the Engineering Union organizer has called a stop-work meeting on Friday morning."

"What? The bloody hell he has!" Jim exploded. He slammed his pen down on the top document.

"Apparently he's got concerns about a lack of consultation. I tried to find out more from Trevor, but he wasn't making much sense."

"That wanker never makes any sense. What does he mean by consultation? There ain't nothing to consult on."

"I know."

Jim picked up his phone and punched a number into it. "Trevor," he growled, "What the hell is going on!?"

Libby could overhear Trevor's stuttering.

"For god's sake man!" Jim shouted into the receiver, "Spit it out!" After a brief pause he added, "Forget it! I'll talk to Matt." Rolling his eyes he retorted to himself, "Who employed that jerk?" before punching another number into the phone.

Libby realized Jim probably employed Trevor. She knew from her consulting experience that bullies, like Jim, usually hired sycophantic 'Yes men' to work for them. She wouldn't let her assessment of Jim to jeopardize the VFM, though. There were bigger fish to fry and Jim was the key to helping her make that happen.

"Matt! What's this BS about a stop work meeting on Friday?"

Libby couldn't hear what Matt was saying but it was clear Matt was attempting to explain or respond as best as he could. She liked Matt, even though she had met him briefly. He impressed her as a natural leader, a guy that would go where nobody had gone, an explorer, who people would gladly follow. He was sincere and honest. The guys knew they could trust he was thinking of their best interests. It was essential for her to win him over to the VFM approach.

"There is no plan to contract out services to VFM, so tell your Union delegate buddy, Dave, to get on with the job we pay him to do, stop shit-stirring and call Grimley off!"

Jim paused while Matt responded.

"Well. Tell him if they are going to start this bullshit I will be happy to contract it out to VFM!" He replaced the receiver with a bang.

He summarized for Libby. "Matt's spoken to the Union delegate in an effort to stop the meeting. He said the delegate insisted the meeting will go ahead as they believe we plan to contract out labor services to your company. You heard my response. No point in talking to the monkeys. We've got some serious work to do here or they will be stalling us around and stuffing up our performance with contract disputes if we're not careful. Jim starting to rifle through a Japanese lacquered box filled with business cards. He quit searching after five seconds and punched his personal assistant's number into the phone.

"Kay! Get me John Grimley, the Engineering Union organizer!"

She called back five seconds later, explaining there had been no answer, but if he wanted to leave a message on Grimley's voicemail it was about to beep.

Looking at Libby he said, "You had better get your pretty little butt over to the workshop again and see if you can find out what's going on. This has the potential to derail things."

Libby paused before replying. She knew this behavior was inevitable. She had promised herself she wouldn't put up with any form of sexual harassment from Jim. She looked him straight in the eye. "Jim, I am happy to go and see if I can find out what's happening, but I'd appreciate it if you would keep the conversation on a professional level."

Jim stretched back into his chair and licked his lips. "I like my women feisty. Don't be so uptight Libs."

"I'm not uptight. If we're going to work together I want you to recognize I <u>am</u> a professional and I appreciate being treated as one." Her voice had grown cold.

"Whoa …okay Libs. Cool it." He replied, adding, "Just get back to me when you know what's going on." He turned away to his computer terminal.

Libby paused, contemplating a comeback. No, she'd made her point. She got up and quietly closed the door behind her.

Later, mid-afternoon, Libby reported back to Jim. She had spoken to Matt, but had failed to get any further information from him. Frustrated she demanded to speak directly to Dave, only to be told by Matt he was on night shift. She left it until 2.00 p.m. to call Dave, at home. He had been insolent, telling her he 'knew her game.' When she had denied any intention to contract out maintenance he had replied 'you can't bullshit me, I have the evidence,' before refusing to say any more.

Libby repeated the conversation to Jim before asking "What does he mean by 'I have the evidence'?"

"Union mumbo jumbo." Jim replied.

"Has the organizer come back to you?" Libby asked.

"Nah. Never does. Arsehole!" Jim mused for a moment. "We'll have to wait until tomorrow to find out what's going on." Jim let Libby think for a half minute before popping the next question. "What are you doing tonight?"

Libby was taken aback by the question. She wasn't prepared for what she believed was a request for a dinner date. "I'll do some work on the project plan."

"Drop it and let's do dinner."

She was correct in her assumption and began to get up from her chair before responding. "Thanks Jim, but I really want to get it finalized so I can present it when I meet with the maintenance team."

"It'll wait" he said.

Libby groaned, inwardly. "I've also got to do a report for VFM and I am afraid it won't wait."

"Make them wait too. Tell them your client has more important issues for you to attend to." He replied, baring his teeth in a lecherous grin. "We do have business and strategy to discuss!"

"Thanks Jim. I appreciate the invite, but not tonight." She headed for the door and said with a smile, "Some other time."

"Yeah, when? I am the customer, don't forget it!?" Jim raised his voice slightly.

"I won't." She left Jim's office gracefully, but at speed.

At her desk, behind closed doors, Libby let her guard down, propping her elbows on her desk and giving herself a massage on the back of her neck. She could feel the stiffness, stored stress from dealing with Jim, the Mornington dairy company, VFM. She wondered, to herself, if the money was worth the effort.

VFM had snapped her up after she received an MBA following a bachelor's degree in engineering. It was an unusual combination for an attractive woman to have, which was precisely her intention. Her university mentor had explained engineering and, in particular the field of maintenance, was an untapped goldmine, with easy money to be made as a consultant. Eighty percent of the world's industrial companies had substandard maintenance programs and were wasting billions of dollars on unnecessary capital equipment investment, spare parts purchases, productivity losses and over-staffed labor expense. Her master's thesis focused on the return on investment for a maintenance excellence program implementation. It had attracted interest from recruiters at a number of the top international consulting firms she already on $250,000US per year salary with an incentive bonus as a result.

She poured herself a glass of Evian bottled water. Was the money really worth the frustration and humiliation of dealing with people like Jim Champion, Trevor and their clones which she continually encountered on her assignments? These people weren't interested in putting a new system in place as much as they were interested in a quick payback or a superficial result that would make them look good in the next two quarters. Afterwards, they would drop the project, or at best, let it slide into decline over the next year or two, usually the length of a VFM contract. Granted VFM was getting what they wanted. Contracts and incentive payoffs for meeting payback targets, but she was concerned about the sustainability of it all. It grated against her personal values.

She enjoyed the international travel associated with the assignments and vacations at exotic spots, the ability to afford expensive clothes. It was a lifestyle she had convinced herself would be satisfying and bring her happiness. There was a potential of making even more money, millions as a partner or leading a consultancy of her own. She was tenacious and resilient, she reminded herself. She could handle anything.

CHAPTER 9

Matt stamped his feet on the rubber mat inside the workshop entrance. He could feel drops of water running down the back of his neck, as he took off his jacket and shook it, watching the spray of water make patterns across the concrete floor. The perfect start to a perfect day, he thought to himself, cynically. He hated days like this and so did the guys. Every time they left the workshop to go to one of the production plants they got soaked. They would avoid leaving the workshop if at all possible, and when they did get into the plant, they would avoid coming back till the end of the day.

At the morning's toolbox meeting, the guys were more inattentive than usual as rain pounded on the corrugated iron roof of the workshop, drowning out the discussion. Matt would have to repeat the specific details to the individuals. What a pain. If they were running Jack's planning system, all of them would be in the plant with detailed instructions for the day on their work orders. They would have known what their schedule was last week instead of this morning.

With the stop-work meeting scheduled for 10.00 a.m., he needed to get as much work done as possible this morning. It was uncertain how long the meeting would last and how easy it would be to get the guys back to work afterwards. The night shift guys would complain they hadn't got enough sleep, and push for a late start. The day shift would refuse to work late. Friday night was pub night. He would be under pressure to fill the gaps.

He told Jan he would be home by 4.30 p.m. on the dot. He couldn't afford to be late for their weekend away. She had been really pissed when he postponed the Thursday start for the weekend, as he had agreed earlier.

Her response to his explanation about the stop-work meeting requiring his attention on Friday morning still echoed in his ears two days afterwards.

"Same old story…..crisis at the plant. Someday they'll bury you out there and nobody will remember you the week after!"

He'd tried to explain about the potential for industrial action, a strike. It was his responsibility, as the Leading Hand, to be there after the meeting to deal with the outcomes.

Jan had shouted, "Workaholic!" and left the house in a fury. She finished up at the gym to "work it off."

After the toolbox meeting, Matt checked in with a few tradesmen about their jobs and then headed for his office. He checked his emails. There were seventeen new messages; notifications of meetings, plant availability updates, quality updates, requests for information, demands for equipment to be fixed, including the site accountant still bleating about a squeaky wheel on his chair. He noticed one email from Mandy

Subject: Uniforms urgent
To: Matt
From: Stores

Miss Prissy wants new shirts ordered for your guys. I need their sizes. Shirts come in S (unlikely for your crew), M (skinny Nathan might fit this), L (your size??), XL (should cover Moke's puku) XXL (Trev size). I need a more accurate measurement. Come on over and I'll size you up.

Matt flicked a quick reply

Subject: Re: Uniforms urgent
To: Stores
From: Matt

too much on today …. grab one of the couriers who's my size.

Before he had time to finish reading the remainder of the emails, a response came back.

Subject: Re: Uniforms urgent
To: Matt
From: Stores

I'd rather grab you, but if you insist I'll see if I can find someone else but they won't measure up to you.

Matt smiled. It was nice to hear something flirtatious from another female, even if it was Mandy. He exited his emails and prepared to head for the weekly production update meeting in the main administration conference room. He wasn't invited to the stop-work meeting as he had been dropped from the Engineering Union membership when he took on the Leading Hand role. Matt had arranged contract coverage for the tradesmen in case of breakdowns during their union meeting.

He was still in the powder plant at noon when his mobile rang.
"Matt. It's Trevor. Jim has asked us to go to his office immediately"
"What's up?"
"I don't know. But John Grimley is there with Dave and that woman."
"I guess it's to do with the stop-work meeting then. I'll see you there."
He wondered why he'd been called in. As a non-union employee, Jim knew he didn't attend Union meetings. It was rare for him to be called to a meeting with Jim. Heading down the corridor towards Jim's office a few minutes later, Matt saw Dave and John Grimley in quiet conversation in the hallway.

John looked toward him as he approached. "Hi Matt. How's it going?" John took Matt's hand in his as he enquired.

"You tell me. You guys are the ones who have been talking all morning."

John inclined his head towards Jim's office saying. "It's about to hit the fan mate! Be prepared to move fast if you don't want any of it sticking to you. We'll be with you just as soon as Trevor gets here."

Matt hesitated. He didn't want to be sitting around in Jim's office, but Dave and John obviously didn't want to stand around and talk with him. He figured they were strategizing.

Jim spotted Matt through his office window. "Come in Matt."

Before Matt could greet the two of them, Jim growled, "Sit down and tell me what you know!"

Matt was stumped by the question. Hesitating he replied, "About what?"

"What reason were you given for the stop-work meeting?" Jim asked.

"Trevor told me there were concerns VFM…" Matt hesitated again. He glanced at Libby before continuing, "Might be planning to contract out maintenance, or at least the trade positions."

Jim slammed his fist down on the table. Matt and Libby jumped. "I decide what goes on around here. Not VFM. I haven't decided to contract out maintenance, but if there's much more of this crap I might!"

At this point Trevor appeared at the door. "Trevor!! Sit down!" Before Trevor had time to sit down he added, "And go and tell those two union jokers we're ready for them."

Trevor returned thirty seconds later. "They said they would be here in a few more minutes."

"Bloody typical!" shouted Jim, "Do they think we have all day to play with? Go and tell them to shift their butts!"

"No." replied Trevor.

Matt looked at Trevor. His face was waxy, an off-white, with a slight gloss from the beads of perspiration. Matt was surprised Trevor had refused Jim's request. He was asking for it. Matt intervened before Jim escalated what was already an extremely tense situation. "I'll go."

Dave and John looked up as Matt came out of the office. John said quietly to Matt, "We heard. We're coming Matt. Just give me a minute."

John walked into a nearby office and picked up an office chair, which he carried into Jim's office. As he came through the door carrying the chair, Jim looked up.

"You don't need a chair, there are enough here already." He barked.

Very deliberately John picked up one of the 'lowered' spare chairs and moved it aside. He replaced it with the office chair. He raised the adjustable chair to hits full height so he could make level eye contact with Jim.

Jim looked at the others and sighed exasperatedly. "Well thanks for the musical chairs session."

John spoke calmly and smiled. "I think there needs to be some leveling in here today."

Matt held his breath. He held a grudging respect for John. In his mind John made too much noise about small stuff, but he had known him to get stuck into his own members when he needed to. A year earlier, Matt had disciplined three union members for poor timekeeping. They had called John in to defend them, but to Matt's surprise John had given them a rev up and told them not to waste his time or Matt's. Clearly he was not going to be intimidated by Jim

"Yeah." replied Jim "Well you had better start leveling with me. What the hell is going on?"

"You tell me. It's about time you started consulting with <u>us</u>," John replied coolly.

"I don't need to consult to call in a contractor."

"No, but you do if you are planning to contract out permanent roles in your engineering services, making people redundant."

"I'm not. So, whatever this guy has been feeding you," Jim said, looking at Dave, "It's bullshit." Jim hesitated for effect and continued. "But I may be looking at disciplinary action against him so it's just as well you <u>are</u> here." Leaning back in his chair after firing the first salve, he picked up a tooth pick from a lacquered box.

"If you aren't looking at contracting out services, how do you explain a letter from VFM saying you are?" John replied, keeping his tone level.

"There's no such letter." Jim looked toward Libby for support. She nodded.

"What do you call this then?!" John produced a photocopy of a VFM letter from his briefcase; like a conjurer pulling a rabbit out of a hat. He slid the letter across Jim's desk.

Jim glanced at the letterhead feigning comprehension. The dyslexia made it difficult for him to understand any written documents, particularly under these circumstances. "It's a letter outlining the work VFM is doing for us. There is nothing about contracting out," he finished, mistakenly. Jim launched onto the offensive to distract Grimley, and buy time to review the letter. "Where'd you get the letter anyway? It's private company correspondence!"

John ignored the question. "It states quite clearly the intention to contract out."

"Bullshit!" replied Jim.

John picked up the letter, turned over the first page and started reading aloud. Jim relaxed, imperceptibly, as John read the letter.

"As discussed, I recommend services are contracted to VFM following a three-month lead in period. We will manage the redundancy and re-employment of selected staff on new rates, as part of the contract to provide services long term."

Matt looked from Jim to Trevor. Trevor's face was ashen, and pools of perspiration made dark patches under his armpits and in a few spots across his stomach where the shirt fell, in folds.

Jim stopped picking his teeth. He threw the toothpick into the trash bin.

"Give it to me." He snatched it from Grimley and read it silently. Then he passed it to Libby. "Where did this come from?"

Libby looked at the letter. She read the second page slowly, before turning back to the first page.

In the silence Matt could hear Trevor's labored breathing.

Eventually she said, "I've never seen this before," and handed it back to Jim.

"Oh, come on!" said John looking at Libby. "You signed it!"

"No." She replied calmly, "I signed a similar letter but it did not include the last two paragraphs."

Jim glared at John. "I told you this was bullshit! I received Libby's letter and it didn't have those two paragraphs. "Where did you get this?!"

"You expect me to believe that?!" replied John.

Jim stood up. Matt noticed Trevor cowering in his chair, like a dog expecting a beating.

Jim turned to the filing cabinet. He pulled out a folder marked VFM, extracted a letter, and handed it to John.

John read it and looked back at Jim and glancing around the room. "Somebody is not telling the truth here."

"Yeah, well you had better start by telling me where this came from!" Jim demanded.

John looked at Dave and shrugged his shoulders. "It's Dave's call."

Matt hoped Dave had himself covered because Jim would fire him on the spot if there was a hint of impropriety.

"Trevor's desk," Dave replied.

Matt's eyes followed everyone else's to Trevor.

Jim challenged Dave. "What were you doing in Trevor's office....... snooping around? You don't have any right to be looking at anything in his office! It is grounds for immediate dismissal!"

Dave appeared prepared for the challenge. "Nope. There's an explanation. Trevor called me on night shift earlier this week, and asked me to go into his office to get a phone number from a list he said was on his desk."

"So you thought you'd just read through his correspondence while you were there?!"

"The email was on top of his desk near the phone, Dave lied. "I couldn't help seeing it. It was an accident."

"This is grounds for immediate dismissal," Jim retorted as he pushed himself back from the desk

"Wait a minute, Jim." John stepped in. "Trevor requested Dave go into his office. There's a potential risk regarding confidential materials in that situation which Trevor was aware of." John turned to look at Trevor, "Who knows? Maybe Trevor planted the memo, intentionally?"

Jim jerked slightly. Exasperated by John's retort to his dismissal threat, but surprised by the suggestion Trevor may have planted the document. Up to this point he figured the Union delegate, Dave, had manufactured the letter. He was momentarily silent.

"OK. I say Dave planted the letter!" Jim's gaze moved from Dave to Trevor.

"I haven't seen it!" Trevor rasped.

"What do you mean you haven't seen it?" Jim demanded.

"The letter," he said, pointing at the copy on Jim's desk.

"Let me get this straight," Jim responded. "You haven't seen this letter with the two extra paragraphs Dave said he picked up off your desk?" He was bearing down on Trevor.

"No." Trevor replied, his eyes fixed on Jim's nameplate.

"And you haven't seen this letter either?" Jim turned to Libby.

Libby shook her head.

"And I haven't ever seen it before. So, where the hell did it come from?" He growled at John.

All eyes turned to Dave.

Matt noticed Dave was scratching his chin. It was an old habit of Dave's which started when he had a beard and scratched it out of nervous discomfort.

"You had better explain, and it had better be good," snarled Jim.

"Trevor asked me to go to his office to get a phone number last Tuesday night. I saw the VFM letter on the desk and had a quick look. I had already asked Matt whether VFM intended to contract services out when I heard they were taking over the maintenance improvement program." Dave glanced apologetically at Matt. "He told me Trevor had assured him they weren't. When I saw the letter, I realized there was a cover-up, so I took a copy and passed it on to John."

Jim jumped to his feet so quickly his desk jerked upward from the impact of his thighs. "You took a bloody copy?!!!"

Dave nodded, looking at Grimley who opened his mouth to offer an explanation.

Jim came around the desk and stood over Dave.

The room was heating up, everyone was breaking a sweat except Libby. Matt got up to open the door.

"Leave the door shut, Matt. This is a confidential discussion." Jim gestured for Matt to return to his seat.

John cut in again. "Dave was asked to go to Trevor's desk by Trevor. Dave couldn't help seeing the letter while searching for the information Trevor had requested, and Dave executed his duty to his union brethren by taking the copy. He was obligated to inform them about the contract out decision."

"Obligated?! My ass! Company policy comes first. John." Jim was adamant.

"Jim. We're probably not going to resolve the issue here, so why don't we park it for now and get back to the core issue of the day. The contract out decision. Is it happening or not?" The union organizer attempted to deflect the confrontation.

Jim stared silently at John, mentally extricating himself from the fight. He walked around the desk and sat down in his chair, and quietly swiveled the chair to face Trevor. Leaning forward, placing his forearms on the desktop and clasping his hands together, staring at Trevor all the while. "Well?"

"I don't know anything about it." Trevor stuttered.

Jim banged his fist on the desk. Obviously, he was not going to let the issue drop as John suggested. "I am not stupid!!" he shouted, swinging accusingly towards Dave. "You saw the letter on Trevor's desk, thought you would stir up some mischief and inserted a couple of extra paragraphs. I'll have you for wasting company time and snooping in areas where you have no right to be!"

"Hold on." said John, quietly. "There was no reason for Dave to do that. Let's look at the facts again. Trevor phoned Dave at night and asked him go to his office. He asked Dave to get a number of a refrigeration contractor. The contractor list was not in its normal place it was on the desk, on top of the VFM letter." John looked at Dave for acknowledgement.

Dave nodded. Trevor did not intervene.

John continued. "Trevor knew Dave would look at it. If the document was confidential information it should not have been left on top of a desk in an unlocked office. Dave said he would phone the cream plant manager directly to share the contractor's number. Trevor insisted he didn't want Dave to do so.. Why? My guess is because Fred, your Cream Plant Manager, did not need the number. If anyone inserted those paragraphs it was Trevor."

Matt now understood why Grimley and Dave had spent so much time together prior to the meeting. They had their story straight, and it was presenting a damning argument against Trevor.

Jim looked at John, coldly. "You should have been a lawyer! But this isn't a court of law." He stood up, towering over them, and added, "Remember I am the judge around here. Right now I am adjourning this meeting. You're free to go, but none of you leave the site. I'll call you when I want you."

Grimley glanced at Dave momentarily, deciding whether or not to agree to the adjournment and Jim's command. Dave nodded imperceptibly, and Grimley turned toward Jim, considering his response.

Matt figured Grimley was barely able to contain himself.

As the two union men rose to leave, Jim nodded to Libby to remain seated, and turned toward Matt and Trevor. "Matt and Trevor. You're excused for the moment. Close the door on your way out."

As the door closed, Jim put the phone on speaker and punched Kay's number into the keypad. When she answered, he asked to be put through to Fred, the Cream Plant Manager. A couple seconds later the phone rang.

"Fred. Jim here. When was the last time you spoke to Trevor?"

There was a long pause. "I'm not sure, Jim. I think it must have been last week when we were having a problem with one of the centrifuges?"

"You didn't call him about a refrigeration problem this week?"

"No? Why?"

"Never mind." Jim left Fred hanging for a moment while he considered further conversation. "You haven't spoken to him this week? You're positive?"

"Yep. I'm positive."

"On the phone?"

"No."

"No contractor requests for Tuesday night?"

"No. I was actually away from the plant on Tuesday."

"Thanks." Jim replaced the phone receiver.

"What do you think?" he asked Libby.

"I'm not sure. Why would Trevor do that?"

"To stop the maintenance excellence project."

"Maybe," she replied. "But he's not silly, is he?"

Jim didn't respond to her query. "We need to work out our best advantage from this situation," he said smugly, adding, "Who do we want to get rid of? Trevor or Dave?"

Libby looked at Jim calculating his level of commitment. There was no hint of humor in his expression. She hesitated.

"Well?" Jim was impatient. "For God sake, don't go soft on me. This is an opportunity to purge resistance to your project. Gross misconduct! But it may be difficult to make it stick for both of them." He rose abruptly from his desk and punched his fist in the air, "Yes, I can get rid of the blathering idiot, no problems! As for the union runt, I'll have him on a final written warning. That'll ensure he doesn't squeak again."

"How will you replace Trevor?" Libby asked.

"Does he need to be replaced? He does stuff all."

"You could do with a good change leader in that position."

Jim waved his hand dismissively. "I could do with someone who knows how to run a bloody maintenance department."

"Matt seems to be competent on the maintenance side of things. You could get him in the role as acting Maintenance Manager while you advertise. That should build his commitment to the VFM maintenance excellence project." Libby's appreciation of the opportunity was increasing.

Jim considered Libby's recommendation. It had merit, but he resented her coming up with the detailed solution. "He can get on and do it, provided he doesn't want any more money." Jim rubbed his hands together. "Now let me get Trevor in here and tell him the good news. You can talk to Matt, when I've finished."

After leaving the meeting, Matt headed back to the workshop and grabbed a sandwich while he responded to his emails and phone messages. He had been tempted to confront Trevor, but Trevor's door was closed. He pictured him sitting, eating his sardine sandwiches. The air would be as putrid as any discussion they might have. He wondered what Jim's next move would be. Glancing up he noticed it was already 2:30 p.m. Where had the day gone? He had promised Jan he would leave on time at 4.00 p.m. They had seats booked to see the hottest new play in New Haven at seven o'clock.

He looked at the weekly plan and shift cover for the weekend. There was information which needed to be passed on to the night shift when they came in at 6:00 p.m. Normally, he would ask Dave to do it, but given the current situation, it would be better not to rely on Dave. He decided to see who was in the workshop. He heard Trevor's office door open and the heavy tread of his footsteps coming down the stairs. He walked straight past Matt without eye contact or acknowledgement.

"What's up Matt?" Matt's thoughts were interrupted by Mad Andy. Matt hesitated for a minute before replying. "Andy, I won't be here for shift change over tonight. If I go through the work orders for the weekend with you, could you go through them with the incoming shift?"

"You didn't answer me, Matt. I asked you what's up?" Andy replied.

Matt chuckled. "And you are avoiding my question. I asked you if you could go through the work orders with the incoming shift."

"What's it worth?" asked Andy.

"Come on Andy, give me a break."

"Well, I may need to consult a union official first, seeing as he's on site."

Matt was about to bite, when he caught the mischievous glint in Andy's eyes. Laughing he replied, "Thanks Andy, I appreciate your help".

"Yeah," said Andy. "And remember it next time I want to get away early on a Friday night."

"I will," replied Matt. "And to answer your question, I'm not sure, but Trevor could be up shit creek with no paddle."

Andy nodded, "Serves him right!"

They were both in the planning office, going through the Friday night plan when the work shop door banged open. Jim strode through the door with Trevor, ashen faced, behind him. Without a word Jim headed for Trevor's office. Trevor followed a few paces behind him.

Andy let out a low whistle and looked sideways at Matt, "Shit creek's gone dry!"

Less than five minutes later, Matt and Andy watched Trevor walk out of the workshop with Jim following behind.

Before following Trevor into the rain, Jim turned at the door and directed a comment to Matt and Andy and anyone else nearby, "Trevor is history. Libby will be here at four o'clock to brief you on the interim arrangements. Matt, make sure everyone in the maintenance department is here to listen."

Matt nodded his agreement. His stomach tightened.

Matt and Andy looked at each other.

"I don't believe it," said Andy as he headed up the stairs to Trevor's office.

Matt, still seated, noticed he was holding his breath. He let out a huge sigh.

From above him, Andy let out a loud 'whoop.' "He IS history!" He shouted, "The briefcase, the family photos, even the sodding sandwich box; All gone!"

Matt heard Andy bounding down the stairs, two at a time, before he appeared back though Matt's office door, grinning from ear to ear.

"Jim was here getting Trev to clean out his desk. There is a Santa Claus!" As he caught his breath, he remembered he didn't fully understand the situation. "But, how come?"

"I'm not sure, but I think Dave may have some answers. We'll find out one way or the other later this afternoon."

After finishing off with Andy, Matt pushed the door closed. Just his luck, the one Friday he needed to be away on time they were calling a meeting for 4.00 p.m. Curious as he was to find out what was going on, he did not need to be curious about what Jan's reaction might be if he was late home and they missed the show. He knew she would be disappointed, and rightfully so. He had promised not to let anything get in the way of their plans this time, and had assured her of Trevor's support. But now, Trevor was gone. He'd have to pay for Saturday and Sunday out of his own pocket if Jan still wanted to go. He realized he should have got things in writing. It was his fault. Bugger!

He took a deep breath and phoned Libby's mobile. She answered on the second ring.

"Libby speaking"

"Libby. It's Matt"

"Oh. Hi Matt." she replied smoothly. "I thought you might be in touch. You've heard the news I suspect?"

"Jim simply said, 'he's gone," Matt replied.

"That's right. Trevor has left the company voluntarily."

"Why?" He wanted to compare her response to Dave's answer, which he would, no doubt, hear very soon.

"I think you had better ask Jim," she replied, adding, "Matt I want to talk to you about your role, since Trevor is gone. I'll be over there at four o'clock, and then we can talk to the team at shift change over."

"That's why I'm calling. I've got a problem," Matt replied. "I was due to leave at four o'clock. I've got commitments at home."

"Can't it wait?" Libby asked, adding with a hint of impatience. "This is important. For the site, and for your future."

So is my marriage, thought Matt before replying, "Libby, I've planned a weekend away with my wife."

"Well surely you can re-schedule. It's not every weekend the Maintenance Manager leaves."

"No." said Matt. Wondering why he was agreeing with her. "No. It isn't every week the Maintenance Manager leaves, but I made a promise."

"I am sure she'll understand," replied Libby curtly. "Just give her a call. I'll be over at four o'clock." She abruptly hung up.

Matt stared at the phone. Bloody woman! How am I going tell Jan? He could imagine her response if he told her a female consultant was demanding he stay late. There was no way he could stay until 6.00 p.m., and make the show. He wondered if they could re-schedule but remembered this was the last week of the show and Saturday night's performance was fully booked.

He weighed up the options. Jan or Libby? Why was his life being turned upside down by domineering women? Weren't women supposed to be soft warm and supportive, understanding of the demands placed on him? Jan needed to come first, but keeping Jan meant keeping a job that paid a decent wage. She was like a machine that needed a lot of maintenance, new parts in the form of clothes and household appliances and regular servicing at hairdressers, beauty clinics and the gym.

Matt loved it when they were first dating, but they had lost their closeness, like they weren't speaking each other's language, any longer. He did all he could to provide Jan with what she wanted; a new car, money for shopping, no need for work, but she didn't seem satisfied. She complained about his lack of emotional availability, or willing to spend quality time with her. What was quality time he wondered? Going to the gym together? Thinking of the gym, Wayne came to mind. He tensed at the idea Wayne might just be doing some servicing of his own. Picking up the phone he dialed home.

A few minutes later he hung up the phone. He had explained to Jan that Trevor had left and the VFM consultant wanted him there for the shift change over. Something in him cautioned him against referring to Libby by name. To his surprise, Jan had taken it quite calmly. She had suggested she call one of her friends and they would go to the show and go shopping together on Saturday, freeing Matt up for whatever he needed to do at the site. Relieved to find an easy solution, he had agreed, apologetically suggesting he join her for Saturday night. Jan insisted there was no need for him to go up to the city on Saturday night, saying she knew he might need to be on call. Matt argued it was their weekend away, but Jan had quietly insisted he should stay home. She realized the site needed him.

Matt found it hard to believe, but a Godsend. Jan sounded happy to carry on without him, and he'd be able to find out what had happened at the plant and what Libby meant about 'his future.'

He was still wrestling with his mixed emotions of relief and disappointment when his thoughts were interrupted by the sound of cheering from the smoko room. He got up and went to see what was happening. The entire contingent of tradesmen was in the room. Dave had just arrived. They were thumping him on the back and congratulating him.

As Matt walked into the room, Andy was shaking Dave's hand exclaiming, "You're the man!"

Dave laughed and seeing Matt approach addressed his reply to Matt. "I'm the man all right. The man on a final written warning!"

"What happened?"

"Jim did me for serious misconduct, for helping myself to supposedly confidential information. John suggested I take the rap with the understanding it would be removed from my file in six months. Jim said he would think about it." Turning to the guys he added "The beers are on you lot tonight."

"Too right!" laughed Andy. "I'll buy the first round." His response was met with loud cheers. A Scotsman through and through, Andy had a reputation for having deep pockets and short arms.

"Seeing as a celebration is in hand, how about letting us off early Matt?" one of the other fitters enquired.

"Sorry guys. No chance. Libby has called a meeting at four o'clock to talk to you day guys and the night shift at six o'clock about what happens next.

"Why Libby?" Dave asked. "Surely now Trevor has gone, <u>you</u> make the decisions?"

"Yeah well …. I've got a meeting with Libby in five minutes," Matt replied awkwardly. "Meantime, I'd appreciate it if you guys could get back to business as usual. There hasn't been much maintenance work done today."

There was a collective groan around the room.

Dave took Matt to one side as the maintenance crew started filing out of the door. "I thought you were off at four o'clock today?" he asked.

"Yeah, so did I……. but …" replied Matt

"Have you told the old lady?" asked Dave.

"Yeah, she's heading up to New Haven with one of her friends. Could be expensive."

"Sorry Mate" Dave said quietly, "Hey look on the bright side you can join us for Andy's shout."

"Sounds good" said Matt. "I'll catch you if you're still at the pub after the shift hand-over at six o'clock."

Back in his office Matt thought about the events of the day. It was hard to believe Trevor was gone. For years he had hoped Trevor would leave, but he didn't share the sense of elation felt by the guys. He realized he'd been on a bit of an emotional rollercoaster during the past two weeks. Jack's audit had provided a renewed sense of enthusiasm. Just when things had started to gain momentum Libby had appeared with VFM's project and now the contracting out threat, or hoax. What did she really want to see him about? She said she wanted to talk to him about his role. What did it mean? What were she and Jim plotting? Perhaps they planned to move him aside and replace him and Trevor's role with VFM people? Should he trust Libby? He hadn't felt comfortable around her from the first moment they met. Not because she was from VFM, but because of her class.

She reminded him of a childhood girlfriend. They were both twelve and attending the same middle school. She was his first 'crush" and he had dreamed of marrying her. She invited him home for tea one Friday. Her father was a manager at the plant where his father, Jukka, worked.

His father had laughed at him when he told him he was going to his boss' house for a meal. He said, "Don't get ideas son, those people will kick you down sooner than they'll pick you up."

Matt had held his head high, while his brothers and sisters had giggled at his father's remark.

When Matt arrived at her house, her father had opened the door and said "What do you want?!"

Taken aback Matt had stammered, "I've come for dinner. Your daughter invited me."

"Well you won't get any here, go home to where you belong!" The door shut loudly in his face.

To this day Matt hadn't told his family what had happened, and the shame of the incident still burned like a hot coal inside him. Contact with Libby rekindled the flame. She reminded him of the girl who never talked to him at school, following the incident.

The four o'clock meeting with Libby went surprisingly well. She told him Trevor's job would be advertised and in the interim period she and Matt would work together to run the department. Matt's confidence increased once he knew his job was not under threat. He suggested the new initiatives Libby had proposed for the Maintenance Excellence project be put on hold. They should concentrate on seeing through Jack's version of the MBP work which had been started, put planning and preventive maintenance systems in place. Libby firmly explained it was not an option. She was here to get results, and with Trevor's departure, she knew they could move more quickly. Matt relented.

They agreed Matt would run the six o'clock meeting to update the guys. The meeting went smoothly and Matt was pleasantly surprised to find Libby providing supportive comments and body language. He left the office at 6.30 p.m. and headed to join the guys at the pub, feeling a sense of relief the events of the week were behind him and there was no need to rush home to Jan.

After the six o'clock hand-over meeting Libby headed for Jim's office to update him. She was happy with the day's outcomes, even though it had been stressful. She had been working on several spreadsheets during the week and could already demonstrate cost savings. Trevor's demise had been a major breakthrough, removing the main blockage to her progress. Her meeting with Matt had gone well. He was pliable. She could get him to do what she wanted.

Jim's door was open, but he wasn't in. Libby walked in and surveyed the set up. His chair stood erect behind the desk, like a mighty throne. One thing for sure, she thought, if he was the only man left in the world, she wouldn't go there. She contemplated taking a seat in his chair, mocking his authoritarian style. She almost laughed out loud.

"Hi Princess. Is the anticipation of my arrival putting a smile on your face?!" Jim said as he entered the room.

Libby stepped back from his desk, realizing she had almost put herself in a professionally compromised position. The smile quickly disappeared from her face. "No. It's the financial results I have to show you."

"Loosen up Libs. You and I have got something going."

She ignored the comment and placed the document on his desk as he slid into his chair. She talked him through the cost saving forecast for the VFM project. "Trevor's departure is a huge bonus. Without him blocking progress and covering up his expenditures we should be able to make even better returns over the next month. I've told Matt you plan to replace Trevor. My personal advice to you is to leave the position vacant. Matt is capable of running the day-to-day operation, and I will drive the maintenance excellence project. I can put Trevor's salary in our savings column."

Jim got up from his chair, walked around the desk and sat on it, facing Libby, admiring her figure slowly without any attempt at disguise. "You'd look great in a low-cut blouse. You've got great tits. Why do you hide them?"

Libby turned away, flushed with anger.

Jim thought she was blushing as a result of his bold compliment, and carried on confidently. "Libby this is good work. You and I make a great team. We can go places together!" He paused as though he expected an agreeable reply.

She stood up to leave without uttering a word.

"I need these figures tidied up so I can present them to the Board. I also need a forecast of the results we are going to get over the next three months and at year end. Make it punchy and get it on my desk by tomorrow morning."

"Fine." Libby replied coldly, not skipping a beat regarding his request for Saturday morning delivery. "What do you think about my idea to leave Trevor's position vacant?" She hoped to deflect any further advances.

"I like it. He was no friggin use anyway."

She headed for the door.

As she reached the hallway she turned just as Jim shouted, "Hey! Princess! If you happen to find a pea under your mattress, just give me a call!"

CHAPTER 10

Matt sifted through his emails on his first day on the job in full charge of the maintenance department. He had to check emails for Trevor as well as his own. Fortunately, the weekend had been uneventful including a great session with "the boys" on Friday evening and no calls for him at the house. He had finished two long rides on his road bike and Jan had returned Sunday night in fine spirits. He had even gotten lucky with her. She had done some shopping, but volunteered the receipts to show she hadn't spent too much. Hard to believe as she had been shopping with Viv, who was notorious for spending heaps. He was in good spirits for a Monday.

He wondered how much time he wasted every day reading and replying to emails. Did any of them get the plant running better? He opened the next one in line.

Subject: Warning
From: Mandy
To: Matt Polaski

Matt. Take care. I have evidence that Miss Prissy is not the lady she makes out. She's a schemer. You don't want to go where Jim has been.
Mandy x

Matt read it again. Bloody Heck! What was Mandy doing sending him an email about Libby and what evidence did she have? Did Mandy mean Jim and Libby were having it on? Libby had more class than that. Libby was another woman in Mandy's territory. It takes a woman to bring out the worst in a woman, he thought.

In the workshop it was business as usual. Moke was sitting at a computer terminal in the planner's office.

Dave was pulling apart a small chemical dosing pump at his workbench

"Hey! Dave! Look-it this! Here on the screen." Moke shouted

Dave put down his wrench and walked over to Moke and the computer workstation.

"Look. The PM's on the drier explosion doors and the pressure tests on the homogenizer lines."

Dave leaned closer to the screen looking for something obvious, not understanding what Moke was so excited about.

"Look at the job status on these PM's. They're listed as complete!"

"So?" Dave couldn't see Moke's point.

"Well look at the dates they're scheduled for."

"Hmmmm." Dave studied the screen then saw the problem. "They're scheduled for tomorrow."

"Well, I'll be damned! You aren't as thick as pigshit!" Moke couldn't help getting a dig into Dave.

"They're scheduled for tomorrow....but they're complete today?" Dave hesitated. "I've never seen anything like this before. I didn't think you could do that with this CMMS system!"

"Yeah. Neither did I. I wouldn't have normally paid any attention except the explosion doors and the pressure checks are part of my area-based PMs. We set them up after Jack's introduction to the MBP program. It pisses me off mate! Somebody's stuffing things up."

"Yeah.....maybe......." Dave still wasn't sure what the story was. "You better talk to Matt. See if he knows anything about a schedule change, or maybe he can talk to the planner and see if there's a stuff-up in the PM software."

Moke nodded and closed off the work order report.

Dave walked back to his workbench. Dave knew Moke had a special attachment to the area, and his concern was real. Moke had spent a lot of time working on the critical plant definitions for the drier area and had asked Matt if he could be assigned to the area he was talking about as part of Jack's recommendation to break the site down to areas where each tradesman could take personal responsibility.

The drier explosion door checks were a key preventive maintenance task along with the pressure checks on the feed lines to the drier. The drier explosion doors were an important safety device. If they failed to open during a milk powder explosion the drier shell could rupture resulting in metal shrapnel flying through the internal building area, a fire, concussion damage and serious bodily injury or death. The doors were intended to relieve the explosion pressure to the atmosphere surrounding the ten-story building.

The only harm following a controlled explosion would be a puff of white powder, maybe a brief fire and an environmental incident complaint from the neighbors near the Mornington plant. They could be back on line in less than a day in the case of a controlled, vented explosion when the explosion doors functioned as designed. Failure of the doors to operate could shut the plant down for weeks or months depending on the extent of damage. Jack referred to such an event as a catastrophic failure. Consequences of the failure were orders of magnitude more costly than the equipment failure. Jack had convinced Matt and some of the staff catastrophic failures could be avoided with a good reliability program.

A couple hours later, Moke, Dave and Matt were huddled around Graeme, one of the two maintenance planners, and his computer terminal.

"You've got to see this, guys!" Moke exclaimed. "I asked Graeme to see if there's a software glitch in tomorrow's Drier PM's. He said there wasn't any glitch!" Moke's voice was tense with anticipation and glee.

Graeme punched a few buttons and pulled up the PM screen showing the Drier Explosion asset numbers and PMs Moke and Dave had been looking at earlier in the morning. "Yeah. Moke's right. I checked the PMs for him, and I noticed they were closed out. I thought it was odd, but there's a simple explanation. Moke just didn't look close enough." Graeme was excited about the discovery as well. Aft

"Shit....the only thing Moke looks close at is a wild pig or deer in his rifle sight," Dave said.

"Cut the crap Dave! You're not gonna believe this!" Moke retorted.

Graeme moved the cursor to highlight the trade group that had completed and closed the PM work order. He double clicked on the area to expand it.

"Christ! What the hell is she doing in there!?" Matt exclaimed.

Moke smiled knowingly, and looked at Dave, whose eyes had widened when he saw Libby Galwaith's name in the trade group slot.

"She's not a tradesman! She can't close a work order!" Dave was nonplussed.

Graeme brought up the second PM work order on the Homogenizer pressure checks. He double-clicked on the trade group, and Libby Galwaith's name came up there, as well.

Matt was speechless. He stood up straight and looked at Dave and Moke, then out the window toward the administration building. He hesitated, weighing up the situation and Graeme's potential allegiance before replying. "How is she able to log into the system on that level?"

"She's logged in as a system administrator." Graeme was certain

"A System Administrator?! Did you set it up for her......or Trevor?"

"Nope. I can't set anyone up as an administrator. Only the jokers in IS support services at head office."

"Bloody Hell! You mean somebody at head office has gone over all of our heads, Trevor's too probably, and set her up like this?" Matt's anger increased as he backed away from the console and the rest of the men.

Moke and Dave gave him space. Matt didn't get angry very easily and they knew it could get nasty.

Graeme turned in his chair, cool and collected. He was used to angry people hassling him, be it irate tradesmen who thought his plan was crap or operations people who were unhappy with the downtime he requested from them to complete work. "My guess is Jim ok'd the access for her. It would have taken his approval for it to happen even if they'd gone through us."

"They didn't bother!" Matt reaffirmed as he thought of another key question. "When was Libby's name loaded into the system."

"It was loaded the day she started, with top level security. She can do anything she wants in the system." Graeme answered. He'd discovered she had more authority than him in the computerized maintenance system. In fact, Libby's level of authority was reserved for the highest-level software developers at head office. "I'd say she knows her way around a CMMS as well," Graeme finished off.

"What's this mean?!" Matt directed his question at Graeme, thinking there must be some sort of mistake.

"I'm not sure. Maybe she wants to show you who's in charge."

Matt stopped at the door, the last of the three to leave. "Thanks for your help Graeme."

"Any time Matt."

The three men made their way outside into the sunshine. The designated smoking area located nearby was one of the few places where it was safe to talk. The noise from the COGEN plant made it difficult for them to hear each other let alone anyone who wanted to eavesdrop.

"You know what this means?!" Moke directed his question at Matt. "It means that bitch Libby is putting all of us in the deep!"

"Yeah.! Those are critical plant preventive maintenance tasks. Time consuming. Aren't they contract jobs as well?" Matt queried.

"Too right. Those checks are outside work. They're worth twenty-five hundred dollars a go." Moke was getting worked up.

"Ok. We've got to think about this. I've got a few more questions that need answers."

"Yeah? Like what!? It's obvious Matt! She's cutting outside work. How the hell else is she gonna save two million dollars?" Dave lit a cigarette as he spoke. As the union rep, he would not allow his work mates to be put at risk. He realized the potential impact and Libby's capability to manipulate the work orders and other aspects of the business.

"Yep. She's already cut our contractor cover down to zero which means we have to work more overtime which isn't covered in our salary agreement. The season's nearly over. What next? She'll probably want to can the outside winter work contractors?!" Moke was on a roll.

"Dave. Gimme one of your smokes." Matt was getting edgy.

"Not for you, mate. You quit. What do you think we should do about this?"

"I'm thinking." Matt stared at the ground wishing he could take a drag on Dave's cigarette, at least.

"I think we should find out what else is getting cancelled. Do you think we can trust Graeme not to squeal?"

"I think so," Dave said.

"Ok. You guys go back in and ask him to do a search on the PMs and upcoming winter work plan and see whether Libby's been mucking around with anything else." Matt hesitated. "And one more thing, get some dates on when the changes were made, and ask Graeme if anyone else could be doing this besides her."

"What are you gonna do?" Dave asked.

"Right now? I'm going to talk to Scott in operations about what'll really happen if those drier explosion doors fail. Then I'm going to wait for you to get the rest of the information to me before I confront Libby."

"Good on you mate!" Dave stomped out his smoke and grabbed Moke by the shoulder. "We'll get onto it."

Moke and Dave headed back to Graeme's office in a hurry, excited to support Matt's initiative.

Later in the day, Matt looked over his shoulder as he walked down the hallway of the administration building toward Libby's' office. Being in the 'shiny ass' section of the site always made him nervous, especially since he might run into Jim who always challenged his presence in the area. He walked up to what he thought was Libby's office and was about to knock when he noticed, through the sidelight, Jim talking to her with his back to the door. Matt continued walking down the corridor.

A moment later the door opened, and Jim turned to walk out. Too late.

"Matt! Good to see you!" Jim exclaimed. "Libby tells me you've slotted into Trevor's role without a hitch. Really appreciate it."

Matt was surprised. Jim had never complimented him before. He was also surprised about Jim's statement regarding the Maintenance Manager's role. Neither he nor Libby had agreed on the outcome and he thought Jim should make the offer since the position reported to him, not Libby.

Jim hesitated. He glanced towards Libby's office and back at Matt, surmising Matt's possible presence in the corridor. His expression changed to one of sage understanding. "Oh, I get it! Your new role gives you an excuse to come and consult with the new lady!?" He cautioned Matt, sarcastically. "Well don't get any ideas……ok mate?!"

Matt took a step forward and stopped. "Yeah. I need to talk to Libby. Is she available?" Matt always hated how conversations with Jim degenerated into one of two topics, sex or ass-kicking.

"Yeah. She's available, but watch yourself." He elbowed Matt and winked as he pushed past.

Matt walked into Libby's office with a folder full of CMMS printouts under his arm.

"Hi Matt. C'mon in. Good to see you."

Matt noticed Libby's exceptionally bright smile. Her full lips were dipped in mauve lipstick and her teeth were a perfect pearl white. She really glowed and Matt caught himself wondering what it would feel like to kiss those lips. He checked himself, certain she might pick up on his thoughts.

"Can I get you a cup of coffee or tea? I'm going to have one myself."

"Yeah. Sure." He couldn't believe she was going to get him a cup of anything. He didn't think people in these sorts of positions did favors for guys off the floor.

"Great. So, what's it going to be? Coffee or tea?" She was still smiling as she moved closer to him in order to make her way out of the office.

He could smell her perfume, subtle but piercingly aromatic. Her blond hair fell straight down her back halfway to her waist. She had a flawless complexion and exuded femininity. Matt was drifting into sensory overload, his primal instincts awakened.

"Matt? Coffee or tea?!"

"Oh. Coffee. Black. Thanks," he said, slightly embarrassed.

"I'll be right back. Have a seat."

He turned and watched her walk out the door. No wonder Jim had the hots for her. Nice ass, nice curves, class. He couldn't believe he was thinking these things. He was supposed to be pinning her down with the evidence Moke and Dave had supplied. He sat down and tried to get back on track.

She returned a couple minutes later, and set Matt's coffee on a coaster in front of him. "So, Matt. Good to see you again, so soon. What's up?"

"Things are going Ok." Matt hesitated, trying to figure out how to bring up the issue of the work order changes as well as his apparent new position in the organization.

Libby cut in while he was thinking. "Matt. I'm really counting on you to help with the maintenance excellence project. You're a natural leader and the guys will follow your example. In fact, it would probably be a good idea for you and me to spend some time really getting to know each other better. Maybe we could meet for dinner to talk some more about our strategy, outside of work."

Matt ignored the suggestion. "Libby. I was wondering if I could talk to you about some things me and the boys picked up on the CMMS today. It's got us worried."

"Sure Matt. Can't afford to have good people like you worried."

"One of the tradesmen was looking at the work orders for the drier explosion vent PM checks which were supposed to happen this week. He noticed they had been marked complete, before the date for release of the work had actually arrived." Matt handed Libby printouts of the work orders and waited for her response, hoping she would fess up, and he wouldn't have to make any accusations.

Libby took the printouts and shifted in her seat. She appeared slightly surprised for a second. After a half minute of thumbing through the work orders she looked up at Matt. "So, what's the concern?"

"Well. The concern is somebody has marked these complete other than Moke. The PMs were meant for him to action and nobody else should have completed them, especially before the date they were to be issued." Matt wasn't sure how to proceed. "Libby, I don't know how to say this…."

"Say what?" Libby's shifted forward on her seat moving her arms onto desk.

"The maintenance planner, helped us look into who closed the work orders since we don't have access to that security level."

"And?" Libby's expression grew more serious.

"And the system indicates <u>you</u> are the one who closed the work orders off, prematurely?"

"Oh? Really?!" Libby exclaimed with a smile.

He knew it. Libby knew what he was going to say. She had made the changes.

"And what if I did close those work orders Matt?" Libby was challenging him, but she didn't seem angry or perturbed.

"Well me and the boys thought it was out of line. We know those drier checks and some of the pressure vessel checks which have been eliminated are critical tasks."

"So, you thought I was just willy-nilly closing out critical work orders and endangering the lives of people here at the plant?"

"Well. We didn't know what to think, but it looked that way." Matt was feeling uncomfortable about the whole thing. She seemed to be turning the tables on him. "We thought if you did it, you would have told us?"

"Matt. I would never do anything to endanger people or the site's performance."

Libby's voice remained relaxed, reassuring and sincere. Matt relaxed slightly. "So, what about the PM checks on the drier...they're going to be overdue?"

"You're right. They are overdue if you go by historic practices here. I've closed out a lot of work orders. Not because I thought the work was unnecessary, but because I want all of us to challenge our thinking about what work should be done and when it should be done."

"But Moke set up those PMs on the drier and the pressure equipment because they are necessary."

"Right. Perhaps necessary in his mind and past historic practices here, but maybe," she hesitated for effect and to make sure he was fully attentive, "maybe the intervals for the checks are too short?"

Matt looked down at the floor.

"How many times have those drier doors failed?"

"Never, that I know of."

"Exactly my point! They've never failed. You don't really know whether you should be checking them every three months or six months do you?"

"All I know is it's just common sense to check them every three months." Matt was losing the argument. She was bringing up considerations which had never been suggested by Jack during his site audit or presentation. They always had done the checks three-monthly. This is what Jack had talked about; basing checks on what tradesmen believed was best. Maybe Libby knew as much about this stuff as Jack did. Maybe she knew more than Jack.

"That's what I want us all to think about Matt. What is common sense? Is it three months or six months? There are ways of getting a real handle on the requirements by identifying the failure developing period, and calculating the checks based on it."

"The failure what?" Matt had heard Jack mention the term. Moke certainly hadn't considered it when he planned the explosion door PM checks.

"Failure developing period," Libby reiterated. She had relaxed into a coaching posture now, sensing the challenge from Matt had been diffused. "It's the time from when you first notice a problem, like a bearing velocity or acceleration reading out of the norm.....until the bearing actually fails. In the case of most bearing failures, it's a month or more."

Matt looked down again. She wasn't really trying to shaft the program he thought. It sounded like he and the guys needed to cut her some slack until she explained where she was going. He'd look like a fool if he pressed any harder, and he was going to look like a fool when he explained to Moke and Dave why he'd backed off. He got up to leave.

Libby stood up and walked around the desk and put her hand on Matt's shoulder as he turned toward the door. "Thanks for coming in Matt. I know some of this stuff is new to you and the guys, but trust me, we're going to improve the maintenance operation and availability of the plant together. I'll get you up to speed on these concepts and we can make it happen together."

Matt walked to the door and turned. "You can understand why we were concerned when Graeme told us you had been on the system, and you had a higher security access than him."

Libby flashed a perfect gleaming white smile. "It's going to be fun working with you Matt."

"Come on in, Libby!" Jim didn't look up. He was concentrating on a spreadsheet report, looking intently through his new half-frame reading glasses. He had just farted, and he smiled as Libby seated herself. He wondered whether she would notice and what her reaction would be.

Libby gracefully seated herself in one of the lowered seats on the other side of his desk.

No sign of any reaction to his flatulence. Jim surmised she must be cool with it or maybe she has a nasal problem.

"Jim. Matt and the guys are getting suspicious."

"Suspicious? Of what?! I thought they were too busy running around chasing breakdowns!?"

"Seriously, they aren't idiots and they've got some good technical people working in the area, like the planner, Graeme."

"So....?"

"So, they've already figured out I've cancelled most of the expensive PM checks for the month, and I have a higher access level to the CMMS than anyone else on the site."

"So?"

"So, they know I've cancelled the drier explosion door checks and some of the pressure vessel checks. I was able to fob Matt off by telling him we could be more efficient by rescheduling all the PMs after an FMECA analysis."

"And he bought it?"

"Yes. But perhaps just for the short term. We're going to have to train them in Reliability Centered Maintenance in order to keep their faith. The training may prove their intervals were correct."

"Keep the faith Libs! Keep the faith. That's why I hired you isn't it?"

Libby ignored his remark. "Matt's a clever guy. He's going to be back with more information and demands to review the work. That will make it difficult to drive all the outside contracts down as rapidly as we want to. I told you we would have to cut almost all of the outside contracts and internal overtime to zero for the next six months to get the two million in savings."

Jim was getting impatient. He stood up and walked around to the chair next to Libby's.

She shifted to the opposite side of her chair.

"Don't worry dear. I'm not going to bite.........yet!" He put his foot up on the arm of the chair next to Libby. The white skin of his leg showed between the bottom of his pant and the top of his threadbare black socks. "I'm counting on the savings. And I am counting on you to do whatever maintenance excellence practice it takes to deliver the savings to me." His tone was threatening. "You need to take Matt under your wing. Train him as you see fit. Buy him some toys to use here at work. Take him out to dinner for bloody sake. Whatever it takes!"

Libby remained poised.

"You need to make sure Matt is ....on our side!" He stopped talking and stared at Libby. He was using his best intimidation techniques, standing over the adversary and stretching the tense silence for effect, letting the words and the tone sink in before he continued.

Libby sat motionless.

He couldn't believe it. She hadn't flinched. He thought to himself, she must be good in the sack. He could feel himself getting aroused at the thought of rooting her until her poised expression turned into a moan of submission.

"Matt's no stooge!"

Libby's remark and her semi-angry tone snapped him out of his momentary fantasy. He smiled. He liked the word stooge and he liked it even more when Libby had mouthed it. He withdrew his foot and walked back around the desk, hesitating, drawing out his response time. He knew, full well, he was going to knock her back with his clever reply. "And neither are you!"

Libby stood up, straightening her business jacket and skirt. She was ticked off but she knew she had to disguise her anger. "Jim. I'm keeping you informed and asking for some advice."

Jim was seated again, glancing at the same spreadsheet report. "You need to give yourself more credit. I'm counting on you Libby. You can do it."

She wasn't satisfied with the exchange. She was looking for some other options and was about to discuss them when his phone rang.

He turned and checked the phone's LCD display. "It's the GM. I'll catch you later." He picked up the phone and turned his back on Libby as he answered the call.

The conversation was over.

"G'day Graham. Great to hear your voice! What can I do for you?"

Jim waved to Libby without looking and launched into a muffled conversation as she left the room.

CHAPTER 11

Matt squirmed in his blazer jacket. The knot of his tie was uncomfortable against his throat.

"You really clean-up well. It's nice to be out with an attractive man instead of eating by myself."

Libby looked radiant. Was it the glow of the candlelight or her? Matt wasn't sure. The conversation was making him feel more uncomfortable.

"I've been here for a month and you're the only other male who's been out to dinner with me, except for Jim. You can imagine what that's like?"

"You mean he's hitting on you too?" Matt shook his head.

Libby flushed slightly. She knew she would have to share some secrets, mutual trials to win Matt's confidence. She felt relieved to think Matt might sympathize with her.

Matt wondered if it was for effect since Libby was seldom uneasy.

"Yes. It's part of the job, part of being a woman in what is still very much a man's world."

"You mean the maintenance engineering world?"

Libby nodded.

"I'm sorry to hear he's hitting on you."

"Yes. Like I said, his behavior goes with the territory." She smiled appreciatively. "Thanks for your empathy, Matt."

He wondered why she was sharing what he considered to be intimate details about her relationship with her boss. Wasn't she worried he might report back to Jim about her? Nevertheless, Matt was beginning to feel more comfortable with her. Her warm smile and soft voice made him feel like she could be trusted. He took another sip of his scotch.

"So, you're really a scotch man, Matt?"

"Once in a while. This stuff is too dear. It's easier on the wallet to stick with Waikato."

"Waikato?" Libby asked.

"Beer."

"Of course. It's the champagne for men?" Libby took a sip of chardonnay.

It was Tuesday evening, a little over twenty-four hours since her exchange with Matt about the PM cancellation issue. She was following up on Jim's advice to engage Matt and prove she could win Matt over, meeting Jim's challenge.

Matt had his own plans. He ordered the most expensive steak and picked a dozen Bluff oysters as an entree at twenty-five dollars a dozen. The Johnny Walker Black label scotch was a treat too; at ten dollars a shot. He figured he'd be into her for at least one hundred bucks before the evening was over. It would compensate somewhat for the risk he was taking, being seen by someone and the 'date' getting back to Jan. He hadn't bothered to tell Jan about the date with Libby. He and Jan had never been in this particular restaurant themselves. He explained to Jan he had a business meeting which could result in more take-home pay.

He didn't want to meet for dinner, but earlier in the day Libby had seemed so vulnerable and sincere when she re-iterated her request to meet outside of work hours. He thought she wanted to talk to him about Jim. He had turned her down initially but her look of disappointment made him reconsider and consent. Jan was away for the evening, so he would have been home alone in any event.

They chatted about Matt's family, and Libby told Matt about her life in the U.K, her career and life on the road with VFM. She was very open about herself and the lonely life of a corporate consultant.

After their dinner entrees had been cleared away she changed the subject. "Matt. I've got plans for you, if you'd like to be involved."

Matt shifted slightly in his seat, but didn't respond.

She poured two glasses of cabernet from a bottle she had ordered to go with their mains. She was having a steak as well. "I think you've got what it takes to be the Site Maintenance Engineering Manager. It's just a question of training and a bit more time. You learn the Maintenance Excellence jargon, how to build a few spreadsheets and graphs and you can run the show at the site."

Matt reckoned she was now focusing on the main reason for the dinner invitation. "I'm not sure. I mean, I haven't thought about it much." Matt was getting a bit giddy from the scotch.

"I'm serious, Matt. You're a natural leader. You're smart and you want to see maintenance excellence succeed as much as I do." Libby was leaning forward and her energy and passion were exciting Matt along with his view of her shapely breasts.

He was surprised. She wore clothes that concealed her curves at the site, but for some reason had decided to expose her womanly features to him this evening.

"I really do believe in it......what it can do for the place, for the boys. We're tired of the crisis day after day. Our families are sick of it as well."

"That's exactly what I mean. Your heart's in it. Not just for the company but for the guys, and that's the reason they'll follow your lead."

"Well. Yeah. You're right." He was feeling the positive energy from her and his confidence about the option was increasing.

"Exactly!" Libby reached across the table and put her left hand on the top of Matt's right hand.

Was there a spark with her?! Matt thought so, but her expression didn't betray it.

"You can lead this crew to maintenance excellence, to a better lifestyle at work and home. I know it's important to you. I want to help you do it. Eventually, I want to hire you to work for VFM and take over for me when I leave."

Damn! Matt was nonplussed. He remained silent thinking about her unexpected proposal. A hint of suspicion crossed his mind as he tried to gauge her sincerity, her motivation. The penny dropped as he realized she would have to find a replacement to enable her to move to the next VFM assignment and ensure the program continued successfully at Mornington.

"Matt!?!" Another woman's voice startled him, from behind.

Matt quickly removed his hand from Libby's grasp as he felt a hand on his shoulder; a woman's hand. He turned, startled at the familiar sound of the voice and stared up at his neighbor, Beverly. Bruce, her partner, was standing next to her with a sly grin on his face as he moved his gaze from Libby to Matt. .

"Oh. Hi Bev ......Bruce. How are you two tonight?" Cripes! Matt thought to himself. He was hoping he wouldn't be seen by anyone he knew particularly these two.

Bev moved toward Libby. "Hi. My name's Beverly and this is my partner, Bruce. We're Matt's neighbors." She extended her hand to Libby.

Libby stood and introduced herself to them, exchanging handshakes. Matt admired her charm and poise while he considered what alibi or explanation would suit.

Libby beat him to it. "I'm working at Matt's dairy site as a consultant. It was my idea to invite him to dinner. I wanted to coerce, bribe, or persuade him into supporting the project I'm introducing there." She turned from Bev and Bruce to Matt. "Am I having any success Matt?"

The three turned back to Matt and he stammered, perhaps slightly discrediting Libby's excellent and truthful cover story.

"I think the wine's getting to me," he said, momentarily at a loss for words. Beverly was quietly taking it all in, he thought. She was better friends with Jan than with him, and he was sure she'd be sharing the details of Matt's rendezvous as soon as she got the chance.

"Everyone knows he's a pushover." Bruce piped in, winking at Matt. "I think you could persuade him into jumping into the Mornington river.........nude!"

Matt blushed again.

Bev took in everything. The food, the expensive wine, the expensive jewelry Libby was wearing and Matt's coat and tie.

"I would say that's a bit off the mark, Bruce. Matt's proved to be very discerning and I'm fighting a bit of an uphill battle. Maybe you two would like to join us for a coffee and desert and we can all work on him together?"

"Thanks Libby, that's very kind." Bev didn't want to get any more involved. It might spoil her interpretive fantasy and what she could gossip to Jan about. "We've got to get home. We told the babysitter we'd be back a half hour ago." She turned to Bruce who nodded in agreement.

"Hey, Matt. Enjoy!" Bruce shook Matt's hand and squeezed extra hard.

The two turned and left Libby and Matt standing together.

"Was that bad, Matt?" Libby enquired.

Matt hesitated before responding. He was kicking himself, mentally, for not fronting up with Jan. It wasn't because he didn't want to tell her, but more because of his dread of her reaction. He realized now he should have explained it to her. Another rev up was in the making, and he deserved it.

"Bev's a real gossip. She's gonna stir things up with Jan." Matt was tense and remained standing while Libby sat down. He glanced at the door and imagined Bev knocking on their back door, after he'd left for work, inviting herself in for a cup of coffee with Jan and then spilling her guts about the Matt and Libby encounter.

Libby looked up at him, giving him time to think.

"I think I better head out Libby. I'm sorry, but maybe if they see me headed for my car alone, it'll help chill the stories she's gonna make up."

Libby got back to her feet quickly and put her hand on Matt's arm reassuringly. "Ok Matt. You go ahead. I'll pick up the cheque."

He turned toward her and extended his hand.

She held it between both of hers. "It's been great talking to you Matt. I'm serious about what I said regarding the Manager role. See you tomorrow."

Matt turned and left the restaurant just in time to see Beverly and Bruce's car heading off. He walked quickly to his car. Maybe he could pass them on the way home.

"Aw, bullshit! I can't believe you fell for it Matt!" Moke slammed his crescent wrench down on the workbench.

Matt had just explained Monday afternoon's meeting and the subsequent dinner with Libby.

"She doesn't want you to be the manager here. She just wants you to stop bugging her about the PMs! She's already called Graeme this morning and told him to can the rest of the outside contracts," Moke was gloating. "Did she let you in on her little secret?!"

"Bullshit!" Matt replied.

"True bro.... true. Go talk to Graeme yourself. She's just playing you Matt. And on top of playing you here at work, she's stuffing up your marriage!"

Moke was right, maybe. She could be playing him, and by now Bev was doing her best to exaggerate last evening's encounter which would make the second half of Moke's comment an understatement. Matt hoped Bev wouldn't get to Jan today, before he did. He could partially pre-empt the rollicking from Jan if he fessed up to the dinner before Bev spilled her story. He hadn't the chance that morning, before coming to work. "Ok. I'm going to see Graeme and what he's got. If it's true, then I'm back in her face.!"

Moke and Dave smirked as he walked off.

Matt was furious. It was only an hour since he'd talked to Moke and Dave. Graeme had shown him the additional one-hundred-fifty preventive maintenance tasks Libby had asked to be deleted from the shutdown and weekly maintenance schedules. She had told Graeme all outside contracts were to be suspended pending further investigation. She hadn't even bothered talking to him or telling him about the changes last night! He figured she was certain she had him in the bag and there was no need for further consultation. Wake up mate! Matt thought to himself as he'd knocked up an email to Libby. He figured Libby was busy with morning meetings. He'd walk up to the admin block after morning smoko and confront her with a copy of the email. It was a good hour and fifteen minutes away. He decided to have a look through the PM files and see if he could find any of the original material used for formulating the PM intervals on the driers, or some regulatory requirement dictating the required intervals. He'd be lucky though. Most of the documentation was in disarray since Trevor made the administrative clerk redundant a year earlier. He looked the email over once more and hit the SEND button.

SUBJECT: Drier Explosion Checks and Removal of PMs
FROM: Matt
TO: Libby

Libby. I have reviewed the additional checks you have asked Graeme to remove from the PM schedule this morning. These changes along with the elimination of the drier explosion vent checks and pressure vessel checks on evaporators and other pressurized equipment are placing people and equipment in danger. I have talked with you last Monday about this, and I have not changed my opinion. As the acting Maintenance Supervisor I must insist that you re-implement the preventive maintenance tasks you have removed or I will be forced to notify OSH.

Thirty minutes later Matt's office phone rang. At first he thought it might be Libby ringing him after reading his email. He checked the phone's message display. Nope it was his home number. A chill ran down through his spine. It was Jan. He thought about not picking up.

"Hello....maintenance office." Somehow, he thought the normal answer might soften whatever blow was coming.

"Matt! Is that you.!?" Jan half barked.

"Hi Jan. Yeah. I'm the only Matt here."

"Well. I just wanted to make sure before I told you what a complete bastard you are!"

Matt gulped. He tried to fend off her anger with some levity. "Well thanks for the good morning. What have I done now?"

"I've never been so humiliated. I went over to the corner dairy this morning and ran into Bev. Before I could get out of the store, with other women present, Bev started ranting and raving about this gorgeous blonde Matt was with last night. And you in a sports jacket at the flashest restaurant in town. You've never even taken me there!!?"

Matt caught his breath. She was practically coming down the wire at him. He thought if he could just buy a few moments, she'd settle. He thought about hanging up. "Jan. Hold on a minute"

"What ....while you think up some lame excuse, like, it was a business meeting?!"

"Just calm down......are you worried about me cheating on you or the fact I never took you there?" Matt thought this was a sudden inspired verbal ploy.

"Oh Matt.....you don't even get it do you?!" Jan hung up, leaving him hanging over the edge of a cliff with no lifeline to claw back.

He put the phone down slowly, the empty dial tone ringing in his ears. The pit of his stomach had just dropped a couple feet through the floor.

He looked toward his computer as he heard a familiar 'bing' which meant a new email message had come through. He slowly lowered himself into the five- wheeler chair and pushed back along the concrete office floor to his computer workstation. He was oblivious to the bright sun shining through the window.

SUBJECT: Re: Drier Explosion Checks and Removal of PMs
FROM: Libby
TO: Matt

Matt. I'm sorry you've decided to react defensively to my initiatives. I thought that you and I had reached an agreement regarding the necessity to halt all preventive work until we conducted an RCM-based review of the PMs and required intervals. My instructions to Graeme and you stand.
The work I have postponed will remain postponed until the appropriate analysis is complete.

Matt re-read the email. Then he hit the delete button. He grabbed a pile of paper sitting next to the computer and flung it across the room. "This place is going to the dogs!!!"

Graeme opened the door from the planner's office and poked his face in.

"Something wrong Matt?"

"Everything! The bitch is pulling the plug on everything!"

Matt picked up his gloves and safety glasses and headed out the door. He seldom left work early, but today was going to be one of those days. On the way home he stopped at the florist shop and bought a dozen roses. He hoped he would soften things up and have a conversation if she saw the roses first.

Jan wasn't there when he got home. He changed into his cycle gear and hopped onto his road bike and headed out for a long ride. On the way down the main street, a couple kilometers away, he peddled past Jan's gym. He was doing about thirty kph when he spotted Jan's car parked outside. He realized she must be seeking refuge with Wayne, her friggin trainer. His speed shot up to forty kph as he headed for the countryside. The bright sunshine was giving way to ominous clouds from the west. He put his head down and rode, hoping to forget his life.

Two hours later Matt coasted into his driveway. He hadn't taken any water and hadn't bothered to stop. He was dehydrated, exhausted. Jan's car was parked in the driveway with both windows lowered. She should know better, he thought, it looked like rain any minute. He could hear Italian opera music playing in the house. He walked in without announcing himself.

Jan was startled, but Matt barely noticed.

"I got home a couple of hours ago. Wanted to have a talk, but you were gone."

"Yeah. You're lucky I wasn't here. It wouldn't have been just talk!" Jan quickly regained the upper hand.

"C'mon Jan. I said there was an explanation. It was a business meeting. I know I should have told you more about the details."

She stopped cleaning and placed her hands behind her, on the kitchen counter, bracing herself as though she was going to swing into him. "I'm tired of this Matt. I'm tired of our relationship. I'm tired of not being loved!"

Matt felt his chest tightening. He shifted his weight subconsciously onto his heels and dropped his gaze.

"I try hard Matt. I don't ask for a lot. And then you put on your best, and take a complete stranger to the nicest place in town."

"She's not a stranger," Matt interjected.

Jan waved her hand, silencing him. "And then you tell me it's nothing. It's a business dinner. Women know. Bev knows. She told me. She could see it in your eyes. It wasn't just business."

Matt shifted and tried to lead the discussion. "Jan. That's not it. Not it at all!"

"Don't interrupt me!" She snapped furiously.

He noticed her hand was near the handle of a frying pan.

She had never hit him, but there was something ominous in her tone. "Matt. Things aren't good anymore. I feel like I'm dying inside. Like I'm missing out on life itself, on love. Meanwhile you are enjoying yourself with a blonde bimbo. I don't know what's going to happen, but I know I don't want you in my life right now." There was a look of resignation in her eyes. "I've been thinking about it all morning. I've packed your bags. I think you should leave the house for a while. Leave me to think it over." She paused staring at him. Staring right through him.

Matt was reeling, caught totally off guard. He hadn't done anything to deserve this magnitude of reaction from Jan. Surely their relationship wasn't as bad as she portrayed it. He couldn't think of anything to say. He felt like climbing back on his bike, peddling back onto the road and into his mental cave. Figure out a response. Understand the logic of what was transpiring, if there was any logic to it.

"Don't you have anything to say?!" Jan demanded.

"Jan. Please. Let me explain what didn't happen last night." He was buying time, while he thought whether an explanation would make a difference and how to structure it. "It was just a dinner meeting. She said she wanted to talk to me about work and opportunities."

Jan allowed him to continue. Her expression was a mix of anger and disbelief.

"Libby is trying to recruit me for her project. I almost fell for it." He knew his tone sounded desperate, pleading. It only served to strengthen Jan's resolve.

She hesitated for ten seconds, measuring her response. "Maybe you are her puppet? Maybe that's why I'm questioning things now, in ways I've never done before."

"I'm not a puppet. I'm trying to look out for the boys and the people at work. Libby's putting everything at risk. I had to find out."

"It doesn't matter Matt! My feelings have changed. I need some time to be alone. I think it's best you move out. Maybe to Moke's or Dave's."

"I can't believe it. It's not as though enough isn't going wrong already!?" Matt was nearly in tears.

Jan was resolute. She walked toward him and put her hand on his shoulder, comforting him like a step-mother sending her naughty boy off to his room. "C'mon, Matt. I've got all your stuff packed. It'll probably only be for a little while. It'll do us both good."

Matt turned and left the kitchen. He walked to his car without a word. Jan loaded his bags into the back seat while he climbed behind the wheel. He was in a state of shock and sat at the wheel while Jan walked briskly into the house. He subconsciously turned the ignition on, backed out the driveway and headed toward the dairy plant. He was on autopilot and didn't bother considering another destination. It was the worst day of his life.

The ring of his phone snapped Matt out of his reverie. He realized he was sitting at his desk and glanced at his wristwatch. It was almost six o'clock. He picked up the receiver.

"Hey! Sunshine! Got time to come over?"

It was Mandy. He reckoned it must have taken Moke and Dave just two minutes to get to the store and tell her what had happened after he returned to the plant. "I'm feeling out of sorts, Mandy. I might drag you under my cloud."

"Yeah. I heard. C'mon over, I've got the jug on."

He hesitated, but realized sitting alone in his office wasn't making things any better. "OK. See you in five."

"Great. You want coffee or milo?!"

"Anything will do."

He had spent the previous hour telling Moke and Dave about the response from Libby, details of the dinner and her effort to recruit him to her project and VFM. He had finished up by explaining the confrontation with Jan. Both men had offered him a place to stay. They encouraged him to get out of the house suggesting absence would make the heart grow fonder.

Moke and Dave expressed their appreciation of Matt's confrontation of Libby. Matt asked Moke if he had any evidence for the establishment of the inspection frequency intervals on the driers. Moke said it was a statutory requirement, but didn't have the documents. It was probably easier to phone the manufacturer or the Occupational Safety & Health ministry to see if they had the regulatory check requirements for powder driers. It would probably take a couple weeks to get the data. The pressure vessel checks were definitely a regulatory requirement. The boiler house guys would have the required intervals in their Code of Practice books. Dave would go over and round up the information during the week. In a couple weeks they'd have the data to challenge Libby.

The most negative result of the recent was changes was the demise of Jack's maintenance best practices program. It was a dead duck as far as they were concerned. Libby didn't have any intention of improving the processes. She'd need to hire outside contractors and she'd already canned them. All the trade training plans including the statutory compliance courses had been postponed as well. That included the fire extinguisher, forklift operation refreshers, hazardous goods and pathogen awareness courses. Not a big loss, but if there wasn't training money for those courses, there certainly wouldn't be funds for reliability centered maintenance courses or the skills development they needed to understand maintenance best practices.

They speculated about the reason for all the outside service cuts. It was pretty obvious this was the easiest way to save money in the short term. It was a way of increasing shareholder payout. They figured Libby might be able to cobble together a couple million dollars for Jim if expenditures could be minimized over the next six months. It would make Jim and VFM look good for the year-end review. They also agreed a six-month delay on the drier checks and all the rest of the critical plant PMs would be a disaster. Maintenance staff and hours would be cut to the bare bones, leaving only the internal company personnel with no extra support for PMs, shutdown planning, or problem solving. Libby had started the clock ticking on a time bomb.

Matt pushed through the outer door of Engineering Stores to see Mandy's bright smile directed at him from behind the counter. The lights in the shop behind her had been turned off. Was it because it was the end of the day, or for effect? He didn't care, but he did notice the dark backdrop highlighted her womanly profile.

She noticed he noticed without him realizing it. "Sorry to hear about the rough day Matt." Mandy walked around the counter and gave him a full-body hug.

Matt didn't return the hug, but allowed her to squeeze him. "Pretty rugged. Yep." Matt picked up the milo drink and took a long sip.

"Just like you like it, eh?!" She had only partially released him from her embrace.

Matt nodded his appreciation, but cautioned her at the same time. "You're crowding me."

"Good." She backed off, sensing Matt's genuine discomfort. "Tell me about Libby and Jan.....or should I tell you?"

He hesitated, but could see Mandy was genuinely interested in hearing his story. He decided she sincerely wanted to help him.

She pulled up a stool and sat down. Matt continued to lean against the counter.

Matt described the day's events, even though he figured she'd already pieced together most of the story from Dave and Moke.

She listened attentively, validating his position regarding the dinner with Libby, the email and response and his unfair treatment at the hands of his wife. It was amazing how much better he felt after sharing the story and hearing her supportive response.

"All better now?" She asked when he finished talking. She leaned forward taking his hands.

Matt flushed slightly as his gaze stopped momentarily on her cleavage. Had she undone the top two buttons of her shirt, intentionally? Matt wondered. "Almost. I'd be better if I was heading home tonight instead of to Moke's place."

"What?! For more of the same treatment!!? You'd be better if you were heading home to a woman wanted you in her bed."

Matt stared down at the floor. He didn't want to encourage her.

"That's right mate. It's pretty obvious Jan hasn't been putting out much for you for some time."

"Oh. Really? How would you know?"

"I'm a woman. Women can tell. In fact, I would say Jan's either frigid or she's got a man on the side."

Matt's guts tightened.

"Bingo?"

He didn't reply.

"All I know, is she isn't having sex with you!" Mandy was defiantly proud of her insight.

Matt was fading out again, after being buoyed by her support. He was sinking back into the depths of despair. He took a seat on a stool.

Mandy sensed his sadness and got off her chair to stand alongside of him She put her hand on his shoulder as he looked down at the floor. "You need heaps of TLC, my boy."

Mandy walked around to face him, pushing in between him and the counter, flush with his stool, pressed between his legs.

"Yeah. I'll be getting a lot of that at Moke's tonight!" He thought his sarcasm would deflect her approach.

Mandy didn't laugh. "That's just my point Matt. You won't be getting any at Moke's tonight." She looked into his eyes.

He could see her pupils were dilated. Was she teasing him or was this for real? He had never been sure with Mandy. He was married and he was already in trouble for having dinner with Libby. What if someone walked in on them now? He stood up, pushing her back gently, and held her hands in his.

"Mandy. This has meant a lot to me. Talking with you. I was really in the dumps. Thanks for your hugs and your caring."

Mandy was still looking into his eyes. Her expression hadn't changed.

He waited for her sarcastic laugh. It didn't come. Matt gave her a kiss on the cheek and headed out the door into the night.

CHAPTER 12

A couple months passed and there was no change in the day-to-day events at the dairy site or in Matt's personal life. Matt continued living at Moke's. Moke's wife had cleared out one of the kids' rooms so he could have his own space. It was supposed to have been a short-term imposition instead of a semi-permanent arrangement. Matt hadn't bothered looking for an apartment. He enjoyed the family life at Moke's and their unconditional support. They had adopted him as part of their extended family. Most of all, he enjoyed Moke's kids. They were fun and innocent and they reminded him of how much he wanted to have a family with Jan. He ran into Jan a couple times, with Wayne, while they were out on the town. It was depressing, and he tried to steer clear of the house and places where he might run into them. Jan hadn't expressed any interest in Matt's return. Giving their relationship another go.

Equally depressing was the increasing number of equipment and process failures at work. A definite trend building as the impact of the contractor reductions and elimination of preventive maintenance tasks resulted in equipment breakdowns. Matt admitted it was unlikely they would have any major catastrophes for another six months, as he and the boys had done what he considered to be a reasonably good job of maintaining the equipment before Libby and VFM arrived at the Mornington site.

The maintenance tradesmen were more frequently asked to stay after hours to deal with equipment problems. It was impacting their lifestyles, but Matt realized, it was also having a favorable impact on the maintenance expenditure which he knew Jim and Libby were determined to achieve. It was a false sense of accomplishment since he knew what had happened at the Riverdale timber mill when VFM had cut back maintenance spending.

They bragged about fantastic cost savings for the first two years, only to find the plant performance drop off significantly with catastrophic breakdowns in the third and fourth years of the contract. Jack, the Canadian maintenance expert, had told them of similar stories at other mills and manufacturing plants around the world.

Matt attempted to remind Jim of the Riverdale debacle on several occasions, but Jim told him he had the wrong data. The Riverdale general manager told him the improvements were valid and backed up his expectations of savings at Mornington. He told Matt to check his sources because they were probably a union misrepresentation.

Matt shut down his computer, turned off the lights in the office which used to be Trevor's. He headed down the stairs to the workshop and switched off the overhead lights. He was the last one to leave as he stepped out the workshop door, as usual. There was a light, misty rain falling and it muffled the drone of the drier exhaust fans and the energy center's normal rumbling.

Suddenly he heard a muffled, dull concussion from behind him. The sensation was accompanied by a screeching, metallic noise like the Titanic brushing and scraping the deadly iceberg. He froze in his tracks while the hair stood up on the back of his neck. A second later, an explosive roar and fire-ball enveloped Matt's immediate surroundings accompanied by the sound of shattering of glass. He instinctively placed his hands over his ears instinctively turned to see a bright, orange flash of light. An electric shock of adrenaline raced throughout his body as he prepared to drop to the ground or run for his life.

He watched glass falling through the air, like a shower of hail, from the main drier enclosure. The drier building was silhouetted by rear lighting, and the destructive display was strangely magnificent with the rear lighting shining through the falling glass particles, smoke and vapor. It was more stunning and terrifying than any fireworks display he had ever seen.

Everything seemed to take place in slow motion. Above the falling glass particles, an orange fireball accompanied by black smoke rose from the drier building. In the blink of an eye Matt realized he wasn't in immediate danger, but he wouldn't have been able to move even if he had been. He was paralyzed by the spectacle. Black smoke continued to pour from a new cavity created in the large stainless steel drier shell. A ten-meter-diameter hole had been blown through the building enclosure surrounding the drier vessel. Matt could see one of the explosion vent doors remained closed.

He caught his breath and went down on one knee. He hadn't been breathing, but now he was hyperventilating and he realized he had to calm himself and get into action. Someone could be hurt or dead inside. He couldn't hear any sounds of life coming from the building, probably a result of impaired hearing from the explosion or the loud hissing from the broken high pressure steam lines and the water spraying from what remained of the automatic deluge system.

He needed to alert the emergency response team. He looked around for the nearest fire alarm box. There was one on the side of the transport garage, fifty meters away and he sprinted to it and broke the glass cover, reached in and pulled the white handle downward. The fire alarm sounded immediately. He was relieved to have done something positive. Help would be on the way as the alarm would be sounding at the volunteer fire station a kilometer away and the fire crew would arrive within fifteen minutes. He pulled his cellphone out of his pocket and dialed 911. An operator picked up immediately and he told her what had happened and to send two ambulances and alert the police department. He turned back toward the building and considered his next move.

The smoke had cleared slightly and Matt started moving toward the drier building evaluating whether it was safe to approach. He could see a fire burning inside the drier building or inside the drier itself. Was it possible? Yeah, it looked like the fire was coming from inside the drier, and the drier was open to the surrounding atmosphere. It was hard to believe. It looked like the drier had ripped itself open in a vertical slit, five meters at its widest point, three quarters of the way up the side, from the first level to the top of the shell at the eighth level. The opening was smaller at the eighth story level near the top of the drier.

He decided to head into the building and make his way to the drier control room. As he pulled open the entry door he was greeted by the sights and sounds of panic and chaos. The emergency alarm was winding up and down rapidly. There was an overwhelming smell of smoke and burned milk powder. The sprinkler system had doused the internal parts of the building. Two of the plant operators were hobbling down the stairway with one of their co-workers supported between them, his arms were stretched over their shoulders and his head was flopping from side to side as they staggered along.

"Is he bad?" Matt asked.

"Got a knock on the head from the explosion!" One of the operators replied. "We're gonna get him outside to some fresh air."

"OK." Matt replied. He didn't want to panic them by telling them how awful they looked. "The fire department and ambulance should be here any minute. I'll get the first responders to come have a look as soon as I find them."

The other operator turned back and yelled, "They're already inside the drier area. A couple of the guys got burned pretty bad!"

He ran up to the second level and into the redline change area. He didn't bother with the hygiene formalities and jumped the changing benches heading for the main control room. Once inside Matt approached the shift supervisor who was standing behind an operator at the control panel, nervously glancing from side to side.

"Hey! John! Anything I can do to help?!" Matt half shouted at the supervisor.

"Matt! Good to see you mate! Yeah. You can help. We think we've got the plant shut down, but we're not sure if the explosion has left steam, hot water and gas flowing anywhere. Would you mind taking this flashlight and two-way radio and checking the drier out on each level with Randy?"

Matt hesitated. He and Randy might be injured if the plant and services weren't secured. The biggest risk besides fire would be exposure to high voltage electricity which undoubtedly would be compromised after the explosion. He didn't want to walk into any live 480-volt cables dangling in the dark. "Are you sure it's the top priority John?"

"Yeah. Matt. The first response team is tending to Viv and Squeek. They were on level three when the drier shell blew. The explosion vent doors didn't open. They must have jammed or something. We had a process problem, a buildup of powder in the bottom of the drier. They were going to have a direct look at it through the viewing port. They must have opened the cover to get a better view and the additional air caused the explosion. It's just a guess for now, but that's why they were up on level 3. Damn! I shouldn't have sent them up there!"

John was taking the injuries to his crew personally. Matt put his hand on John's shoulder. "I'm sure it was the right call, John. If the explosion vents had opened things wouldn't be this bad."

"They got serious burns. I had a look," John continued. "We think everyone is accounted for, but there may have been some lab techs in there as well. We're checking the sign-in sheets to be certain. We just need to secure the plant now and get it safe before any gas leaks or steam leaks hurt someone else. I know it's dangerous to ask you to go, but if you buddy-up with Randy, you can cover each other." He hesitated for a moment gauging Matt's willingness and added, "You should wear the SCBA's too."

Matt looked up from the floor while he'd been mulling over the proposal, "OK John. We'll put on the SCBA's. Just in case." He knew somebody needed to check things out. It might as well be him and Randy.

Matt pulled a self-contained breathing apparatus pack out of the cabinet and slipped his arms through the harness while lifting the heavy cylinder onto his back. As a member of the volunteer fire department and a trained advanced first aider, he had practiced for situations like this before. Randy was a member of the volunteer fire brigade as well, so between the two of them they should be able to handle the assignment. "Have you called Jim and Scotty?"

"Yep. They're on the way. Fire department's just around the corner at last report a minute ago. What's it look like from the outside."

"Like a bloody plane crashed into the side of the building! I called 911 and they're sending two ambulances and the police."

"Yeah. That's the way it looks inside. Watch yourself. There could be missing railings and walkways. Don't' take any chances. Keep your RT on transmit position the whole time you're out there so we can hear you."

"OK. We'll work our way up from the bottom."

Matt and Randy walked out of the control room into the main drier hall, at the bottom of the drier. It was dark, almost black, except for the faint glow of the emergency lighting system. Matt decided they should check the burner control room where the main gas line fed the combustion air heater for the drier. They should also check the steam heat exchangers at the base of the drier in the high pressure pump area as well as the steam heating units in the CIP rooms. Those were the two main concerns along with any high voltage cables that may have been severed and present an electrocution hazard. He'd have to check the motor control center to make sure there weren't any fire hazards or obvious problems with the power supplies. They would go there first and ensure the main power was disconnected to everything but the control room. Just in case the ERT team had skipped that step.

The first emergency response team was four levels up. Matt could see the flashlight beams moving in the darkness where they were probably tending to the two burned operators. Matt got on the RT and asked John to call in Dave and all of the sparkies and fitters he could get in touch with. They would be required for clean-up and securing the plant.

He couldn't believe how calm he felt. It was as though he had been through this before. He imagined the certainty he, Moke and Dave had regarding this potential eventuality and the consequences might be the reason for his feeling of 'déjà vu.' He couldn't believe it had happened in such a short period of time. So much for Libby's challenge of Moke's interval calculation, he angrily reminded himself.

He glanced up toward the hole in the side of the building where the remaining half of one of the explosion vent double doors was dangling. It was obvious it hadn't released. It was a miracle nobody had been killed, but that fact wasn't a certainty, yet. Libby and Jim were going to have a lot to answer for.

Matt and Randy finished their reconnaissance an hour later, without incident. Matt broke away to help coordinate the Mornington site tradesmen and contractors who had arrived to support the shutdown of the plant along with installation of temporary lighting and power supplies. He developed a plan to work safely while assessing the hazards, as well as investigating damage to the plant and reporting their findings.

The hours passed quickly and Matt was surprised when 5:00 a.m. arrived. Dave arrived to relieve him as they'd agreed and Matt passed on the details of the explosion and status of activities before wearily heading to the parking lot. He returned to Moke's for a few hours' sleep before the scheduled update meeting with the Jim, Scott and the General Manager.

Six hours later, Matt was on his way to the administration block for the update meeting. He hadn't had a chance to catch up with Dave before the meeting. Getting some much needed sleep had been more important. Moke's kids hadn't even bothered him when they took off for school. He had been absolutely exhausted.

He was surprised by the din of activity and amount of people at the site as he walked into the main conference room which had been converted into a crisis management center. Colin Grey, the CEO, and Graham Chambers, the General Manager, were both huddled with Jim Champion in one corner of the room. Libby, Scott, and the other plant managers, along with the corporate and site safety engineers were talking in another cluster. Matt could see the operating union organizers and site union delegates were are all present in yet another corner of the room. The electronic whiteboards were covered with heaps of scribbling, calculations of plant throughputs, losses. Charts of process flows, damage estimates, and safety assessments were taped to the conference room walls.

Everyone looked haggard and tense. Pots of coffee were bubbling on portable warmers and the trash cans were almost overflowing with Styrofoam cups and paper plates. A cartload of sandwiches and fruit was sitting in the corner which reminded Matt he hadn't eaten during the past twelve hours. The main meeting table was covered with paper, laptop computers and a host of notebooks and planning materials along with a replica of the site drier buildings.

He picked up a sandwich and an apple while he watched Jim nod to the CEO and GM and then turn back to face the room.

"Ok everybody. Listen up!" Jim half shouted to silence the room. He paused for a few seconds as he surveyed those present and continued. "I've got the official report outlined here." He paused again as half the group took seats, facing Jim

Libby had moved alongside Jim, in support, a step behind.

The top two buttons of Jim's shirt were undone and one of his shirt-tails was hanging out of his pants at the back. "My thanks to all of you who have worked through the night to support the operations staff, our investigative team, the emergency response team and members of the union and management. We've got a major problem on our hands here,

155

but we've worked out a plan to get the site back up and running within two weeks."

Several people let out a gasp.

"Which is amazing given the fact there is an estimated twenty-five million dollars in repair work to be completed." Jim half-turned toward Libby, who nodded her agreement.

"There have been three injuries associated with the explosion last night which I sincerely regret. Fortunately none of the injuries has resulted in fatality, but two of the operators are in hospital with third degree burns on twenty-five percent of their bodies. The prognosis is for a full recovery, but they'll be out of action for six to nine months. The third injury was a concussion, and the operator has been released from the hospital. So that's good news!" Jim hesitated again, looking around the room to gauge people's reactions.

Scott was looking at the floor.

Matt figured he didn't want Jim to see the anger simmering in his eyes.

"Of course, we'll be doing everything we can to address any mental or physical trauma impacting our colleagues, their families or their friends as a result of this accident."

Matt jerked reflexively at the mention of the word accident.

Jim turned toward Libby and said, "Libby has run through the numbers for the drier repair and plan to get back into production."

Libby looked around the room confidently. "This has been a huge shock for all of us at VFM. My heart goes out to the injured people and their families."

Matt marveled at her tone of voice, the sincerity and feeling Libby projected, given the fact her decisions were probably the cause of the so-called accident.

"Jim has asked me to compile a brief review of the detailed plan the project team and I have put together to rebuild the drier system so we can get back into production. We already have the major stainless-steel fabricators moving into action with materials and personnel to affect the necessary repairs on a twenty-four-hour schedule." She went on to clarify the project would be headed up by more VFM construction and contract personnel.

Matt guessed VFM's work and invoice to the company had just

quadrupled as a result of this event. He doubted whether they'd be able to get the plant back on line within a month much less two weeks. There were still too many unknowns from the explosion impact. But it wouldn't hurt to promise two weeks and it would give Jim the whip to drive the contractors and Matt's trade colleagues.

Libby wrapped up her review of the recovery plan and turned to Jim for final comment.

"Preliminary assessments by our operations and project engineering team indicate the cause of the explosion was a process fault which allowed powder to build up at the bottom of the drier into a massive smoldering chunk. The explosion occurred when the two operators opened the viewport to inspect the build-up and inadvertently allowed a sufficient amount of oxygen to enter the chamber. The increased oxygen supply resulted in a spontaneous explosion which the explosion vent doors were not able to respond to, quickly enough, causing physical damage to the drier."

Matt was incensed, ready to explode himself. What did Jim mean the explosion vent couldn't respond quickly enough? Jim was lying through his teeth! Matt had worked in the drier operations area himself, and he knew there wasn't any explosion the vent doors couldn't respond to, as long as they were in good condition, especially an explosion emanating from the base of the drier. Matt raised his hand to challenge Jim's comment.

Jim looked at Matt and then looked away, intentionally ignoring his raised hand. "So that's it everyone. We won't take any questions now since I'm sure you all want to head home for some sleep. Libby will make further project plans in the project offices adjacent to the engineering building. Before she goes though, I'd like to express my thanks to VFM's project team for getting here in the wee hours to begin assessments and to Libby for her excellent work in coordinating the response project. I'm confident she and the team will deliver and minimize the impact of this unfortunate accident."

Matt looked at the CEO. He was the first to raise his hands and initiate the applause for Libby. Jim had obviously fed him a line of bullshit. Matt pushed past the union organizers and out the door as quickly as he could, so the rest of the people in the room wouldn't see how furious he was. He let out a shout and threw his hands in the air as he hopped down the steps and hurriedly walked to the engineering workshop.

"Bloody Hell!" Matt yelled as he angrily slammed open the door to the engineering stores room. His yell and the sound of the door slamming against the wall startled Moke, Dave and Mandy who were chatting at the stores window.

"Damn Matt! You trying to wake the dead?" Moke retorted. Matt's behavior had set adrenaline pumping in all three of them. There was a hole in the wall where the door handle had smashed through the gib board.

"Jim up to some new tricks?" Mandy couldn't muster a smile to go with her remark, but she hoped a little humor would diffuse Matt's anger.

"You got it! You won't believe the bullshit story I've just heard."

"Uuhhh huh! We wouldn't? Try us babe." Mandy walked around to the shop side of the stores window to stand closer to Matt.

Dave filled a cup of water from the cooler and offered it to Matt at the same time.

"That wanker just told the CEO and everybody else the drier explosion was an accident! He congratulated Libby and the VFM crew for doing a great job of preparing a response plan and reacting to the crisis! What a total load of crap!"

"You set them straight?" Moke demanded.

"I tried to."

"What dya mean? Mate?! You were there. You didn't tell them?" Moke was getting testy and Matt put down his drink of water. "Hey watch it, mate! I was going to tell the CEO and everyone else there the explosion doors failed because Libby canned the PMs, but Jim cut the meeting off the minute after he made the announcement. He wouldn't let me speak."

"So! Does that mean he cut off your tongue too? You could have talked over him." Moke retorted.

"Yeah well maybe you could have, but if I'd started talking I would have gone over the table after him." Matt's fists subconsciously clenched as he spoke.

Moke looked down at Matt's hands and realized he was pushing too far.

Mandy saw the gesture as well and stepped in between Matt and

Moke, facing Matt, grasping his forearms in her hands. "Hey c'mon you guys. You need to chill. Jim should be feeling your heat, not each other."

"Yeah she's right. I'm gonna head out of here, it's getting too hot." Dave who had been standing by, watching the exchange, turned and headed for the door. He didn't want to hear any more about the crap coming from Jim "I've got to get back up to the fourth floor and help direct the riggers putting up the scaffolding."

"Ok Dave. Catch ya later." Mandy waved, and turned back to the two men. Neither of them acknowledged Dave's departure.

"I'm sorry Matt. You must be buggered. I can't believe that wanker!" Moke was apologetic.

"It's ok, mate. I should have spoke up anyway. I hate the way the asshole cut me off. He didn't even acknowledge I had something to say."

Mandy interjected, "Yeah, maybe babe. But do you have solid proof?"

"It wouldn't have mattered. It would have raised doubts in the CEO's mind."

"Or maybe Libby or Jim would have used your response to put you down!?"

Moke moved away from Matt and Mandy, thinking out loud, "You should send the CEO an email telling him the real story, mate. Tell him about Libby, the PMs, the outside contract and cost cutting." He was talking strategy now.

"I'm not sure the CEO would say it was a bad thing. Besides I'm not sure how much of this Jim knows about. Libby may have done this on her own initiative." Matt replied.

"I still think the CEO needs to know more. What's the worst that can happen? He'll tell Jim and you'll get a rev up?" Moke wouldn't let this one go.

"I don't know, but I've got to have a solid story to go to the CEO."

"Yeah....well I can tell you about something solid right here." Mandy interjected as she stopped and pressed her fingers in a massaging motion into Matt's shoulder muscles. I think you should stop talking and thinking about this for a few hours."

Matt paused considering Mandy's recommendation and the tension she exposed with her fingers.

"I've gotta get back into the drier building myself. I'll catch you later." Moke turned and tossed his leftover coffee along with the foam cup into the trash.

"Ok mate, see you later." Mandy replied. She looked at Matt, wondering whether she should offer a hug or leave him alone. Before she could make a move Matt turned away, lost in thought, and headed toward his office, without a word to her or Moke.

CHAPTER 13

"Ok gentlemen, you can carry on with your plans for the demolition work without me. I'll check back on your final figures in an hour. I've got to meet Jim for lunch." Libby took the papers lying in front of her and stacked them together in a folder labeled DRIER ACCIDENT RECOVERY PLAN.

The four design engineers nodded and settled back to work as she left the project engineering room.

It was nearly noon, and Libby was simultaneously exhausted and energized. Exhausted because she had been at the site since midnight when Jim called to inform her of the accident. Energized because of the adrenaline rush associated with a high profile, high stakes project, where everyone at VFM sensed the urgency and the financial prize.

Her boss, Tor Johannsen, emphasized the need to keep a lid on the cost cutting exercise before she arrived at the Mornington dairy site. When she phoned him immediately following the drier incident he agreed with her estimation VFM could triple the year's income at Mornington with the twenty-five million dollar repair of the drier. This was a huge windfall for her VFM assignment, and if the job went well it would set them up for other high stakes project work as well as the maintenance contract for the rest of the dairy company's sites. He wanted Libby to make sure no negative publicity got out about the preventive maintenance cutbacks or any other cost cutting exercises prior to the explosion. His admonition created a negative, gnawing sensation in her stomach.

She needed to talk to Jim about her feelings and make sure their stories were aligned before she talked with any more strangers, especially site personnel who had intimate knowledge of the night's events. She knew why Jim had failed to acknowledge Matt's raised hand at the morning meeting.

She walked through the automatic doors to the administration block lobby and headed toward Jim's office. He was sitting with his back to the door, feet up on the credenza, talking on his landline phone when she tapped politely at his half-open door.

"Be with you in a sec Libs," Jim said, as he turned and gestured for her to sit down. He kept talking with his back to her for several minutes before hanging up. "Big things happening in China, Libs! Might be some work up there for you and VFM if you play your cards right."

Libby opened her mouth to speak, but Jim cut her off with a hand gesture as he leaned forward with both arms on the desk in front of him.

"Libs, you are doing a great job on this response planning."

She was taken a bit off guard. This was the first compliment Jim had paid her without an attached sexual innuendo. She waited a moment before responding.

He stared at her, waiting for a response, with a grin.

He was oblivious to the severity of the drier explosion, she thought. How could he be so detached, so arrogant and indifferent?

"Thanks Jim," she finally responded. "There is something I want to talk to you about."

He cut her off again, "Yeah, we've got a bunch to talk about."

She sat back in her chair, clasping her hands together, mirroring his body language to a degree, "Some of the project engineers are expressing an opinion that the damage to the drier was avoidable. The explosion vent doors are designed to operate in any type of explosion."

"And?"

"And I'm worried they're correct. Maybe deleting the PMs on the doors was the root cause of the damage to the drier. I'm worried somebody in the maintenance department may tell the project engineers, or they may get more inquisitive and ask somebody like Matt to explain whether there were any anomalies prior to the explosion. Besides the powder buildup and operator error."

Libby had let down her guard and exposed the fear she was feeling about her potential contribution to the explosion. She was also concerned about Jim's exposure, potentially, though she doubted he would be. She continued, "I thought you and I should talk about the situation. Perhaps there is some way of explaining the PM changes as a possible contributor so we wouldn't be culpable if someone finds out? I'm worried."

Jim rapidly pushed back from his desk and jumped to his feet as Libby finished her sentence. He leaned over his desk toward her. "You heard my announcement in there didn't you?!" His eyes burned into hers, and his sour breath flooded her nostrils. "What have you said to the project engineers so far?!"

Libby cringed and shrunk back to escape the smell of his breath. She hadn't anticipated his emotive response, though she had expected him to challenge her suggestion. She hesitated.

"Well! You told them they were wrong didn't you?"

"No. I didn't tell them anything. I ignored their comment. I don't know how the drier explosion doors operate. I wasn't in a position to challenge any technical arguments they may have put forward."

"Bloody hell! You are the boss! You are in a position to tell them anything you want! It is your prerogative! You heard me in there! We made a joint statement about the cause and repair of the driers. I praised you and your company. You <u>will</u> live up to that statement and your role as a representative of VFM!"

Libby <u>was</u> intimidated by Jim. She had dealt with workplace bullies in her career and thought she had the ability to maintain her balance. It was evident he demanded complete loyalty to his approach in any interactions, be it with the project engineers or anyone else who challenged his position.

"You and I are like a captain and first mate, sailing through a Fijian lagoon, escaping the pursuing cannibals. We've only got one direction to sail. If we tack port or starboard we run out of wind and the cannibals catch us." Jim admired his analogy of their situation to the heroic escape of Captain Bligh from the locals when he was set adrift from the HMS Bounty.

Libby cringed at the analogy. This situation was nothing like his analogy which she recognized from the film, Mutiny on the Bounty. She wasn't surprised Jim admired the captain of the Bounty. The color drained out of her face.

Jim could see he had over-estimated Libby's nerve. He thought she was on the verge of breaking down in tears. Too friggin' bad, he thought to himself. Maybe she really wouldn't be so good in the sack. "We have made a statement to the CEO we have to live by. If I'm not mistaken, your boss at VFM, the dork from Sweden, will want you to support the position as well. Am I correct?"

"Yes. Jim. Mr. Johannsen has made it clear he wants VFM to support one hundred percent!" Her voice was quivering.

"So what is the fuss about? You'll just have rein in those techno-wimps and get on with it!" Jim shifted gears as Kay walked in, breaking into a smile. "Hey! Here's our food!"

Kay struggled with the large tray at the office entry. Instead of helping her, Jim just motioned for her to put the tray on a small meeting table. "Just push aside those papers Kay. That'll be fine." He picked out a section of a club sandwich and turned to Libby as Kay closed the office door. He fingered out the tomato slice and tossed it into the trash.

Libby bit her tongue. She wasn't comfortable challenging the engineers on the explosion door operation. She wasn't comfortable challenging Jim. He was staring at her breasts again, and for once she didn't mind as it gave her some time to collect her thoughts. "I'll have to get myself up to speed on the explosion door operation. I don't feel confident challenging the engineers until I do."

"You do that Libs. You take all the time you bloody need, take a year if you want. By then this thing will have blown over and nobody'll give a damn about whether the doors should have operated."

"Ok." Libby's response sounded submissive.

Jim took her reaction as an opportunity to make a move on her. He grabbed her by the shoulders, forcefully pulling her close. Her breasts brushed his chest and he could feel the rush of heat to his genitals. He was aroused by her scent, her youthful athletic body and her vulnerability. She was like putty. He thought about locking the door, forcing her to the floor. He was certain she wouldn't resist. She was too frightened.

She could see the hairs in his nose. His stone-cold eyes were focused on her lips.

Jim looked into her eyes. The pupils were small, fierce.

Libby thought he might be considering raping her.

His hesitation prolonged the invasion of her personal space, breathing into her mouth and nose.

She felt like vomiting.

He spoke slowly and forcefully. "You get comfortable, Libs. You know the options."

She could feel her knees shaking as she pushed away from him. She prayed he wouldn't notice as she walked to the door and closed it behind her.

Jim picked up another section of club sandwich. A few morsels of food tumbled from his mouth to the floor as he smiled to himself.

Matt surveyed the empty milk tanker reception area as he headed for the administration block at 4:00 p.m. There wouldn't be any milk tanker deliveries to the site for at least two weeks, perhaps even a month. Instead, the tankers would be going full tilt to pick-up and divert milk to other dairy sites. The diversion costs would be hundreds of thousands of dollars for extra fuel and overtime. There would be delays in pickups at the farms and angry phone calls to the dispatch office and the CEO from irate farmer shareholders. He had decided to follow up on Moke's dare. He was going to confront management. He was going to confront Libby face to face.

He was still angry, but not as livid as he had been after Jim's remarks at the update meeting. He was fairly certain he knew more about the vent door operation than Jim or Libby. The explosion door pins would be sheared rapidly by an explosive force and the pressure would be vented to atmosphere. He was certain the failure to check the shear pins and the door mounts was the root cause of the drier explosion. The mechanism could get bound up by atmospheric dirt and corrosion, and it needed to be re-lubed, rotated and visually inspected at least four times a year. He had found problems once before when he was doing the PM, and he had recommended a re-design of the mechanism to avoid the problem. He wasn't sure what Libby knew about the explosion prevention device. She might be up to speed and could possibly counter his argument. She might simply refuse to listen to him.

"You should be easier on yourself!" Matt jumped at the sound of Libby's voice.

"Oh. Hi Libby," Matt said awkwardly. "I was coming to see you." He noticed she seemed a bit disheveled and her face was wet like she'd been splashing water on her face.

"Ok. Do you want a coffee or tea before we talk?" She was making more of a demand than a polite request.

"No. I'll wait for you." He waited in her office doorway while she went to the break room.

She kept her distance as she entered the office and invited him to sit down. The office was full of drawings, vendor manuals and stacks of paperwork. H cleared off one of the seats before seating himself. "You've been up for a long time today."

He wasn't sure if her comment was one of caring or observational small talk.

"So have you."

"I'm sure you didn't stop by to chit chat, given the fact you're due to head home for some rest."

"Yeah." He was searching for a way to challenge her, without sounding childish. "I don't know quite how to put this Libby."

"Put what? Matt?" She had regained her composure and confidence after meeting Jim.

He forced himself to get it out without mincing his words, "To tell you the truth. I think either you've been bullshitting Jim or he's bullshitting the rest of us!"

Libby's eyes flared slightly.

Matt was surprised she hadn't jumped down his throat as he expected following his accusation.

"That's a rather harsh statement Matt. What are you getting at?" She remained calm, confident, challenging.

"I think you know what I'm talking about Libby! I'm talking about the story you and Jim put forward about the explosion doors! The statement he made this morning about the explosion to the CEO was a lie!" He realized his story wasn't coming out the way he intended. He felt like he was painting himself into a corner.

"Matt, I'm about one second away from asking the HR representative in here to have you repeat your statement. I can have you disciplined for defamation even though I'm not a company employee if you don't have evidence to back up your statement!"

Matt could see the veins standing out on her neck.

She moved forward in her chair. "Well? Do you have evidence Matt?! What do you want to say next?!"

Matt hadn't realized how quickly he could get himself into hot water. He hesitated. He realized his accusation was premature. He'd told Moke confronting Libby without evidence was dangerous, but he had proceeded since he wanted to show Moke and the guys he wasn't' a whimp.

"Do you know what a jerk you are? I worked through the night putting a plan together! You're wasting my time. She stood up, ready to escort him out of her office.

Matt sat still, looking at the floor. Maybe she was right? Bull! She wasn't right! But she was right about his lack of evidence. He was on shaky ground.

"I'll tell you what Matt. I'm in a generous mood. You're tired. You don't know what you're doing. You're emotional. You leave now, and we'll forget this discussion happened." She paused to let Matt consider her offer.

She had backed him into a corner. He wanted to challenge her, keep up the fight. He had planned to walk out of her office with her admission of guilt so he could confront Jim. It would have been a vindication of the maintenance department. He had failed. Heather, the site HR manager, wouldn't allow Libby to sack him unless he violated company policy, but he would be reprimanded, perhaps formally disciplined. More people would know he had lost the argument. He couldn't think straight. He looked up at Libby. She was focused on him, poised to punch in Heather's number on her phone. No empathy or fear was manifest in her expression. "Yeah I'm tired," He relented. "Must be the stress."

Libby replaced the telephone on its cradle. "Yeah Matt. We're all tired. This has been a very tough day."

"Yeah." Matt repeated. "I'll see you later."

Libby heaved a sigh of relief as Matt left her office. She had taken Jim advice, acted like 'The Boss' with Matt, and it had worked, for the time being. She was worried. If he got together with the project engineers there was bound to be trouble. With better evidence and an engineering analysis he would return. She needed to talk to Jim, again. He had to accept Matt was a serious threat. If the truth came out about the preventive maintenance cancellations being partly or totally responsible for the explosion her career with VFM would be finished. Feeling a wave of nausea, she got up, opened the window and inhaled. The air was cool on her face but the acrid smell of the lingering smoke from the fire caught in her throat. She looked across the car park towards the maintenance workshop and engineering stores building. She was about to close the window when she noticed somebody approaching the entry to the stores building. She recognized Matt, silhouetted in the entry lighting. Closing the window, she sat at her desk and started typing.

Subject: Maintenance Leading Hand
To: Jim Champion
From: Libby Galwaith

I have just met with Matt Polaski, Maintenance Leading Hand, and I wish to formally advise you of concerns I have regarding his performance. Whilst not wishing to preempt the outcome of the enquiry into the explosion I feel it is my duty to raise these concerns with you.
Since the Site Engineering Manager left, Matt Polaski has been in sole charge of the maintenance department. During this time he has been doggedly resistant to the Maintenance Excellence project. This has been evident in his failure to implement systems and procedures or to instruct maintenance team members to do so.

As you are aware, the preliminary assessments have indicated the explosion was caused by a build-up of powder in the drier. This build-up ignited when the view port was opened, introducing oxygen into the drier chamber. Given the catastrophic results of this occurrence and the assumption all powder driers are fitted with explosion vent doors designed to release should an explosion occur. Why did the doors fail to release?
I can find no evidence of either preventative maintenance or routine safety checks being carried out, despite procedures being in place to ensure them. Matt Polaski is responsible for ensuring these checks are carried out. His failure to

do so is either due to gross incompetence or a deliberate attempt to subvert the maintenance excellence project.

I understand his wife has left him, since she learned of his affair with Mandy Smith, the Engineering Stores Clerk.

Libby hesitated. Was this taking it too far, she wondered? She'd overheard the maintenance guys talking about Jim hitting on Mandy. She figured if Jim had tried and failed, he'd bear a grudge toward a successful suitor. She continued.

Whilst this should be a personal issue, he is openly conducting the affair after hours in the Stores. This is most unprofessional behavior, given his position.

I believe Matt is emotionally unstable, and, were it not for the importance of his involvement in the investigation and clean up, I would recommend he be given leave of absence.

Libby Galwaith
VFM Project Manager

Libby re-read the email, made a couple of minor changes and hit the SEND button.

CHAPTER 14

Contrary to Libby's perception, Matt's visit to the Stores was simply a shortcut to his office. As requested, the guys had done an initial assessment of the spare parts they would need to get the plant operational and left the list on his desk. Anxious to get things moving he phoned Mandy, who promised to wait for his request.

He talked her through the list before she asked how the meeting with Libby had gone. He knew his reply had sounded harsh as well as his refusal of her offer to share a drink after work. She reacted angrily.

Exhausted and lost in thought on his drive to Moke's, he had nearly turned into the driveway of his own house when he realized he didn't live there any longer. Turning the car around to leave, he thought about his row with Moke earlier in the day. He couldn't face Moke now either.

Suddenly the desire to turn the clock back and return to normality was overwhelming. He would reverse direction and go home and talk to Jan. He'd try to make up and get things back on track with their marriage. He turned back toward the house and he was pleased to see the lights were on and Jan's car was parked in the drive. He pulled his car behind hers, shut off the engine and bounded toward the door. As he reached the top step he took out his key and hesitated. Should he just walk in? He rang the doorbell instead.

Jan answered the door. "God, Matt, you look awful. Are you alright? I heard about the explosion.

"I'm ok," he said wearily. "Just tired."

"Don't tell me you are working around the clock?"

Matt attempted a joke, "Yeah. How'd you know?"

He smiled, but Jan didn't find his remark humorous.

"So, what do you want?"

"I want to talk, about coming home. A lot's happened in the last couple months."

"It's not a good time."

"Jan." His voice had a pleading tone. "I could have died up there. Some of the guys nearly did. Life's too short to wait for a good time."

She hesitated before moving aside, "Go and sit down, I'll make some coffee."

Matt walked into the living room and sat down on the sofa. Feeling a wave of fatigue rush over him, he removed his boots and put his feet up on the ottoman.

A niggling pain in his hip woke him. In the darkness it took him a few minutes to work out where he was. He rolled over and turned the light on, realizing he had fallen asleep before Jan had returned. A mug of coffee and sandwich were sitting on the table and a blanket had been thrown over him. He touched the mug, it was cold. Switching the light off again, he rolled onto his back. She still cares, he thought. He contemplated crawling into bed bedside her, and nestling into her. Unsure whether it was weariness or wariness that kept him on the sofa, he drifted back to sleep, momentarily, unaware of Jan's giggle and a man's voice coming from their bedroom.

The sound of the water running in the shower woke him. He checked the time on his cellphone. 6:30 a.m. He lay back and let his mind drift. His thoughts were distracted by Jan's footsteps in the hallway followed by the sound of the front door open and footsteps going down the path. Damn! She's going out. Jumping off the sofa he opened the curtains, making ready to open the window and call to her. His hand froze as he reached for the window catch. A tall, athletic man, wearing a tracksuit, was opening the gate at the end of the driveway. As Matt watched, he closed it behind him and jogged off down the road. Wayne! The bastard! While I've been sleeping on the sofa, he's been in my bed!

He steadied himself, willing himself to remain calm, to think clearly. He settled back onto the sofa as he heard Jan enter the kitchen and fill the jug. Should he confront her now? She could hardly deny it. Deny what? Sleeping with Wayne. It was probably what she wanted, to have a row over it. Get him out for good. He jumped to his feet and headed for the entry to the kitchen. He felt a flash of anger burn through him. He swung his fist into the wall. The searing pain through his knuckles temporarily blocked out all thoughts.

"Matt! Did you fall?! Are you alright?" Jan rushed into the hallway from the kitchen. "What was that noise?"

"Yeah," Matt replied quietly.

"Go and grab yourself a shower, and I'll make some coffee and breakfast."

Feeling the anger rise again, Matt checked himself. He couldn't trust himself to stay in control of his emotions. He had to get out before he took a swing at her. "No, I've got to go," he replied. He picked up his keys and phone from the coffee table. "It was wrong for me to come over last night."

"Don't rush off Matt." She hesitated.

Matt couldn't understand why she wanted to talk. "There's nothing to say Jan. I shouldn't have dropped in on you last night." His voice was bitter. He walked toward the door to leave.

Jan put a hand on his arm.

Shrugging her off, he pushed past her.

"Matt? Is that you, Mate?" Moke called from the fitters' locker room.

Matt switched off the shower and started toweling himself dry. "Yep."

"Good, I've been trying to find you. Listen mate, I know I was leaning on you yesterday, but it doesn't mean you don't have a bed at our place. Ngaire was worried about you." Seeing Matt come out of the shower he added, "She gave me a right earful. Where have you been?"

"You don't want to know, mate."

A broad grin spread across Moke's face. He chuckled "Doesn't she have a shower?"

"She?! Is not the she, you are thinking of. She is my wife and she just happens to have another guy using her shower!"

"Crap!" Moke shook his head and then noticed Matt's right hand. "What happened Matt? Where did you get those knuckles?"

Matt looked at his hand. His knuckles had disappeared beneath the swelling and blue bruising was starting to show through. The pain was pulsing, a dull ache throbbing upwards through his arm. He rubbed his hand before replying. "A combination of the stores door and the living room wall," adding wryly, "I should be ambidextrous!"

"Looks bad. bro. You should get it x-rayed."

"Nah. I've got better things to do. If the HR manager hears about this she'll me to do an anger management course."

"Matt, I shouldn't have lost it with you yesterday. Squeek and Viv are injured and the bloody consultant woman is getting away with it. I went to see the two boys in hospital last night."

"How are they?"

"It's not pretty. Squeek was laughing and joking, saying he always wanted curly hair. Viv was real quiet. He's hurting big time."

"I bet you cheered them up?"

"Yeah, we had a laugh. Took my guitar and played some songs. Got the nurses singing along too!" Moke grinned, "There are some legs and bums up there that would cheer any man up!"

Matt smiled. "Sounds like I should pay them a visit."

"That would be good. Take them a couple of beers and forget the flowers." Moke's voice got serious. "The only thing is, Matt. They'll ask you why it happened. They're expecting you and Jim to front with a believable explanation."

"Not going to happen."

Moke pushed up his cap and scratched his head. "Well. I don't envy you. Let me know if I can help, and I'll tell Ngaire to expect you for tea tonight."

"Thanks mate."

"Got your email!" Jim's voice grated her nerves as Libby listened to his voicemail. She could faintly hear him, down the long hallway, in his own office, as he continued to leave the message on her phone.

"I don't give a damn what you are in the middle of! Get your arse over here!"

Libby knew he didn't like leaving messages. He expected people to pick up his calls regardless of what they were doing. She didn't pick up.

Jim banged the desk in frustration. Where the hell was she? He had left countless messages on her mobile before phoning VFM's downtown office and being told she had left to return to the site. Since then, he had left several more messages. He re-read her email, before banging a response in sheer frustration.

Subject: Re: Maintenance Leading Hand
To: Libby Galwaith
From: Jim Champion

I have a maintenance leading hand who is shagging around and you are shagging around not answering my calls.
Smart move, making Matt responsible. Grounds for dismissal. Can he fight it? Catching him in the act shagging the stores tart would be good.

Jim smiled. He'd like to teach both of them a lesson. If anyone was shagging on his site, it should be him.

I've got a better idea. You get him coming on to you. I'll step in and we'll have him on sexual harassment charges.

He smiled again, realizing his personal brilliance. Matt could be sacked on the spot, and it would be easy to lay the blame for the explosion firmly on him. He added *'call me'* and hit SEND

Matt finished going through the spare parts orders, with Mandy. It was mid-morning. She must have worked half the night doing the orders and had contacted all the suppliers demanding delivery dates. Once again Matt was impressed by how much Mandy could achieve when the heat was on. "Thanks Mandy," he said. "Did you work all night?"

"Not quite," she replied shrugging her shoulders. She was still hurt by his refusal to have a drink.

"I really appreciate it," he said reaching out and touching her arm.

"Nothing else to do Matt," she said reproachfully.

"Moke saw the guys in hospital."

"Yeah he told me."

"You've got to do something."

"I know. I just don't know what. I tried to confront Libby and she tied me in knots."

"How?"

"She turned it all around on me. Accused me of defamation! Threatened to call HR and get me sacked."

"Damn," exploded Mandy. "There are some things you are stupid about, but not that. You know what happened!"

Matt hesitated, wondering what he else she thought he was stupid about. "Yeah, I know what happened. I don't have any evidence."

"You must have the evidence. You knew she had been in the systems canceling out the PMs. You told me."

"Yeah, but she'll have covered her tracks."

"Did you talk to her about it?" Mandy asked.

"Yeah. Even emailed her."

Mandy jumped off the stool she was perched on. "Bingo! You emailed her! The email is the evidence."

Matt shook his head. "I'm afraid not. I was so mad I deleted it."

"It'll be in your sent items file."

"I guess it is but her email response to me, denying her actions were dangerous is deleted as well. It's gone."

"Bugger!" Mandy was exasperated at the missed opportunity.

"You can say that again."

"Interrupting something? Am I?" Moke's voice startled both of them.

"Shit! Moke! Don't sneak up on us like some sleuthful warrior!" Mandy exclaimed. "Where'd you come from anyway!?"

"Through the door, like most people do," he replied with a grin.

"We were just talking about Matt's next move."

"I don't think I need to know. Do I? Is it dragging your pretty butt into the dark recesses of the stores?"

"Not that kinda move! For Christ sakes!" Mandy grinned at them both.

"Oh. You mean the other move on the VFM lady?" Moke hesitated. "Personally, I'd like to get Jim's balls in my benchtop vice."

"Only if you let me watch," Mandy egged him on.

Matt heaved a frustrated sigh and stood up, preparing to leave. "Until you two can come up with a sensible suggestion I'd better go and get some work done."

Mandy watched Matt walk out of the door. She turned to Moke with a pleading expression. "We've got to do something."

"Yeah" said Moke.

Mandy hesitated, considering her next words. "How's he been?"

"What do you mean?"

"Well. He's staying at yours. How's he been? He was pretty down when he left here last night. How was he when he got to yours?"

"Ahh" said Moke hesitating. "He didn't stay at ours last night."

Mandy looked up sharply. "Where was he?"

"He went back to his."

Feeling a sharp pang, Mandy asked "To Jan?"

'Yeah."

Mandy felt tears welling up in her eyes. She brushed them aside quickly hoping Moke wouldn't notice.

He put his hand on her arm.

"Leave me alone, you letch!" She pushed his arm away and moved down the counter to her computer screen.

Moke let out a long slow whistle. The silence was awkward and lasted uncomfortably long.

"Now I forgot what I came in for," Moke admitted awkwardly. "Can you let me have a seal for a Fristam pump?"

Moke followed her as she disappeared into the store's maze of shelves. Mandy and Matt? He wondered. Would they make a good pair? Better than Jan, for sure. Jan didn't appreciate Matt. She always wanted him to be something better. It would be good to see Matt happy, but was Mandy ready to stop playing around? Matt needed a good woman who wouldn't mess with his head.

"Things aren't good with Matt and Jan!" Mandy shouted from several aisles back in the stacks.

"Looks like she might have another bloke," he responded.

"Yeah, I figured something like that," she agreed as she returned to the counter.

"He could do without extra grief right now," Moke added and with a veiled challenge to Mandy, "He could do without being dicked around."

Mandy returned his accusing look. "I wouldn't do that."

"Well. Just take it easy then."

Mandy remained at the counter, as Moke left. She stared dreamily toward the inward goods receiving area, tapping her pen on the sheet-metal counter top. She was thinking of Matt, and how she genuinely cared for him, desperately wanted to help him. She had almost admitted it to Moke. It had been a long while since she had expressed her feelings about a man to anyone. She realized she might be falling for Matt. She could feel the tension and excitement, the rush of energy and love as she thought about the possibility of her and Matt together. The crisis of the drier explosion had made her realize it. It was frightening as well, because she realized she had allowed herself to be vulnerable. She could be hurt. But most of all, it felt good, true, real, full and warm. She smiled to herself as she thought about what she would do to Matt given half the chance. She would absolutely smother him with love. Would he return her affection? She wasn't sure. She didn't care. She was committed and she knew it was real. She yearned to see him, to hold him.

"Damn!" She said aloud to herself. "Got to get him outta trouble first!" She glanced around the room to see if anyone heard her talking to herself and went back to tapping her pen, thinking about a solution for Matt's dilemma. 'Ding,' the audible alert signal coming in from the computer network email server sounded. Another email had arrived. Mandy grimaced. She didn't want to be looking at any emails. She wanted to work out how to get Matt off the hook.

'Ding.' Another email arrival. Irritating, she thought. Mandy had slipped back into her daydream. Suddenly the penny dropped. "That's it!" Her eyes were bright with inspiration. "Email….that's it!" She jumped out of her seat. Energy pumping, she reached for the phone and dialed. "Shane? That you?" She half shouted into the phone.

"Hey, you told me the porno stuff I sent you could be seen by others and it was saved on the server?! Ok ok….I'll talk softer, but I'm bloody excited mate! You have to help!"

Shane replied, guardedly admitting he might help her, but first he needed to know what she was proposing.

"Matt's in trouble with Jim and Libby. They've said the drier explosion and damage was an accident, but Matt told her it was because she cancelled the PMs on the drier vent doors. Jim is supporting her. I think they're both after Matt."

Shane said it wasn't his, or her concern.

"Yeah, I know I shouldn't know, but Moke and Matt explained it all to me, in detail. So, listen up. Matt says he deleted an email from Libby which would help protect his position. Serve as evidence of her responsibility for the explosion."

Shane didn't follow.

"Don't you see?" If we can get the deleted email back, then Matt has the proof. He can prove he warned Libby about the vent system, and it's her fault! You gotta help me find the email. Please, Shane."

Shane was sweating. He'd be violating company policy. He was supposed to get the Site Manager or the Regional HR Manager's permission to go snooping for anything damaging to another employee's reputation. "I don't know Mandy. I could get into some serious grief."

"C'mon, Shane! I'm gonna come down there and bust your chops if you don't come through for me!"

"You can't threaten me, Mandy!"

"I'm not threatening you Shane. I'm pleading with you. This is Matt's job on the line."

Shane didn't respond. Why should he help Mandy or Matt? Neither of them had really done him any favors.

"Shane! You still there?!"

"I'm thinking. What you're asking me to do. It could get me sacked."

"It could get you into the sack too! When the women around here learn what you did to save Matt's job. You'll be a hero!"

"I don't need to be a hero, and I don't want anyone to know I've helped you."

"Do it because it's the right thing to do?"

Shane went silent again. "I'll think about it."

"You think about it and then come back to me with the email! Ok?" Mandy was frustrated Shane hadn't agreed immediately, but she knew she couldn't expect an immediate response from him. He needed to get into his mental cave. Men! They were frustrating!

She hung up the phone and jumped in the air. She couldn't wait to tell Moke and Dave about her plan.

In the IT office, Shane considered his options. It was easy for him to search the deleted emails. All he had to do was log onto the system as a system administrator and search in the archived database of the email system. Searching by Jim or Libby's name, or Matt's for that matter, would turn up all their emails for any time period he decided to search. The only problem was his log-on as the System Administrator would be noted on the corporate database and it would be highlighted in the daily and weekly system reports. There was a chance the corporate IS manager would question his actions. There was a chance he wouldn't ask him at all. Shane logged on as a system administrator once or twice a month, as part of the troubleshooting process. If they were busy enough at the head office there was a good chance they wouldn't notice.

He decided to log on and have a look. Matt was a good guy and Mandy gave him a buzz. More than a buzz, she frightened him. He had fantasized about her, and he was sure she was aware of it and he felt guilty. He was married with two young kids. He shouldn't be fantasizing about Mandy or any other women.

Shane had no previous interaction with Matt. Apparently, he never got into any predicaments with the computerized maintenance management system since he'd never asked Shane for support. He didn't seem to need Shane. Maybe that was part of the reason Shane wasn't motivated to help Matt . He'd never formed any sort of a bond or relationship with Matt.

On the other hand, Shane didn't want to violate Richard's trust. He had hired Shane for a role that paid twice as much as he'd ever made as a contractor and Shane felt Richard had his back, his best interests at heart.

His fingers seemed to be on autopilot as he typed in the appropriate system administrator login and password details. He accessed the archived email database in a matter of seconds. Instead of sifting through hundreds of emails from Libby, he went directly to the past three months of emails from Matt, which numbered under a hundred. After five minutes he found the email Mandy wanted.

SUBJECT: Drier Explosion Checks and Removal of PM's
FROM: Matt
TO: Libby

Libby. I have reviewed the additional checks you have asked Graeme to remove from the PM schedule this morning. These changes along with the elimination of the drier explosion vent checks and pressure vessel checks on evaporators and other pressurized equipment are placing people and equipment in danger. I have talked with you last Monday about this, and I have not changed my opinion. As the acting Maintenance Supervisor I must insist that you re-implement the preventive maintenance tasks you have removed or I will be forced to notify OSH.

He saved the email in a folder where he could retrieve and share it with Mandy and others, if he decided. He continued browsing the emails. Not much else in Matt's archives.

Shane decided to look at emails following or prior to the date Matt replied to Libby, only this time he looked at Libby's emails. He didn't' find anything else on the day Matt replied to Libby. Shane was just about to exit the database, when he saw a couple of emails with Matt's name in the Title addressed to Jim.

Subject: Matt / PM Concerns
From: Libby Galwaith
To: Jim Champion

Jim. Matt is continuing to challenge the reduction of PM's that I'm making in the system. He may be correct with his assessment, but I can't afford to leave the work orders in the system and make the R&M savings you have requested. I need to talk to you urgently about how to diffuse Matt's campaign and discredit his arguments, if possible.

"Hmm." Shane said to himself aloud. He appreciated the company confidentiality protection policy but this appeared to violate employee rights. He checked over his shoulder, reflexively, since he realized he shouldn't be looking at the email. He decided to close the door to his office, briefly glancing up and down the hallway before pulling the door shut. He checked through the rest of Jim Champion's emails and found Jim's response to Mandy's email about Matt.

Subject: Matt / PM Concerns
From: Jim Champion
To: Libby Galwaith

Get a grip. You're the expert. Don't bother responding to him. I have got to have the savings or it's your butt!

"Damn!" Shane said, aloud. This potentially confirmed suspicions about Jim and cost reductions. It meant the rumor he heard about an IT department downsizing was likely to be true.

The phone rang in Shane's office. He could see Richard's name on the caller display. He froze suspecting for a split second Richard had noticed what he was doing in the email archives. He picked up the phone. "Hi Richard. What can I do for you?"

Richard wanted Shane to get over to the drier area and see if he could help out with any of the programming re-implementation following the drier explosion.

"Yep. Sure. I'm not busy. I'll log off and get over there."

He hung up the receiver and reviewed a few more emails from the past two days, one from Libby to Jim. Both Libby and Jim had deleted their emails immediately after sending them, demonstrating a need for cover. Jim opened his Sent file and deleted his own emails. Shane was too curious to log off without further investigation.

Subject: Matt
From Libby Galwaith
To: Jim Champion

Jim per earlier phone conversation. I'm positive Matt is preparing to tell the CEO about PM and contractor reduction on the drier. He practically accused you and I of causing the explosion here. I put him off with a threat to call HR. He is about to expose the PM reduction program and he has documented proof.......or at least he did have it unless he's deleted it. I don't think we can wait any longer to act. I strongly suggest you neutralize Matt asap.

"Uh oh!" He scrolled down the deleted email to see if there was a reply message from Jim to Libby. There was.

Subject: Matt
From: Jim Champion
To: Libby Galwaith

Ok. I'll make it happen. Announcement this avo. Matt's suspended.

"Bloody Hell!" Shane logged off the system as fast as he could. He knew if Jim or any other managers on site, including Richard, knew what he was doing and what he'd found he would get the bullet. He wasn't sure what scared him the most, getting caught snooping or the potential outcome for Matt and the site. He wanted to get clear of the computer workstation as soon as possible. He didn't bother saving the email from Jim or Libby.

Five minutes later, Shane cut through the engineer's workshop on his way to support the drier data archiving and implementation.

"Hey! Shane!"

He cringed at the sound of Mandy's voice. He had hoped she wouldn't be in the stores, or at least, wouldn't see him taking the shortcut.

"You got any good news?! What happened with my idea?"

"I'm in a hurry Mandy."

"So. Can't you answer a simple question? Did you find anything? Any useful deleted emails?" She was walking toward him as he reached for the exit door.

"I looked, but I don't have anything, and you shouldn't be talking to me about it." Shane didn't look her in the eye.

She pulled up short, suspicious, but he was already half out the door.

"You had better!" She shouted as the door closed

Matt had been sitting in Trevor's old office for an hour after leaving the engineering stores area. He still didn't think of the office as his own. There was a good chance it might never be his office. He didn't really care. The whole place was turning to shit. Best maintenance practices! What a joke, he thought to himself. How could they have a best maintenance practice when the site manager didn't know the first thing about maintenance practices, himself, and in addition, was willing to sacrifice the whole program for short term profits to make himself look good? Libby knew the basics but was defying the fundamentals to achieve immediate bottom-line results.

Matt reckoned their behavior was probably the reason there weren't any best practice operations in the dairy industry or anywhere else in the country. Too many site managers had the same attitude. They were looking out for number one and short-term results. They weren't willing to learn about what needed to happen or make sacrifices. They were fooling themselves and their shareholders.

Matt doubted whether anybody achieved maintenance best practices anywhere. Maybe it was just a bloody pipe dream, something to entice tradesmen into trying to get better when they never had a chance. A pie in the sky, flavor-of-the-month program to get a little extra effort out of the workforce. Or maybe just an opportunity for high-priced consultants to make money off companies, while giving the board of directors the impression improvements were underway. There had been plenty of other programs in the past that had come and gone like world class manufacturing, total quality manufacturing, total safety. They lasted for three to six months before getting dropped for the next big idea. How had he allowed himself to be convinced this maintenance best practices program was any different?! "Damn! I must be nuts!" He shouted aloud, to himself.

No. It was Jack. He was the reason. Matt reminded himself, Jack had actually 'been there.' He had worked at a best practices plant. Jack was a tradesman and he had told them too many real-life stories for the concept of maintenance best practices to be a false illusion. But Jack said he was successful at sites where the manager knew about maintenance and supported the program <u>and</u> the culture change required to make it happen.

There was no longer any question about maintenance best practices only the question about whether he would remain employed. It was time to go along with the new VFM project, time to be realistic. If he chilled out, backed off on the quest to expose Libby maybe things would cool off. Maybe if he got back on a more realistic track he'd be able to win Jan back? He would pay more attention to her, cut out the distractions and concentrate on making her happy. Letting his mates down was a concern, or was it? Moke and Dave would be disappointed, but he'd never promised them he'd be their advocate. The other guys didn't really care. They expected the program to fail like the rest of the management's improvement initiatives. None of them had come up to talk to him or thanked him for standing up to Jim and Libby.

He was on his own. Why? Was he some sort of bleeding heart? And whose heart was bleeding anyway? His certainly was. Maybe that was his true concern, fixing his own bleeding heart. No more crusades. He would pull his head in and support Libby with the rebuild and her project. He might get a shot at the maintenance manager role, but if it didn't happen, he would be happy being one of the boys.

Matt felt relieved. He had made up his mind. He could feel the weight lift off his shoulders. He felt hopeful about getting back together with Jan. He prepared to leave for the day when he heard the audible notification for an incoming email. He hit the 'Enter' button on his computer, awakening it from its sleep mode. The Outlook screen was still active and it showed a message from Jim had just arrived. He clicked on the email.

Subject: Drier Fire – Further Actions
From: Jim Champion
To: All Site Personnel

It is with regret, that I have to inform you Matt Polaski will be suspended until further notice. Please contact Libby Galwaith regarding any maintenance matters.

"What do you mean we've got to hold fire?!" Mandy's eyes were blazing from her position behind the counter. Moke and Dave were on the opposite side. It was the morning after Matt's suspension announcement, and Matt had rung Dave early and suggested they wait to see whether the suspension was going to be upheld before doing anything stupid. Dave had just finished explaining Matt's recommendation to Moke and Mandy.

"Of course, it's going to be upheld if we don't do anything!"

Dave held up his hands, encouraging Mandy to back off. "Listen.

There is a chance HR will overturn the suspension. Everyone knows it has to be done in person, with a third person, HR, or union delegate in attendance. Jim suspended him with an email!"

"Yeah. Right! Jim will follow it up, and it will stick!" Mandy was on fire.

Moke and Dave were silent.

"If you guys are the mates you say you are, you will dig deep for more info to nail Jim and that consultant bitch."

"She's right Dave." Moke moved to sit on a stool. He looked at Dave for a response.

Dave shrugged his shoulders in agreement, "Ok. So, what do we do?"

Mandy relaxed slightly, recognizing Matt's two friends were finally open to a pitch about her plan. "I've already got it started. You guys just have to make Shane deliver."

"Deliver what?" Moke moved forward on his stool.

"Deliver the emails Matt deleted from Libby. They prove she knows the deleted PM's may have been the reason for the drier explosion and Matt warned her before it happened!"

"Are you sure?" Dave asked

"Yep! Matt told me about them. He said he deleted them a couple months ago after a fight with Libby. He thought the proof was gone. I remembered Shane could retrieve anything including my soft-core pics." Mandy said continued with a grin. "So, I asked Shane if he could find the emails end of last week."

"And?" Dave queried her for more feedback.

"He hasn't come up with anything, yet." Mandy hesitated. "But I think he's scared. I'm sure he's got something and won't tell us."

Mandy was certain Shane was lying when she confronted him. "If you guys put a little pressure on, I think he'll come up with the goods."

"Sounds like you've got it sussed, Doll." Moke got off the stool ready to make a move.

"The least we can do is round up the computer nerd," Dave agreed. "We'll go check in with the boys and tell them the plan. A couple of the guys are pretty hot about what's happened. If they know we've got a plan, it'll keep them from going off half-cocked."

Mandy nodded as the two men headed for the door. She was pleased. "Be back for smoko?"

"More like lunch."

"Don't be too hard on Shane." She smiled to herself, thinking what Shane would feel like when these two guys confronted him. They wouldn't take no for an answer. Not now.

The group of tradesmen stopped talking as Dave and Moke entered the workshop.

Crazy Andy was the first to speak. "I'm about ready to kill the sonofabitch Champion!"

"Yeah this is bullshit! What're we gonna do?!" One of the sparkies spoke for the group of electricians who were standing together, separate from the mechanical fitters.

"Listen guys. Keep a lid on it for now," Dave cautioned. "Moke you head over to Shane's office. I'll join you in ten minutes."

"What's he going to 'Nerd-o' for? He's not going to help us?!" Andy was red as a beet.

"Go on Moke. I'll catch you in ten. No time to lose."

Moke nodded and quietly slipped out the workshop door.

Dave turned back to the guys. "I think it's great you guys are so ticked off. It would really warm Matt's heart. But the last thing he wants is for you guys to get suspended as well."

"I don't really give a rat's ass," Andy said.

Another fitter piped in, "Yeah. We're bloody tired of working here. First they get VFM and the blonde in here to stuff up things. Then they blow up the drier and blame it on Matt. What's next?!"

"Maybe an opportunity to move the blonde and Jim outa here?" Dave suggested.

"Oh Yeah, right. How?" Andy smirked.

"It's tied up with Shane. That's why I asked Moke to get over there. I wanted to fill you guys in on the plan."

Moke was seated in Shane's office, leaning forward in his chair, slightly crowding Shane who sat facing him. He thought he'd get to work on Shane before Dave arrived. "This is the way I see it. Matt knew the PMs weren't being done."

Shane nodded as Moke paused.

Moke had a way of speaking in short bursts, getting a couple of sentences clear in his head before opening his mouth. "Matt knew it was dangerous. He could have looked the other way. That was the easy option. He didn't." Moke paused again. "He told that woman, and backed it in writing. She ignored it. Now Viv and Squeek are badly burned and Matt's suspended, maybe lost his job."

Shane shifted in his chair. He knew Mandy had sent Moke over to pressure him, but he was preparing himself to stay the course and protect his manager and himself.

Moke carried on. "Call me soft but it doesn't seem right to me? Worse still, who is to say there won't be more of the same? It wasn't just the driers that weren't being maintained. Who's going to be the next victim?" Moke paused again looking down at his hands.

Shane sensed Moke was honestly pouring his heart into this. He realized he had a point about the potential for more injuries as a result of plant failures.

"Doesn't matter how hard us guys shout, they won't listen. There is only one guy who can stop that happening. The guy who has the proof." Moke looked up at Shane.

Shane's face was white, dark circles dimmed his normally bright blue eyes.

Moke continued to look alternately at Shane and down at his hands, waiting for a response from Shane. Minutes seemed to pass.

Shane mulled over the options, glancing out the window of his office and back at Moke. "Okay. Moke. I've had enough sleepless nights as it is. Pull up a chair and I'll show you the emails."

As Moke pulled a chair towards the computer workstation, Shane got up, and put his 'NO INTERRUPTIONS, GENIUS AT WORK' sign on the outside of his office door. He closed the door and wedged a large box against the back of the door from the inside.

Moke smiled to himself. This must be some serious shit if he's blocking the door. He watched intently as Shane typed a series of passwords. A series of emails from Jim Champion to Libby came up on the screen. "Can't you get the one from Matt to Libby?"

"Have a look at this first," Shane replied

Subject: Re: Matt
From: Jim Champion
To: Libby Galwaith

Ok. I'll make it happen. Announcement this avo. Matt's suspended.

Subject: Matt
From Libby Galwaith
To: Jim Champion

Jim per earlier phone conversation. I'm positive Matt is preparing to tell the CEO about PM and contractor reduction on the drier. He practically accused you and I of causing the explosion. I put him off with a threat to call HR. He is about to expose the PM reduction program and he has documented proof....... or at least he did have it unless he's deleted it. I don't think we can wait any longer to act. I strongly suggest you neutralize Matt asap.

Moke stared in astonishment at the email.

"Is that what you want?" Shane asked.

"Geez, did they stitch him up or what?!" Moke shook his head in disgust.

"There's more, " Shane said, once again scrolling through the emails before stopping at another.

Moke squinted at the screen.

Subject: Matt / PM Concerns
From: Libby Galwaith
To: Jim Champion

Jim. Matt is continuing to challenge the reduction of PM's that I'm making in the system. He may be correct with his assessment, but I can't afford to leave the work orders in the system and make the R&M savings you have requested. I need to talk to you urgently about how to diffuse Matt's campaign and discredit his arguments, if possible.

"Christ! It's worse than we thought! Can you find the email Matt sent to her? He told me he deleted it when he got her reply."

"Yeah, I need to go into Matt's deleted files. Hold on a minute." Shane punched the keys while Moke leaned back in his chair, trying to work out his next move.

Shane had let him see the emails, but would he be prepared to share the evidence? Shane interrupted his train of thought.

"I think this is what you want."

SUBJECT: re: Drier Explosion Checks and Removal of PM's
FROM: Libby
TO: Matt

Matt. I'm sorry you've decided to react defensively to my initiatives. I thought you and I had reached an agreement regarding the necessity to halt all preventive work until we conducted an RCM-based review of the PM's and required intervals. My instructions to Graeme and you stand.
The work I have postponed will remain postponed until the appropriate analysis is complete. I apparently have over-estimated you.

SUBJECT: Drier Explosion Checks and Removal of PM's
FROM: Matt
TO: Libby

Libby. I have reviewed the additional checks you have asked Graeme to remove from the PM schedule this morning. These changes along with the elimination of the drier explosion vent checks and pressure vessel checks on evaporators and other pressurized equipment are placing people and equipment in danger. I have talked with you last Monday about this, and I have not changed my opinion. As the Maintenance Supervisor I must insist that you re-implement the preventive maintenance tasks you have removed or I will be forced to notify OSH.

"That's it mate! Well done!" Moke was excited there was so much proof.

"Did he notify OSH?" Shane asked.

"No. Or at least I don't think so. If he had, we wouldn't be sitting here."

"Shame. Is there any more?"

"Probably, but I'm not keen to spend too much time digging around in the files. My work is traceable too."

"I guess there's plenty there as it is,"

"You want me to print it for you?"

Moke's face lit up. He hadn't even asked. "You can do that?"

Shane let out a small chuckle. "Of course." Shane hit the PRINT button.

Moke laughed, relieved Shane had broken the tension. "You forget. I'm just a dumb fitter."

"So, what are you going to do with them?" Shane queried as he handed the printed copies to Moke.

Moke's smile disappeared. "I don't know. I'll talk to Dave. He's the ideas man." Hesitating, he scratched his head again. "Shane, if we use these, they'll know where they came from."

Shane smiled wryly. "Yeah, I already worked that one out."

"You could lose your job."

"No <u>could</u> in it. Look what they did to Matt. Unless Jim goes, I might as well pack my bags now. I've broken the IT Code of Conduct. That's grounds for dismissal."

Moke looked at the emails in his hand. Why should Shane lose his job? He put heaps of free overtime into the company. He had a young family. If he were sacked from his job for gross misconduct how would he get another? Moke put the emails on Shane's desk and stood up. "Nah mate. It's not worth it. Matt's lost his job, there's no need for you to lose yours too. We'll work it out another way."

Shane was torn. On one side he felt like insisting Moke take the printed copies. On the other hand, an inner voice told him to let Moke go. He said he would find another way and Shane could keep his job

Minutes later, Moke returned to the workshop.
All eyes turned toward him.

"Sorry I didn't get over to Shane's, mate. How do you go?' Dave asked.

"It's no good."

"What do you mean?!" exploded Crazy Andy.

"I mean we've got to find another way!"

"Bastard! I told you he would be no fucking use!!" Andy kicked his steel-toed boot into the table leg. "I'll sort him out!" Grabbing his wrench, he started for the workshop door.

Moke shouted but before Andy reached the exit, Mandy entered.

Seeing the fury in Andy's face and the wrench in his hand she froze in her tracks. "Hey Andy, where you off to?" she asked in a calm voice.

"Get out of my way woman!" he shouted at her.

Dave grabbed him by the arm. "Hold on Andy. Moke isn't finished."

Before Moke could say anything the workshop door opened again, and Shane walked into the workshop, clutching the printed emails.

Everyone held caught their breath.

"This is what you need," he said passing them to Dave. "Use them however you want. I'll back you."

Dave released his grip on Andy in order to take the emails and the big man swung toward Shane and grabbed his shirt at the collar before pinning him against the wall.

Moke who reacted first. He stepped in behind Andy, locking his right arm around Andy's throat. He pulled Andy's head back, hissing through his teeth, "Let him go!"

Andy, struggling for breath and released his grip on Shane.

"Jesus! You're friggin nuts!" Shane was visibly shaken.

Moke backed away, dragging Andy with him.

Nobody moved while Shane recovered. Moke slowly released his hold on Andy.

"Lemme go!" Andy sputtered.

Moke gave Andy a gentle shove toward the locker room. "Go wash your face!"

Andy grumbled incoherently and staggered away.

Dave and Mandy looked over the emails, as though the incident with Andy was a common occurrence, which it was, unbeknown to Shane.

Moke turned to Shane. "You all right? That boy can get wound up like a cornered boar with three pig dogs on him."

"Yeah, I'm ok." Shane looked slightly embarrassed.

"Right." said Dave decisively. "That's enough drama for one day." Addressing the maintenance team, he added, "If you jokers are happy to leave this to us, I suggest you go and do some work, and we go and sort out what to do next?"

The rest of the crew nodded their assent, happy a plan to support Matt was in the works.

An hour later, Dave, Shane, Mandy and Moke were busy at the engineering stores counter discussing their plan of attack. They considered directly confronting Jim with the email evidence and decided against it. Jim was a survivor and if surviving meant drowning a few other people to stay afloat, he wouldn't hesitate. He could easily dismiss them and get the evidence destroyed by the IT Manager.

Going direct to Colin Grey, the CEO, seemed like a better option until they thought about implementing it. Dave explained he had heard there was more likelihood of getting by the Queen's guards in all their bearskin busbies than there was of getting past Colin's secretary. They weren't high enough up the ladder to warrant a meeting with the CEO. His secretary would call Jim after she reviewed the email copies and the cat would be out of the bag.

Moke suggested confronting Libby directly, getting her to spill the beans. He believed Libby was the weakest link and might break.

Dave disagreed and reminded them about Matt's description of her presentation of the recovery plan. She was too professional; cold and hard. They couldn't break her.

Mandy agreed explaining Libby was the one who recommended Matt's suspension.

Dave asked, 'What is the worst thing that could happen if they went to Libby?' They contemplated the question and Dave suggested Libby would likely go back to Jim with their plan to expose them both.

Mandy surprised the men by saying she didn't think Libby would go to Jim. She explained her women's intuition told her Libby was fed up with Jim, and she needed to protect her position as well. Mandy suggested Libby might throw Jim under the bus. Implicate Jim as the ringleader of the cuts and the resulting explosion?

"That's it then, eh?! We'll confront Libby. Smoke her out. Get her to break down and spill her guts." Dave summarized

"Yeah. But leave the kid out of it." Moke said gesturing toward Shane.

"I agree," said Mandy. He's too sweet and he's done enough already. With a bit of luck he might duck the fallout."

"Wait a minute." Shane piped in. He expressed his disappointment about their intention to leave him on the sidelines since he'd produced the evidence.

"Nope. It's decided. You're out! Sorry mate," Dave stated.

"No time to waste, let's go and see her now!" Mandy was eager.

"Not a good idea, to go over there," Dave cautioned. "If Jim sees the three of us heading for Libby's office, he'll be in there in a flash."

"You're probably right," Mandy agreed. "Can we get her over here?"

"I'll give her a call," Dave replied as he picked up the phone, pressing down the speaker button while he punched in her number.

Libby picked up on the third ring.

"Libby? It's Dave. We've got something we want to show you. Can you come over to the workshop?"

"What is it?" she replied with a semi-perturbed tone.

Dave shrugged his shoulders, looking to Moke and Mandy for answers. Mandy silently mouthed "PMs."

"PMs," he said leaning closer to the microphone on the telephone console.

"What about them?" she demanded.

"We've got some information related to the explosion we think you should see."

"What sort of information?" Her tone was guarded and angry.

Dave paused, lost for a response again. Seeing Matt's name on the email he ad-libbed, "Information Matt left."

The pause on the end of the phone was audible. After several seconds she replied, "Well you had better bring it over."

Dave sensing a turning of the tide replied, "We think it's a better idea if you come over here to the workshop."

Her reply was sharp. "Dave, I have no intention of playing games. If you have something you want to show me, bring it over. Otherwise stop wasting my time." There was a click as she hung up.

Dave put the phone down and looked at his compatriots.

"Bitch!" Mandy exploded.

"What now?" Moke asked quietly in an attempt to calm the group.

"We smoke her out!" said Shane, his eyes bright. "We send her one of these emails, letting her know there are more to come. That'll get her running out of her office fast enough."

Dave's eyes lit up. "I like it!" He grinned, thumping Shane on the back.

Shane nodded. At least he had an opportunity to help out and maybe he would keep his job in the process.

They agreed the email should be sent from Matt's computer. Shane headed back to his office. Ten minutes later Matt's computer pinged indicating an incoming email.

Subject: Matt
From Libby Galwaith
To: Jim Champion

Jim per earlier phone conversation. I'm positive Matt is preparing to tell the CEO about PM and contractor reduction on the drier. He practically accused you and I of causing the explosion. I put him off with a threat to call HR. He is about to expose the PM reduction program and he has documented proof....... or at least he did have it unless he's deleted it. I don't think we can wait any longer to act. I strongly suggest you neutralize Matt asap.

Mandy looked at it. "Good man! I wonder how he did that? Look there's no trail to where this email's from!"

"What do you mean?" asked Moke.

"Shane's forwarded Libby's email to Jim from the deleted files archives to Matt's computer. Normally the header would show who forwarded the email. This one doesn't. She won't know it's Shane who's dabbling in the system." Jumping into Matt's office chair, she clicked the 'FORWARD' button and punched in Libby's name. She also clicked on 'HIGH PRIORITY' to add a bright red exclamation mark. "What shall we head it?" she asked.

Dave's eyes gleamed. "ONE OF MANY, in capitals. In the text box tell her she's got five minutes to get over here."

"Sounds like blackmail to me," Moke understated.

"Yeah. And it feels great!" Dave grinned.

"You reckon she'll come?" asked Moke.

"Yeah. I give her four minutes after we hit the send button, " replied Dave.

"One minute to read it twice, and three minutes to get here."

"Shall I send it?" asked Mandy.

"Yeah, go for it. I've got the stopwatch running." Dave adjusted his watch to time the event and placed it on the desk.

Three pairs of eyes watched the seconds ticking by on the stopwatch. Two minutes and forty-seven seconds later they heard the workshop door open and close. Glancing nervously at each other they listened for footsteps. None came.

Letting out a long breathe of air Mandy said, "Maybe she won't come?"

"She will." Dave focused on the watch.

After three minutes and thirty-three seconds the workshop door swung open again, this time they could hear footsteps coming across the workshop.

Moke was the first to speak. "That isn't a pair of steel capped boots! She's faster than you thought."

Dave chuckled and nodded, knowingly toward Moke. "Hunter's ears!"

Seconds later the door to Matt's office burst open.

"You better have an explanation!" Libby blazed. "And it had better be good!"

Dave leaned back in his chair and calmly responded. Years in heated company union negotiations had steeled him for situations like this. "You might like to take a seat and turn down the tone a bit. You're doing the explaining this time."

"I'll stand!" she replied angrily, "And I have nothing to explain."

"You'll sit! And you have everything to explain!" He pointed to the copies of the emails sitting on the table.

Libby glanced at the email copies on the table. As her eyes caught the email headers, the red blush highlighting her cheekbones seemed to blend in with the angry, embarrassed blush spreading across her face. She looked as though someone had put a pin in her balloon and she deflated before their eyes, sinking into the chair as she looked more closely at each email.

After a minute of silence Libby asked, "What do you want?"

Dave nodded toward Mandy.

"We want Matt's name cleared." Mandy was insistent, struggling to contain her anger. She hesitated, searching for words to describe her next request but blurted out, "Why, Libby? Just tell me why!"

Libby didn't respond. She kept her head down, eyes averted from theirs, pretending to look at the emails. She was considering the situation, their demands; her options. She decided against an immediate response. She needed to consider alternatives, perhaps go back to Jim. She would have to consult with him before making any moves, as well as her boss at VFM. These people have inappropriately accessed emails. There wasn't enough evidence to trap either she or Jim. The emails could be suppressed as contrived or manufactured. At least she and Jim could make that argument. Although somebody, probably in IT, had pulled them out of the archives. That person would have to be neutralized.

Mandy, Dave and Moke were surprised when Libby suddenly rose to her feet. Her demeanor had regenerated and color had returned to her face. She picked up the emails and shuffled them into an orderly pile to take with her. "I'll get back to you."

Dave opened his mouth to speak, but Libby cut him off.

"I'm just a consultant here. I'm sure you understand I can't make any decisions without talking with my client, Jim Champion."

Mandy's mouth dropped open. This wasn't what she or the others had expected. She thought they'd be able to bully her into an admission of guilt.

"I'm sure you've got copies of these, so I'll take these along." Libby gestured to the emails in her hand, calculating her next words, "I'm not sure they're authentic, to be honest."

Her conclusion had an air of finality, implying she wouldn't entertain any further discussion. She pushed the chair back from the small, circular table and made her way out of the engineering office. She had left the workshop before they could say anything.

Ten minutes later, Libby considered her next step. She stretched her neck from side to side. The tension she had first felt, ten days ago, was now locked solid through her shoulders and neck, generating an intense headache. The situation at Mornington had slowly paralyzed her soul and now it was threatening her career with VFM. She decided it was time for a change. She couldn't violate her principles any longer, but she wouldn't approach Jim. She wouldn't tell her boss at VFM, nor would she talk to Matt. She would focus on the recovery plan, and let the emails, rumors and the rest take their course without her input. She knew one thing, for sure. She wouldn't be compromising or lying, any longer, to protect Jim or VFM.

Mandy, Moke and Dave sat in stunned silence for a few moments following Libby's abrupt exit. It hadn't been a complete surprise, they agreed. Libby hadn't taken the bait. She wasn't weak, and she would be looking out for Number One. They were certain she would be shaking in her boots. They agreed they should talk to Matt. With the email evidence provided by Shane, they believed Matt had a strong case for re-instatement. They should take it to Colin Grey, the CEO. Dave suggested Matt could fill in the blanks and put an approach together for a meeting with Grey.

Moke piped in. "He won't do it."

"What do you mean, he won't do it?" Mandy asked, desperately.

"He says it's time he moved on."

Mandy shook her head sadly. "He's giving up?"

"He's gone back up North," Moke explained.

"Where?"

"Home. He said he needs time to clear his head and decide what to do next." Moke knew the only way to sort yourself out in these circumstances was to get back to your roots, to your family.

"He'll have to come back!" Mandy exploded.

There was a short silence before Mandy spoke again. "Maybe he would think differently if he could see the bits and pieces we've collected?"

"I don't think he'd look at it right now. Besides, we've no way of getting it to him."

"I know where to get him, "Dave piped in. "His brother will know. He's probably at their fishing bach out at the Heads."

Mandy grabbed Dave by the hand and pulled him out of his chair. "Let's go make some phone calls."

Dave followed and Mandy made several calls with his direction. Sure enough, Matt was there. Horst, Matt's brother was curious to know what was going on, but Dave declined to explain, knowing Horst would likely give Matt grief if he knew the details. He told Horst just to get him to the pub tonight and he'd make travel arrangements to meet the two of them.

Mandy booked flight tickets for Dave and by 3.30 p.m. he was airborne. He promised to phone both Mandy and Moke as soon as he had a response. They decided to head over to Moke's place after work. They wouldn't relax until they had word from Dave.

At 8:30 p.m. Mandy's cell phone rang.

Looking quickly at the display she said, excitedly, "It's Dave!"

Mandy talked briefly and hung up.

"What did he say?" Moke was worried since the call was so short.

"He'll be on the first flight back! With Matt!" She grinned and high-fived Moke.

"Sweet! Things are looking up!" He shouted.

Mandy finished her drink, and gave Moke and his partner a hug and headed for home.

Matt was still reeling from the past few days. Being back in his home town always generated mixed emotions. This time more than most. Horst had demanded to know what was going on. Matt had told him, about his suspension and about Jan's relationship with Wayne, the gym instructor.

Horst, laughed saying "You want your big brother to come and sort them out?"

Matt had felt a surge of anger. Horst had never been a good listener or counselor for him. His way of sorting things out was with his fists. He had followed Horst's advice on several occasions with negative results and he realized he needed to deal to his problems his own way.

He was energized by the interest and support he felt from Dave and Mandy during their phone call and it had inspired him to think differently about how to resolve this conflict. Dave was correct. He couldn't give in to Jim, Libby or Jan. That's what he had always done in the past, compromised to smooth out the arguments. He was always the only one who compromised. Jim had never budged and Jan had always put herself and her interests ahead of his. He and Dave had a heart-to-heart discussion.

It had been an epiphany. Aided by a couple "cold ones," to help him get out of the box and commit to a different approach, he decided on an 'all or nothing' approach for the first time since he'd joined the dairy company and married Jan.

CHAPTER 15

The next morning, Matt returned to the Mornington site. Dave, Moke, Mandy, and Shane were gathered in Trevor's office. At first, Matt had been hesitant about coming to the site since his suspension hadn't been lifted, but Dave had convinced him otherwise. They reckoned neither Libby nor Jim would raise an issue since Libby had seen the copies of the emails and would undoubtedly make Jim aware the maintenance crew knew the suspension was illegal.

"I've made an appointment to see Colin Grey at eleven o'clock, this morning." Matt explained.

"I'll come with you," Mandy replied, reflexively.

"And me," added Moke. Dave didn't say anything, since he knew Matt's feelings, expressed to him the night before.

"No." said Matt firmly. "I'm doing this on my own."

Moke, Mandy and Shane argued Matt shouldn't go to see Colin alone. There was strength in numbers. He listened for a while before telling them politely to get out of the office so he could get his thoughts together for the most important meeting of his life.

They relented and filed out.

A few hours later, Matt walked to the administration block where he'd arranged to meet Colin Grey in the board room, alone. When he had called Grey's office the afternoon before, his personal assistant had informed him the CEO would be at the Mornington site to meet with Jim about the recovery plan.

Matt had specifically requested Jim not be involved when he requested the meeting, and the CEO had called him back to protest the request. Grey explained he would be violating management protocol by talking to Matt directly, without Matt first having gone through the site chain of command. Matt had asked him to support his request. The reason would be apparent when they met.

Now, as he walked into the meeting room, Grey's reception was frosty.

Matt opened the discussion with a direct accusation. "I want you to know the explosion of the drier and subsequent damage was a direct result of Jim Champion's actions and fully avoidable. I am telling you this to prevent further incidents."

As Colin started to speak Matt put up his hand and produced a pile of emails, "Let me show you the evidence."

Ten minutes later, after the CEO had finished reading through the emails twice, Matt reiterated, "As I said at the start, the explosion and subsequent damage was completely avoidable."

Colin sat back in his chair and considered Matt's statements and the evidence. "It paints a picture Matt, but it's not damning evidence. There isn't an absolutely clear relationship between the explosion and the preventive maintenance cancellations."

Matt began to argue, but the CEO cut him off.

"What I'm equally concerned about, though, is your suspension."

Matt relaxed slightly and waited for him to continue.

"We pride ourselves on our company culture and treatment of our employees. Your dismissal was unsubstantiated and in direct conflict with our company policies."

Matt could see the cogs turning in the CEO's head, but he wasn't sure he had a handle on what he was thinking. He didn't' feel confident Grey was making a strong enough connection between the drier explosion and the preventive maintenance task reductions. Maybe he needed to go into more detail to convince him.

Suddenly, Grey gathered up the email evidence and tapped the stack into a single neat pile. He was finished talking. "Leave it with me, Matt. You were correct in your request to meet with me privately as this human resource matter wouldn't have been appropriate to discuss with Jim."

"What about the drier explosion, the PM task evidence?"

"I'll get back to you. As I said, there isn't a clear case, though I understand what you are driving at." The CEO extended his hand to Matt. "Consider yourself re-instated Matt. I'll sort it out with Jim, and he'll be getting back to you to confirm. Thanks for bringing this to my attention." Grey escorted Matt into the hallway.

Matt waited in the hallway while Grey returned to the meeting room. He knew other employees in the administration block were watching him from their offices, or had seen him and the CEO together. Word would be getting back to Jim, but he didn't care. What he cared about was what action, besides his re-instatement, the CEO was going to take. He wanted to suggest Jim and Libby both get the sack, but the discussion with Grey hadn't provided the opportunity to discuss it. The CEO had focused on the policy violation more than the explosion's possible cause. Matt didn't get it. Why wouldn't Grey be more interested in solving that issue and punishing the responsible parties? He was proud of himself for fronting the CEO about the incident, and for getting himself re-instated, but it was a partial victory. He didn't want to continue working with Jim and Libby, and they certainly wouldn't be interested in working with him, now that he'd done exactly what Libby had warned Jim about. He shuddered slightly. He felt he was lined up in some hunter's crosshairs and he didn't know which way to run. He should have insisted on Jim's or Libby's dismissal. Grey seemed like he had already made up his mind. He guessed Grey would expect him to report back to work, even though his two bosses, one official and one contractor weren't informed. Bloody Hell! He thought and turned toward the main entrance. He pushed through the door and walked toward the workshop.

He felt a new strength and resolve in his step and a sense of well-being even though he was uncertain about his future at the dairy plant. For the first time, he had truly taken charge of the situation and faced a personal demon. He was no longer afraid of the site manager. His had overcome his fear of Jim and he felt energized. A load had lifted. He had faced his own weakness, his inability to deal with conflict and bullying that had plagued him, he realized, for much of his life. He'd also done something nobody had done before, to the best of his knowledge. He'd gone over Jim's head, Jim's worst nightmare, directly to the CEO and the CEO had agreed Jim had violated company policy. He had reclaimed his job, a considerable victory.

Nobody had seen Matt return to the workshop or the grin on his face as he walked into what was now, truly his office. He pushed the door shut and sat down at his desk. Time for the next face-off, he thought to himself.

He punched Jan's mobile number into the desktop phone keypad.

She picked up on the second ring. Her response set him back on his heels. "Hi. Matt. I'm so glad you phoned!" Her voice was cracking, trembling.

"Why? What's happened?" he asked, coldly.

"I've realized what a fool I've been," she replied. "I'm sorry"

"Sorry?"

"Sorry, I haven't been there for you. I just wanted some fun. To be loved."

"Ok," he said, hesitantly, wondering if she was sincere and what event had occurred to change her state of mind.

She hesitated and then cautiously said, "Oh, I'm so glad. When will you be home? I want you to come back to the house, our house."

Matt took a deep breath. He couldn't believe how vulnerable she sounded. It was disarming. He considered changing his mind, but realized he needed to confront her directly, not on the phone or with a text message. "Where are you Jan?"

"At home."

"I'll be there in twenty minutes." His tone was neutral. He didn't want her to feel everything was suddenly resolved between them.

Jan didn't pick up on his tone or at least didn't react to it. "Good. I'll be here." She sounded almost cheerful.

He hung up the phone. He didn't care about leaving the site in the middle of the day. It was probably best he made himself scarce while the CEO sorted out whatever he was going to do with Jim, if anything. He needed to talk with Jan face to face.

Matt pulled into the driveway twenty minutes later,.

Jan was waiting at the back door, holding it open as he got out of his Hilux truck. Her expression was mixed, a half-smile, biting her lip slightly.

She looked drained. She held her arms out as he came up the steps and gave him a desperate hug.

Matt didn't return the hug, but allowed her to hold him before following her into the house.

"I made you a cup of coffee and baked some muffins. Blueberry," she said warmly.

Matt didn't say anything. He moved through the kitchen to the small round table in the alcove where they ate most their meals. He sat with his back to the windows and took a sip of coffee. Jan sat down in the chair alongside of him, instead of her usual chair, on the opposite side of the table.

"Do you like the muffin?"

Matt nodded. He couldn't help feeling suspicious. Part of him wanted to believe something significant had changed and there was a chance for an improvement in their relationship. "So, what's up Jan? Why the change of heart?"

Jan sat back in her chair, catching her breath. "What do you mean Matt?" She was still vulnerable, not defensive or aggressive like she normally would have been after such a direct question.

Matt couldn't believe it. "Well. For months I'm at Moke's and I don't hear boo from you. What happened?"

Jan didn't say anything, just turned her head and looked past him, out the window.

Matt's mind clicked and the anger welled up in him as he realized the possible cause. He blurted, "Something went wrong at the Gym? Wayne, your instructor, dump you or something?!"

Jan turned back to him, with tears in her eyes, and then dropped her head into her uplifted hands, shaking her head from side to side.

He instinctively moved to put his arm around her, but caught himself. He hoped she had ended the affair, not Wayne. That would provide the only reason for a resolution between them, he thought. If the hotshot gym instructor had simply dumped her and she was on the rebound there was less hope. He waited for her to respond.

"It's not what you think Matt," she mumbled.

He could feel himself softening up, but caught himself, checking his typical rescue behavior. He was surprised he had prevented himself from responding as he usual. Looking for a reason, a tidbit of hope, which would give him false justification for relinquishing his self-esteem. He recognized the feeling, the caving in, the desire to take her in his arms and forgive and start over. Instead, he waited.

"I was going to call it off," she hesitated.

Matt sensed she was measuring her words now, rather than responding spontaneously.

"I realized it was a mistake. I'd been selfish and unfair."

Matt sensed she was constructing a defense. "Unfair?" He asked.

"Yes." Jan sensed he was looking for something, the meaning of the word. "It was mean as well."

"Oh?!" Matt realized Jan had seldom, except at the beginning of their relationship, used the word, love. She used the word to describe how she felt about things he did for her in the early days, but not about how she felt about him.

"Yes. Mean. I didn't put myself in your place. I accused you of things you didn't do."

Matt realized how true her words were. She had usually been on the attack, keeping him back on his heels. That's when she seemed the most confident and in a strange way, happy. He remembered how she'd explained it as a tactic she used with her father, keeping him on the defensive as a means of blocking his abuse. "So? What's the story? Did he dump you or did you dump him?!"

"What's the difference Matt? It's finished." Matt noted a hint of defiance in her reply. Her energy was shifting back toward Jan's default character.

"Big difference, or, like you say, maybe no difference. Either way, what's different about you and me? How is our relationship different? How is it going to be better, more promising than the next gym instructor, or the milkman?" Matt could feel the anger rising as he spoke.

Jan wiped her eyes, and sat up straight, staring at him. Her hands now pressed flat on the table

"Maybe you're right Matt. I tried just now, to be open and vulnerable, and you're just throwing it back in my face!"

"What about me, Jan? While I've been at Moke's, you've been here bonking Mr. Six Pack without a thought of me until you got dumped!

What about my vulnerability, my pain, my suffering? I pleaded to talk with you, to come back."

Jan didn't reply. She pushed back from the table and stood up, walking slowly into the kitchen.

Matt leaned forward in his chair. He realized nothing had changed between them. Jan was merely on the rebound. He realized he needed to continue with the break she'd initiated. A different basis for change in their relationship was required rather than the end of her affair. "I'm not coming home Jan." He spoke with resolve and without anger.

"What do you mean?" she asked, her voice rising, slightly panicky, as she turned toward him.

"I mean I'm not coming back to the house we used to live in, together." He paused.

"I've thought a lot about this, and I don't believe we're a good match. I don't think we were ever a good match."

"No, Matt! Don't say that." Jan moved toward him, imploringly. "You've got to give us a chance! I've admitted making a mistake."

Matt was torn between taking her in his arms and fending her backwards in order to maintain his resolve. It was torture. "Maybe, Jan. But I've learned a lot about myself these past couple months, and it would be a mistake for me to move back in here now." He thought her eyes appeared to tear-up as he continued, "I'm going to find my own place." He stood up and moved around and past her to the hallway where he turned.

Jan remained standing near the table, staring out the window.

"I'll be in touch about clearing out the rest of my things."

He didn't wait for her response as he pushed out the door and headed to his truck.

Matt lifted the glass to his lips and swallowed half of the golden ale without taking a breath. It was cold and refreshing. There was a euphoric rush from the alcohol as it spread through his body and surged into his bloodstream. He heaved a sigh of relief. It was over. The days, weeks, months of mental torture were nearing an end. He didn't care about the outcome. He was elated by acting from a new, more powerful position and self-image. He wasn't clear about the psychological mechanics, but he felt more courageous and confident than he had ever before.

It was 4:00 p.m. almost quitting time at the Mornington dairy, and he was in a corner booth at the Cosmopolitan Club. He was unaware of any outcomes at the dairy site following his departure to meet Jan at midday. Mandy, Dave and Moke would be joining him soon, but for now he simply wanted to lean back and breath, relax, and enjoy the effect of the beer and his newly established independence.

As he drained his glass, he noticed the entry door open. Mandy, Dave and Moke heading toward his table. He got to his feet as Mandy rushed toward him and buried her head in his chest with a powerful hug.

She looked into his eyes with a bright, admiring smile. "You did it Matt!"

Moke and Dave were standing behind her, grinning and nodding their agreement.

"Did what?" Matt wasn't sure which action they were referring to. They weren't aware of the details of his discussion with Jan.

"Jim's on his way out!" Mandy shouted.

He held Mandy away at arm's length and slapped her outstretched palms with his hands. He didn't believe what he was hearing.

Mandy could see the doubt in his eyes as she pulled a piece of folded paper out her pocket and handed it over to him. "Read it. The CEO put it in writing."

Matt took the paper and sat down.

Mandy pulled a chair up close to him and Moke took a seat across the table straddling the chair back to front.

"I'll go get some drinks. What's your fancy, Mandy?" Dave asked.

"Same thing you and Moke are having."

"That'll be Waikato!" Moke said with a wink.

Matt unfolded what he expected was an email from the CEO. He was right.

Subject: Site Transition Changes - Effective Immediately
From Colin Grey
To: All Site Employees

Effective immediately, Jim Champion, Mornington Dairy Site Manager, has agreed to take a new business development role in China. Jim has served the company well in his twenty years in operations and I am sure he will be an asset to the company in his new position. Please wish him the best.

Effective immediately, the VFM Maintenance contract and services of Libby Galwaith, VFM Project Manager, have been terminated.

Effective at Noon today, Scott Simpson will assume the role of acting Site Manager until a selection process for a permanent Site Manager has been completed. Please give Scott your full support.

Scott will make further announcements regarding selection of a new Maintenance Engineering Manager. In the interim, Matt Polaski will be the acting Maintenance Engineering Manager.

I appreciate the response that all of you have made following the recent events, and I will do all I can to support your efforts to return business and operations to normal.

"Shit!" Matt exclaimed. "I didn't think he was going to do it!"

"Somebody must have done a damn good job of convincing him he needed to do something," Moke looked Matt directly in the eyes. "Somebody like you, mate! Good on you!"

"Yeah. Matt. The shop is humming. The boys are on a high!" Dave had returned with the drinks.

"And Scott is looking for you Matt. He wants to talk to you," Mandy said, beaming at him.

"I can't believe Jim's still with the company. He's got a job in China?!" Mandy slid a fresh glass toward Matt.

"Yeah. It's bloody awful all right," Moke agreed "Why didn't Grey just give him the sack and boot him into the parking lot?"

"It never happens that way with the higher ups," Dave explained. "Champion probably said he wouldn't go quietly and Grey had to cut him a deal."

"Grey knows if they didn't get him out, OSH might be coming down on him." Matt was attempting to explain Grey's actions to himself, aloud.

"Yeah it's the type of card Champion probably played."

"Or he could have told Champion he'd expose VFM and Jim's cost cutting plan? Put Jim in the shit with the Board?" Dave conjectured.

"What kind of management is that?" Mandy was gob-smacked.

"It's real-world management. The higher up you get the curlier it gets," Dave explained.

They looked at each other, shaking their heads in unified exasperation.

"Aw Hell mates! Let's talk about the positive. Here's to us and breaking-up the dynamic duo." Moke raised his mug toward the other three.

They clinked glasses.

"Yeah. We're on the upward trail now. Champion can go blow up a storm with the Chinks," Mandy looked thoughtful. "I think the women over there carry knives. He better watch his pecker!"

The three men looked at each other and laughed. Mandy put her hand on Matt's forearm. She was happy she made them laugh, especially Matt.

Moke and Dave looked at Mandy's gesture and then at each other.

"Hey, you two! If you'd like to have a little more private celebration of the events we can move to another table," Dave suggested.

"Yeah. Or another bar!" Moke quipped.

The two friends got up as if to make a move to leave.

"Sit down you guys," Matt retorted. "We just need to sit here and gloat, together."

"Yeah. Gloat, and drink and laugh," Mandy agreed. "And talk Matt into taking the Maintenance Manager job. Scott's all for it." She squeezed Matt's arm again.

He seemed relaxed about her attention, for a change.

"Alright? Let's get another round of drinks." Moke held up his empty glass.

"I'll second that, and take care of it!" Mandy jumped up, pushing Moke aside while she collected the empties and headed to the bar.

The three men watched her graceful walk and voluptuous figure.

She looked back over her shoulder, as though she had eyes in the back of her head, and winked at them.

"I don't know what's holding you back, mate?" Moke said, turning to Matt.

They all laughed.

The next morning Matt was on site, walking down the administration block hallway. The receptionist had greeted him, guardedly and a couple of the accountants had looked up from their desks and nodded at him as he walked down the hallway toward Jim Champion's office. Funny, he thought to himself, the people here should be acting more cheerful following yesterday's announcement from the CEO. He was certain Jim had been tough on everyone in the administration area, and they'd be feeling a sense of relief about Jim's departure for China. It definitely didn't seem to be the case. The reason was immediately apparent.

Jim was in his office, as usual, beavering away at his desk. He looked up, feeling Matt's disbelieving eyes staring at him. "Matt! C'mon in!" Jim exclaimed energetically as he came from behind the desk. "So. Surprised? Eh?! Thought I'd be on my way to Beijing by now?" Jim paused for the full impact of the surprise to sink into Matt's psyche. Jim was gloating about the apparent reversal of Matt's expectations.

Matt was speechless.

Jim continued. "Actually, I'm surprised to see <u>you</u> here! I thought I had suspended you? Guess you talked that wanker, Colin Grey, into giving your job back?." He patted Matt on the back as he returned to his seat. His expression became serious. "You were right to do what you did Matt! I mean talking to Grey about what was happening here. I needed a bit of a rev-up from him, for not being completely honest about what happened, and suspending you the way I did."

Matt was completely non-plussed. He felt physically and mentally dis-oriented.

"It was Libby's fault! She convinced me she knew the risks and what was going on. All her RCM talk! I never thought she'd screw-up and cause the drier explosion! After it happened, she said you were the one to blame. I didn't know you'd warned her about the consequences. I'm sorry mate. I took her word for it."

Matt couldn't believe what he was hearing. He felt like he was in an episode of The Twilight Zone. He felt disoriented and slightly nauseous.

Jim carried on. "Libby is history. So is VFM! They made promises they couldn't keep, led me down the garden path, so to speak. I think you were right." Jim hesitated and corrected himself. "We were right, when I sent you and Trevor off to see that Canadian guy...........what was his name?"

"Jack." Matt muttered, wondering where Jim's tangent was headed.

"Yeah! Jack! He was a common-sense sort of guy, and maybe he was right. It <u>will</u> take longer to put the program in place and save some dosh. Libby and VFM were bull-shitting us."

Matt continued to stare at the floor.

"So, what do you reckon Matt?! I totally agree with the CEO. You should be the maintenance manager. Scott's totally behind you as well. He confirmed it this morning. How about you head up the program?! Get Jack back in here. Take over the Maintenance Manager's job. Get the boys in behind you?" He hesitated, gauging Matt's neutral reactions. "This VFM deal was just a hiccup!"

Matt realized Jim hadn't skipped a beat. He couldn't look him in the eye. He was torn between incredulity and outrage. Part of him wanted to rip Jim apart, the other part wanted to run and hide. He said nothing.

"Ok Matt. I can see this isn't the time for you to make a decision! There's been a lot going on."

Matt looked at Jim for a moment, half-nodding his head.

"You go off and think about this. Talk to your partner. Talk to the boys. Then come back to me."

Matt smiled. Jim wasn't aware he had split up with Jan. After working with Matt for eight years, he didn't even know his partner's name. He replied half-heartedly, "Yeah. I'll have a think on it."

Matt rose slowly from the lowered chair.

Jim walked around his desk, and slapped Matt on the back. "Good on ya mate! I'm sure you'll see this has worked out for the best, and you can make a better job of it than the blonde bimbo!"

Matt felt stunned like one of the snappers he often hauled into the dingy and miss-hit with his iron baton. He took a right turn after leaving Jim's office, on auto-pilot. A few seconds later he was passing Scott Simpson's office.

"Hey! Matt! Hold up!" Scott jumped up from behind his desk. He could see Matt was in dazed, and surmised he had just talked with Jim. He walked into the hallway and took Matt by the shoulders steering him to the right and into his office. "Have a seat mate. You look like you just saw a ghost!"

Matt hesitated before responding. "I thought he was supposed to be on his way to China?"

Scott pulled out an unopened bottle of water from his backpack and set it on the desk in front of Matt as he walked behind Matt to close the door to his office. "Yeah. I kinda felt the same way this morning, especially after the CEO called me yesterday afternoon and asked me to take on Jim's job."

"So. What happened between yesterday and this morning?!"

"The Chairman of the Board came to Jim's rescue!" Scott smiled sarcastically and continued. "Guess you didn't know how tight these farmers are?! Jim and Chairman McCoy go back a long way. Rumor has it they are actually relatives, uncle or something. Jim never talks about it."

"So?"

"When Jim got the bullet from Colin yesterday, he got on the phone to McCoy."

Matt was putting it together in his mind as Scott explained.

Scott could see the penny drop for Matt, judging his expression change.

"Yep. You got it. Then McCoy makes a call to Grey, who he semi-despises anyway, and tells him to back off Jim."

"And?"

"I'm guessing McCoy gives Grey a rev-up for making a hasty decision without consulting the Board or the marketing group in China. I'm not sure why Colin did it anyway. There was no hint of sending Jim to China. You have any idea why?" Scott had a hunch Matt knew more than he was letting on.

"Yeah. I had a chat with Grey yesterday morning about the whole thing, explosion and the preventive maintenance program tasks and my suspension." Matt knew he could confide in Scott and carried on. "I was surprised how big a deal Grey made out of the suspension instead of the explosion. I didn't think he'd make a move on Jim."

"Yeah. I figured you might have done something like that. Good on you for not taking it lying down." Scott stopped for a moment, piecing his theory together to explain to Matt. "There's no way Grey was going to make a big deal about the explosion because he wants to avoid negative publicity."

"Then why'd he go after Jim on the suspension? Sending him to China seems pretty heavy."

"Grey knows Jim wants his job, and McCoy's been trying to push Grey out as well. The rest of the Board is the only thing stopping it, so far."

"So, if Grey sends Jim to China, he's less of a threat?"

"That's the way corporate politics work. You're learning fast!" Scott figured Matt would loosen up if he could add a bit of levity and support.

"What happened to Libby and VFM?"

"I wouldn't worry about them. They can take care of themselves. VFM and Libby know what happened. It's a risk they take doing contract maintenance. There's always the chance they'll be made a scapegoat if something goes wrong."

"You mean their contract's finished?!"

"Yeah. Neither VFM or the dairy company want any negative publicity as a result of the drier explosion. The dairy company will make Libby the scapegoat, along with VFM, on an internal, need to know, basis. It won't be publicized." Scott looked at his watch. He needed to cut the conversation off so he could make the morning production meeting. "I think the most important thing is for you to decide what you want. You've got a promotion out of this and you deserve it. I told Jim I support you for the role when he asked me this morning."

"Shit! What a bloody let down. The boys are going be ticked off, no end, about this reversal!"

"Yeah. We all are. But what are we going do, mate? I suggest you take it easy today. I hear there's a new contract engineering group coming in to carry on with the rebuild project. People we used before VFM came on the scene."

Matt rose from his chair and took Scott's extended right hand in his own. "Thanks for the explanation and the timeout Scott. It's making more sense, not that I like it."

"Take it easy Matt. Stop back later today or first thing tomorrow. It'll do us both good."

Ten minutes later, Matt pushed through the workshop door. Moke was on his tools, disassembling a pump at one of the workbenches. Dave was standing nearby, chatting with a couple tradesmen.

Moke put his tools down when he saw Matt's forlorn expression, and the other three men stopped talking as well. "What's up Matt? You look like a possum's backside."

Matt explained what's happened with Jim's re-instatement and Scott's summary of company politics.

"You've got to be shitting me?" Dave exclaimed.

"Yeah! Hey! What the frig?!" One of the tradesmen shouted.

"So.........that's it? Everything's just happy chappy then?" Moke was sarcastic, shaking his head, clenching his fists. His dark skin flushed a tone darker with anger.

"I don't know. Jim wants us to carry on with the maintenance best practices program, this time with Jack supporting us like we originally planned."

"Hah!" Dave responded. "Fat chance it'll last!"

A couple of the other tradesmen looked Matt in the eye as Dave spoke, and then shifted their gaze away, half turning toward the back of the workshop. Their body language spoke louder than words. Two of them shifted toward the workbench where they picked up tools, trying to distract themselves from the uncomfortable scenario.

"Yeah. Scott also told me I should take on Trevor's job, permanently. There's going to be an interview process, but Jim told him I'm going to be the only one interviewed."

"Typical." Dave criticized the failure to follow company policy. "Will you take the job?"

"I don't know. I want to support the program, but I don't trust Jim."

"You'd be on a hiding to nothing." Andy advised.

Matt was silent. He looked at the floor, averting their eyes, awaiting an epiphany, a word of hope or enthusiasm to surface from someone, an indication of whether or not the maintenance improvement initiative and the manager's job were worth pursuing.

Moke cleared his throat, and took a couple steps toward Matt. The rest of the crew looked on, intently. Moke announced with a tone of accusation and resignation, "It's just gonna be another BOHICA."

Matt cocked his head glancing from Moke, to Dave and then back to Moke for an explanation. The expression's meaning had slipped his memory.

Moke was surprised and exasperated. "It's simple mate! It's another B...O....H....I.....C....A.......Bend Over, Here It Comes Again!" He put his right thumb toward his butt to illustrate. Like all of management's bright ideas and politics! Us little guys always get it up the backside!"

A couple of the tradesmen half-smiled and grunted their agreement.

The tension dissipated slightly as Moke turned and headed toward the smoko room.

The rest of the tradesmen slowly followed him.

Matt realized they wouldn't get their hopes up again.

THE END

RESOURCES

1. smrp.org website - Society of Maintenance & Reliability Professionals
2. IDCON.com Christer Idhammar, Founder of IDCON INC
3. terrywireman.com
4. KITA: One More Time: How Do You Motivate Employees? By Frederick Herzberg, Harvard Business Review Classic, January – February 1968
5. The Knowing Doing Gap by Jeffrey Pfeffer and Robert I Sutton.
6. From Good to Great by Jim Collins.
7. Making Common Sense Common Practice by Ron Moore
8. Skills4work.org.nz

ABOUT THE AUTHOR

Rob Probst has forty years of industrial manufacturing experience, working in engineering and operations management roles as well as reliability engineering, consulting and training. A mechanical engineering graduate from UC Berkeley, he has authored articles about operational behavior, maintenance, and engineering practices. Rob and his colleagues at Bay Milk Products initiated a reliability improvement program that achieved world-class accreditation in 2009, and he subsequently co-created a software program that predicts the return on investment for best-practice maintenance reliability program implementation. He recently completed a Master' of Business Studies degree at Massey University and is a certified maintenance and reliability professional. He lives at Ohope Beach in New Zealand, where he works as a consultant and pursues study and writing projects related to organizational behavior.

Printed in the United States
by Baker & Taylor Publisher Services